Mortal Remains

Emma Page first began writing as a hobby, and after a number of her poems had been accepted by the BBC and her short stories began appearing in weekly magazines, she took to writing radio plays and crime novels. She was first published in the Crime Club, which later became Collins Crime.

An English graduate from Oxford, Emma Page taught in every kind of educational establishment both in the UK and abroad before she started writing full-time.

By Emma Page

Kelsey and Lambert series

Say it with Murder
Intent to Kill
Hard Evidence
Murder Comes Calling
In the Event of My Death
Mortal Remains
Deadlock
A Violent End
Final Moments
Scent of Death
Cold Light of Day
Last Walk Home
Every Second Thursday
Missing Woman

Standalone novels

A Fortnight by the Sea (also known as
Add a Pinch of Cyanide)
Element of Chance
In Loving Memory
Family and Friends

Mortal Remains

Emma Page

HARPER

This novel is entirely a work of fiction.
The names, characters and incidents portrayed in it are
the work of the author's imagination. Any resemblance to
actual persons, living or dead, events or localities is
entirely coincidental.

Harper
An imprint of HarperCollins*Publishers*
1 London Bridge Street
London SE1 9GF

www.harpercollins.co.uk

This paperback edition 2016
1

First published in Great Britain in 1992 by Collins Crime

Emma Page asserts the moral right to
be identified as the author of this work

A catalogue record for this book is
available from the British Library

ISBN: 978-0-00-817178-0

For B.D., G.G., J.C., *et al*,
For all the happy hours

CHAPTER 1

All summer long the local children played on Whitethorn Common, a sizeable tract of land on the edge of Cannonbridge. The common didn't present a flat, exposed terrain but a landscape of diversity and unexpectedness, swelling into hillocks, dipping into hollows; secluded spots, open spaces, trees and shrubs, smooth stretches of turf.

Now, in the caressing warmth of this golden Tuesday evening in September, the shadows had lengthened by eight o'clock. The blackberrying youngsters were departing with their pickings, the pensioners heading for home and television.

A young couple still strolled over the emerald slopes, their arms around each other. The girl, Jill Lingard, was nineteen years old, pretty enough in an everyday fashion, an air of robust common sense. Her boyfriend, Norman Griffin, seven years older, was a virile-looking young man with a stubborn set to his jaw.

They paused from time to time to survey one or other of the half-dozen houses, of varying sizes, dates and styles, dotted about the common, each in its own garden. They climbed a grass-covered eminence and stood looking down. 'That's the kind of house I'd like one day.' Jill nodded in the direction of a substantial late-Victorian dwelling standing on gently rising ground a little distance ahead. The name on one of the tall gate pillars read: Fairbourne.

The house fronted the common, its large garden screened on three sides and a good part of the fourth by trees and shrubs.

'That's the sort of place to bring a family up,' Jill added. 'It's got character. And space.'

'We could never afford anything like that on what I earn,' Norman said. He was a driver for Mansell's, a local building firm. 'There's only one way it might be possible and that would take luck and years of hard work. Start off small and trade up. Find some run-down property dirt-cheap, work on it, sell it. Find another, work on it, sell it. The same again. And again. The real difficulty would be getting the money to buy the first property. We'd be lucky to get any mortgage at all on something like that. And we'd need cash for materials, all the way along.'

She looked earnestly up at him. 'If we did find an old place cheap, do you think Tom Mansell might lend us the money to buy it?' Tom Mansell was his boss. 'You've always got on well with him. We'd pay him back every month, exactly the same as a building society, we'd have it all properly drawn up.'

He shook his head. 'Mansell would never put up good money for us to buy some clapped-out property, he'd tell us to buy one of his starter homes. That would make a lot more sense. We could get the maximum mortgage on one of those, with both of us working.'

She pulled a face. 'I'd hate one of those poky little boxes.'

He gave her a considering look. 'I notice you don't mention your grandfather. If we were trying to borrow from anyone, surely he'd be the obvious person. I wouldn't mind betting he's worth a lot more than he ever lets on.'

It was Jill's turn to shake her head. 'We'd be wasting our time. Granddad wouldn't lend Gareth a penny when he was starting up.' Gareth was her brother, several years older, married, with two small children; he lived some distance away. In spite of the age difference he and Jill had always been close. A few years ago Gareth had set up with another young man in the business of contract gardening. In the event he had managed without help from his grandfather; his wife's parents had come up with the necessary backing.

'Wouldn't do any harm to ask the old man,' Norman persisted. 'He's very fond of you. Catch him in a good mood, he might surprise you.'

She shook her head with finality. 'He'd never do it. You know what he'd say: "If you want something you must work for it, save for it, the same as I had to do.'' But she wasn't defeated yet. 'What about your mother? Has she got anything she might lend us?'

He laughed. 'You can forget my mother. She's got a few pounds in the post office and that's about it.'

Jill's face broke into a rapturous smile. It had just dawned on her that here they were, discussing properties, loans, mortgages, as if they were definitely intending to get married. They had been going out together for some months—on a strictly so far and no farther basis, by Jill's express diktat. Norman had never mentioned marriage and with Jill it would have to be marriage, she could never settle for the casual arrangement of simply setting up house together, seeing how things went from there. Only the full commitment, the traditional set-up, would do for her: a settled home for children, security, stability. Norman was well aware of her views; if he was talking about buying a house together, then he was talking marriage.

As she savoured her moment of realization a girl of about ten years old came running up the grassy incline, a spaniel frisking at her heels. She was a rosy-cheeked child, chubby-faced and bright-eyed, her long fair hair taken back in a plait tied with red ribbon. She gave Jill a warm smile.

'Not another dog!' Jill exclaimed, laughing. 'It's a different animal pretty well every time I see you.' She often came across the girl about the common, exercising a pet belonging to some relative or neighbour. Jill reached down to pat the spaniel; she began to chat idly to the girl.

A bus turned into the road running alongside the common and ground to a halt. Norman stood watching as a woman alighted and crossed over on to the common, towards Fairbourne. Not very tall, a slim, supple figure. A wealth of naturally curly hair, golden chestnut, beautifully arranged. Delicate features, a face lovely enough to arrest the eye. She was dressed with casual elegance in a light summer suit. She wore a shoulder-bag, carried a number of books. Norman's gaze remained fixed as she let herself in through the wrought-iron gates of the dwelling.

As Jill straightened up from playing with the spaniel she caught sight of the woman turning to close the gates. Norman's intent expression vanished abruptly.

'There's Mrs Holroyd,' Jill exclaimed with lively admiration. She watched the graceful figure move away along the path. 'She always looks so smart, she has such marvellous taste.' There was a note of professional assessment in her tone, she worked as a sales assistant at York House, the high-class department store in Cannonbridge where Mrs Holroyd bought many of her clothes. 'And she always wears such gorgeous perfume,' she added without a trace of envy. 'It must cost a fortune.'

Inside Fairbourne, ten minutes later, Claire Holroyd came downstairs and went along to the spacious sitting-room, attractively furnished, immaculately kept. Some handsome old pieces, part of the original furnishings; an atmosphere of solid comfort. Petit-point cushion covers Claire had embroidered, fresh flowers she had skilfully arranged. The walls were hung with Victorian watercolours—one of her husband's hobbies was restoring neglected paintings he picked up at sales.

She paused by a table to glance through the books she had earlier set down, then she crossed to the fireplace and rested her hands on the mantelshelf, staring down into the hearth with its summer screen of garden blooms.

Through the open window came the chirruping of birds, the murmur of traffic. She raised her head and contemplated herself in the mirror above the hearth. A look of glowing happiness shone from her eyes, a smile curved her lips. After a moment she leaned forward and gazed searchingly at her image. Her smile faded.

She raised a hand and passed the tips of her fingers lightly over her mouth, cheeks, brow. Surely the scars were almost gone now? In this evening light she could scarcely make them out. As she tilted her head this way and that a look of anxiety crept into her blue-grey eyes.

The sound of the side door opening and closing pierced

her absorption—her husband coming in after his evening stint in the garden. He managed the garden himself, large as it was.

She left the mirror and dropped into her chair. She switched on a table lamp, picked up one of her books and opened it at random. By the time Edgar had changed his shoes and washed his hands, had come along the passage and opened the sitting-room door, she was leaning comfortably back, reading with an air of studious attention. She glanced up at him with a smile of calm friendliness.

Edgar was tall, strongly built and fit-looking, ten years older than his wife. Dark hair already thinning, gaze level and controlled. A narrow, ascetic face, deeply carved lines running from nose to mouth. He was a local government official, number two in the department of housing and the environment.

He went up to her chair. Her perfume rose up at him as he stooped to give her a kiss. She turned her head slightly so that the kiss landed on her cheek.

'How was your class?' he asked as he crossed the room to switch on the television.

'Very interesting,' she told him with animation. 'Some of the students are very bright.' She smiled. 'I shall have to watch out they don't leave me behind.' It was the beginning of the autumn term at the Cannonbridge College of Further Education; Claire had just attended the first class in her local history course.

She had made a start at the college shortly after her marriage four years ago, choosing, that first year, a single afternoon class. She had added a second afternoon class the following year. In the third year she had in addition signed on for one evening class. This year she had dropped her afternoon classes and enrolled for three evening courses, the other two being in literature and drama. 'The lecturer is very good,' she added. 'Enthusiastic and lively.'

'Sounds promising,' Edgar commented as he sat down and gave his attention to the television.

Shortly after half past nine Claire said she was tired, she

would have a bath and go to bed. She went slowly up the wide staircase with its ornamental balustrade. The house had been built by Edgar's great-grandfather, a prosperous merchant; it had been modernized over the years.

Outside the door of the large bedroom she shared with Edgar, Claire paused with her hand on the knob. She turned her head and looked along the landing to where a narrower flight of stairs rose to the next floor. Up there were the nurseries with their barred windows, silent now for many a year. Her face fell into melancholy lines, then she gave her head a brisk little shake and went into the bedroom.

Left alone in the sitting-room, Edgar switched off the television. The evening paper lay on a table beside him but he didn't pick it up. He sat staring ahead, then he got to his feet and went to the bureau. He took out an old leather-bound album and returned to his chair. He opened the album and sat studying the photographs, remembering, reflecting.

His mother, fair-haired and pretty, delicate-looking, gently smiling; Edgar, her first-born, her treasure, had greatly loved her. She had died at the birth of her second child, his brother Lester, born after a gap of twelve years. Their father, dark-haired, an austere cast of countenance; he had died ten years after his beloved wife. Edgar was then twenty-two years old; the task of rearing his young brother to manhood had fallen to him. He had gladly embraced it, seeing it as a service rendered to the mother he had so dearly loved and never ceased to mourn.

He turned the pages of the album: Lester as a baby, a toddler, a schoolboy. Lester in his first long trousers. Lester as a young man.

He turned another page: Lester as a bridegroom, smiling confidently into the camera—five years ago, now. Beside him his bride, a striking brunette, radiant with health and vitality, twelve months younger than her groom: Diane Mansell, only daughter of Tom Mansell, the local builder, the apple of her father's eye. She had been the star of the

Cannonbridge tennis club in her teens, renowned for her mighty smash. She and Lester had met at the club when they were both still at school.

Edgar looked down without affection at Diane in her bridal finery, her hair looped up under a filmy veil, her handsome face with its strongly moulded features, her habitual expression of self-will plain even then, on her wedding-day. Edgar had wanted Lester to take some further course of study or professional articling after leaving school but Lester would have none of it. He had walked out through the school gates for the last time on a Friday afternoon. On the following Monday morning he started work at Mansell's. Three years later he and Diane were married.

Edgar gave a sigh as he contemplated the bridal couple. He had been against the marriage, had considered them both too young. But it had been more than that: in his official capacity he hadn't welcomed the Mansell connection. He had never been able to put a positive finger on it but he had long had the feeling that Tom Mansell sailed close to the wind in his business dealings. Mansell for his part had heartily approved the match, had done all he could to encourage it. Edgar couldn't help thinking this was at least partly because Mansell believed it could do him no harm to have an in-law high up in the local housing department, it could set a seal of respectability on his activities.

But Lester had needed neither Edgar's approval for the match nor his financial assistance. As soon as he reached the age of twenty-one he came into a substantial legacy, his share of their father's estate; he could do exactly as he pleased.

In a secluded rural spot four miles from Fairbourne, Lester Holroyd put his car away in the garage and walked towards his house, well designed and soundly constructed, built by Tom Mansell as a wedding present for his darling daughter and her bridegroom.

Lester was as tall as his brother, somewhat better-looking than Edgar. He had a rangy, athletic figure, a fine head of fair hair. Where Edgar closely resembled their father, Lester in some respects took after the other side of the family, inheriting his mother's colouring, her eyes and smile.

Whatever Tom Mansell's motives had been for encouraging the match, he had come increasingly over the last few years to value his son-in-law's services, to rely on him as an able assistant and deputy. Lester was now indisputably Mansell's right-hand man; he had hopes of more formal promotion before long. He had a shrewd notion changes were in the wind; he was certain they would be to his own advantage. Mansell always kept his cards close to his chest until the last possible moment but Lester believed he knew the next objective Mansell was contemplating: the opening of a second yard.

He let himself into the house. Diane would soon be home. She was a trained nurse, employed in that capacity at a large factory in Cannonbridge. She was currently working the second shift, two till ten, she had done so for a few months and had found it suited her, she liked the long, free mornings.

Lester went into the sitting-room and settled himself down to watch the news. But it had been a long day, his eyes began to close. Before long he was asleep, slipping shortly into a spell of vivid dreaming.

He was driving an open sports car in sparkling sunshine, at tremendous speed and with great exhilaration, along a steeply twisting road, the wind whistling through his hair. He shouted in exuberance as he rounded a bend with a swooping roar. All at once he saw before him a precipitous drop, down on to jagged rocks, into a boiling sea. He slammed on the brakes. There was no response.

The car whirled off the road, hurtling out through the brilliant air, describing a soaring arc before it began to fall. Down, down, faster and faster, towards the vicious rocks, the churning waves.

He started up in his chair, wide awake, his face running

with sweat, his heart pounding. As he strove to steady himself he heard Diane drive up.

She came into the room a few minutes later, smiling cheerfully. She wasn't unduly fatigued after her stint at the factory, she found it far less demanding than hospital work.

They greeted each other with affection. A little later, over coffee, Lester remembered something he had to tell her. 'I ran into one of the Acorn committee today. He said the tickets for the dinner-dance will be ready tomorrow.' The Acorn Club was a prestigious association, founded one hundred years ago by a group of local businessmen—among them Lester's great-grandfather—with the aim of raising money for charity. The annual dinner-dance, always held on the last Friday in October, was the outstanding event in the Cannonbridge social calendar, a fund-raiser on an impressive scale. There was always a rush for tickets; this year, because of the centenary, it was likely to prove a mad scramble.

'I'll get the tickets in the morning,' Diane promised. They always looked forward to the event, they both enjoyed the big local social occasions. Diane had arranged some time ago to have the evening off work.

Her expression suddenly changed to a frown. 'I suppose Edgar and Claire will be there?'

'Yes, of course they will,' Lester responded. 'Edgar's expected to go, in his job. And Claire's gone with him every year since they've been married.'

Her frown deepened. She was three years younger than Claire, no small gap during the years of growing up; they hadn't known each other in those days. Claire had married Edgar—much to everyone's surprise, not least that of Edgar himself—twelve months after Lester's marriage to Diane. The two women had never taken to each other. Relations between the households had teetered along on a shaky footing, finally petering out altogether a few months ago.

Diane's tone was sulky. 'If Claire's going to be there,

then I'm not going.' Ill humour gave her face a tigerish look.

Lester was astounded. 'Of course you're going! Your father's making a big donation this year. His evening will be ruined if you're not there to see it.' The donation ceremony, with its formal announcing of names and amounts, punctuated with drum rolls and storms of applause, was always the highlight of the evening. 'If you don't go, I can't go. It would look very odd if I went without you.'

Her face remained mutinous.

He tried another tack. 'Stuart will be there this year, now he's old enough to go.' Stuart was Diane's younger brother, they had always been close. And Lester had always got on well with Stuart. 'It would spoil all his pleasure in going if you stayed away.'

He detected a faint softening of her expression, his tone grew cajoling. 'I honestly can't see why it should bother you in the least if Claire's there. The hall's big enough in all conscience, there isn't the slightest need for you to go anywhere near either of them all evening.'

'No, I suppose not,' Diane grudgingly acknowledged.

He delivered his masterstroke. 'You go out and get yourself something really stunning to wear, guaranteed to knock Claire's eye out. Never mind what it costs, I'll pay.' Diane had always envied Claire her style of looks, her easy elegance.

She began to smile. 'All right,' she conceded. 'You win.'

He jumped up, went over and flung an arm round her. He gave her shoulders a squeeze, bent his head and planted a jubilant kiss on her cheek. 'That's my girl! We'll have a great evening! You'll see!'

CHAPTER 2

A mile or so from the dwelling he had built for his daughter and son-in-law, Tom Mansell's splendid modern residence stood on the brow of a hill in a superb situation with magnificent views.

On Wednesday morning Mansell woke even earlier than usual. His brain, ever active with plans and enterprises, even during sleep, roused him to full wakefulness before five. He knew the moment he opened his eyes it was all settled, his mind was definitely made up.

He pulled on a dressing-gown and made his way silently from the room, along the corridor, past the bedroom of his son Stuart, eighteen years old now, learning the ropes at the yard—under his own careful supervision—since leaving school over twelve months ago. Past the flight of stairs leading up to the suite of rooms set aside for his housekeeper, a highly respectable widow, good-natured and motherly, in her sixties now. She had kept house for him for the past fifteen years, had ably and cheerfully assisted in the upbringing of his two children. The last ten of those years had been spent in this house, the house he had built for himself and his children, the kind of house he had always dreamed of.

He went down the stairs, towards the kitchen. He was a muscular man, forty-eight years old, a little over medium height, very striking in appearance. His hair was already snow-white, though still thick and wavy, but his heavy eyebrows had remained jet black. His skin was deeply tanned, his eyes a piercing sapphire blue. He exuded a feeling of raw power.

In the kitchen he made himself a pot of tea and carried it along to his study. He sat down at his desk and addressed himself to the matter that had been occupying his thoughts for some time now: the desirability of opening a second yard. Wychford, yes, that was definitely the place; he was getting more and more work these days over in that direction.

He smiled as he drank his tea. He would deeply relish the challenge of setting about cutting himself a second slice of the cake. He would move Lester over to take charge of the new branch. Lester would do well there, he had a good head on his shoulders. He had never traded on his position as the boss's son-in-law, had always pulled his full weight, he had more than earned his promotion. And he might very well find a spot in the new set-up for Norman Griffin. A useful and loyal henchman, the right stuff in him, the backbone to start taking on a bit of responsibility.

He stood up and went to a wall map. Pins and flags marked current developments, projects still under discussion, sites of possible future interest, and, most mouthwatering of all, likely locations for the second yard. He studied the map closely, then he moved on to consult the calendar—his own trade calendar, expensively produced, beautifully photographed, portraying the best of the firm's work over the previous year. It bore the correct name of the firm, Dobie and Mansell, though the business was known everywhere these days simply as Mansell's.

Dobie was now retired, living abroad. The firm had been started by Dobie's father after the First World War, Tom Mansell had come in fifteen years ago. Dobie had taken no active part in the management since his retirement. As long as his share of the steadily increasing profits kept rolling in, he didn't bother his head about what went on in the business.

Mansell fingered back the glossy pages, considering dates: September . . . October . . . November . . . His face broke into a smile, he jabbed a finger down. 'That's it!' he said aloud. Sunday, November 11. He'd have them all here together for a slap-up lunch, Lester, Diane, Stuart, he'd make his announcement then.

It pleased his fancy to choose the anniversary of the day he had taken over sole active control of the firm. Dobie had left the yard for the last time thirteen years ago, on November 10, at the end of the working day. Early next morning, before anyone was about, Mansell had driven into the yard. He had walked about the entire place with a great grin on his face, knowing it was all before him, tasting the powerful sweetness of the moment.

He picked up one of the framed photographs ranged along a shelf, one he particularly liked: Diane and Lester, strolling in the rose garden here, holding hands, smiling at each other. He'd taken the photograph himself one Sunday afternoon when they'd come to tea, not long after they'd got back from their honeymoon.

He gazed fondly down at the smiling pair. How right he had been to encourage the match—in spite of the opposition from that brother of Lester's. Edgar always struck Mansell as a dry stick, though still a couple of years away from forty. His thoughts were briefly side-tracked by a vision of Claire, beautiful and elegant. The question rose in his mind, by no means for the first time: Whatever could have persuaded a woman like that to marry such a man?

He dragged his thoughts back to Diane and Lester. No sign yet of starting a family. He drew a deep sigh. Time enough, Diane always told him whenever he raised the matter with her. Another year or two, she'd said the last time he'd brought it up, then I really will settle down to it.

He replaced the photograph and picked up another, more recent, more formally posed: Stuart on his eighteenth birthday. It was like looking at a portrait of himself as a young man. I suppose it might not be all that many years before we have Stuart thinking about getting married, he told himself with a lightening of his spirits. Not that Stuart had any steady girlfriend as yet. Mansell fervently hoped that when the time came his son would have the sense to find himself a girl with old-fashioned ideas of a home and babies, not some hard-nosed modern female with her sights set chiefly on a career.

He put the photograph back and returned to his desk. He sat staring ahead, lost in thought.

Children, grandchildren, great-grandchildren, they were what gave life and substance to it all, made the whole shooting-match more than a dance of shadows on a flickering screen. The unbroken line of one's own flesh and blood stretching into the misty centuries ahead, that was what took away the sting from the stabbing thought of one's own mortality, that must in the end prevail, struggle against it as one might.

Over in Fairbourne, Edgar Holroyd's day didn't begin quite so early. At six-thirty precisely he opened his eyes in the spacious front bedroom looking out over the common. Never any need for an alarm, he always woke at the same hour, winter and summer; he had trained himself to that useful habit long ago, as a lad.

A still morning, little sound of traffic as yet. Pale streaks of light stole in around the edges of the curtains. From the trees screening the garden the collared doves murmured their ceaseless calculation: Thirteen six, thirteen six.

He glanced across at the other bed. Claire lay with her back to him, curled in a posture of deep sleep. He moved his covers gently back, eased himself noiselessly out, silently drew on slippers and dressing-gown.

With barely a whisper of sound he let himself out of the room and went stealthily along the landing, into the small bedroom he had used as a dressing-room since his marriage. He got into jogging gear and went down to the kitchen where he drank a glass of orange juice and ate the single piece of rye crispbread he allowed himself before setting out.

He went for his early-morning jog in all but the worst weather. Every evening, if at all possible, he took a brisk walk. He had begun these habits years ago, they were by now deeply ingrained. Claire never accompanied him on either sally, it had never occurred to either of them to suggest it.

His watch showed his customary time as he let himself

out of the house and set off at his customary pace to cover his customary route.

Upstairs in the front bedroom Claire caught the sound of the side door opening and closing. She had surfaced to full consciousness before Edgar left his bed but she had lain motionless and kept her eyes closed while he was still in the room.

She switched on the light, flung back the covers and sprang out of bed. She pulled on a robe and slippers, darted across to a mirror. This morning it was her hair that occupied her attention. Time for a new style—making her third in as many months. Before that, she hadn't changed her hairstyle since her marriage; she smiled now at the thought.

She lifted her shining tresses, pinned, unpinned, pursued a fresh inspiration; another and another, arriving at last at an effect that satisfied her. She gave a decisive nod; at her next hair appointment she would definitely suggest something along those lines.

She turned from the mirror and went to the wardrobe, she ran her hand along the rail, appraising. The first day of autumn was only a little over a week away. Some new clothes for the new season. Her blue-grey eyes sparkled. She began to hum a tune.

The area immediately to the north of Whitethorn Common contained a variety of dwellings: terrace houses, red-brick semis, large Victorian and Edwardian residences turned into flats; here and there an old cottage clinging to its original garden, reminding the district of its rural past.

A little further out, a fair-sized council estate had sprung up after the First World War. It had seen several changes; many of the houses had passed into private hands.

In one of the more attractive parts of the estate a small grove of trees separated a group of dwellings from their neighbours. One of these dwellings, a semi occupying a corner plot in a pleasant cul-de-sac, was the home of Harry Lingard, Jill Lingard's grandfather. It had been his home since boyhood, he had lived there alone since the death of his wife three years ago. They had had one child, a son, father of Gareth and Jill; he had been carried off in his thirties by a virulent form of pneumonia. His widow had married again two years ago and lived now with her second husband in a northern city.

Harry had been up since five-thirty, endlessly busy as always, every moment of his time structured and purposeful. A wiry little man, nimble and vigorous for his seventy-two years, a teetotaller and non-smoker, with an alert eye, a weathered face, a fringe of sparse, iron-grey hair surrounding a gleaming pate.

He had been a regular soldier, a driver, never rising above the rank of private but never disgracing himself either; he had served throughout the Second World War. When his army days were over he found himself a job as a driver-porter with Calthrop's, an old-established firm of auctioneers and estate agents in Cannonbridge; he stayed there until he retired at sixty-five. He had immediately found himself another, lighter job as a yardman at Mansell's, where he was still working.

During his time at Calthrop's he had always done a bit of dealing—perfectly legitimate—on the side, mainly buying in the saleroom old items of furniture in a dilapidated condition at knockdown prices, working on them at home, putting them back in the saleroom later; he had always shown a worthwhile profit. He still kept up this practice, nipping along in his dinner-hour on viewing day, leaving his bids with a porter.

He owned his council house, he had been the first tenant on the estate to exercise the right to buy, exercising it in the teeth of entrenched opposition from the forces of local bureaucracy. The house was his pride and joy. Since the purchase he had modernized and extended, refurbished every inch, carrying out all the work himself.

On this calm September morning he ate his customary sparing breakfast while listening with keen attention to the business news on the radio. It was broad daylight by the time he set off a little later to fetch his morning paper. He glanced ceaselessly about as he strode along, keeping a citizen's eye open for broken paving-slabs, blocked road drains, overflowing litter bins, overgrown hedges, graffiti, acts of vandalism. He halted now and then to jot down anything worthy of attention in the notebook he always carried.

As he rounded a corner he caught sight of someone he recognized going into the paper shop: Edgar Holroyd. He quickened his pace, he wanted a word with Holroyd and he intended to have it here and now. Repairs to tenants' houses on the estate were falling behind again. Though no longer a tenant himself, Harry still fought the tenants' battles for them, orchestrating every campaign. He was a well-known figure at the local library, thumbing through legal tomes and consumer manuals in the reference room.

Inside the shop, Edgar turned from the counter with his newspaper and saw with annoyance that Harry Lingard had stationed himself in the doorway, blocking his exit. Harry's expression told him plainly he was about to be tackled.

Harry wasted no time in greeting or preamble but launched at once into a spirited attack on the council's procrastination and penny-pinching. He pulled out his notebook and embarked on a rapid recital of individual cases.

Edgar was humiliatingly aware of the shopkeeper, the other customers, cocking sharply interested ears. He kept his expression, his voice, civil and detached. 'This is hardly the time or place,' he began.

'It's never the time or place for you jacks-in-office,' Harry broke in.

A ripple of amusement travelled over the watching faces.

Edgar's jaw tightened. 'If you'd care to make an appointment,' he said, still deliberately courteous, 'I'll be happy to see you in my office.'

Harry gave a snort of disdain. 'You'll dodge it again,' he averred with conviction. 'I'll be fobbed off with that assistant of yours.'

All commerce in the shop had now ceased. Around him Edgar felt the intently listening silence. He strove to lighten his tone. 'I'll make it my business to deal with you myself,' he promised.

Harry waved the assurance aside and plunged into a fresh chapter of complaints.

Would-be customers appeared behind him in the doorway. 'We're holding up traffic,' Edgar pointed out, polite to the last.

Harry stood reluctantly aside and Edgar was able to make his escape. As he took himself swiftly off to the shelter of Fairbourne, Harry's parting shot winged after him: 'You haven't heard the last of this.'

In a cottage not far from the council estate, Norman Griffin, Jill Lingard's young man, lived with his mother, a widow in her fifties. Norman was an only child. His father had also worked in the building trade, in a casual fashion; he had been a good enough workman when he was sober and not engaged in picking fights. He had died not long after his son started school. For the greater part of Norman's existence he had been accustomed to being king of the castle.

No early-morning jogging for Norman, he got all the exercise he wanted in the course of a day's work. And he certainly didn't start his day with a paltry piece of rye crispbread, he tucked into a substantial breakfast every morning, set before him without fail, eaten and enjoyed without haste.

This morning, as he reached the half-way point of his meal, his mother ceased her bustling about and poured herself a companionable cup of tea. She sat down opposite him to drink it.

He looked across at her. 'Jill and me, we seem to have decided something last night. We're getting engaged on her birthday, the first of December.'

A smile of genuine pleasure flashed across his mother's face. 'That is good news! She'll make you a good wife, she's got her head well screwed on. When are you thinking of getting married?'

He shrugged. 'When we can settle on somewhere to live.'

She jumped in at once. 'No reason why the pair of you can't live here with me, to start with, at any rate. Your bedroom's a decent size and you could have the front room to yourselves.'

By way of reply he gave an indeterminate grunt. There was no mistaking his meaning but she wasn't offended, her suggestion had merely been a spur-of-the-moment notion. She took another drink of her tea. 'Harry Lingard's house,' she said reflectively as she set her cup down. 'Who gets that after he's gone?'

'Half to Jill and half to Gareth,' Norman replied at once.

'It could be many a long day before Jill gets her share,' his mother commented. 'Harry's as fit as a flea, he could live to be a hundred.' Another thought struck her. 'What are you doing about a ring? Anything decent's sure to cost a fortune. And Jill's not a girl to wear any kind of cheap rubbish.'

He laughed. 'I wasn't thinking of giving her cheap rubbish. She likes old things. I thought I might find her a nice old ring, something with a bit of quality. There's an antiques market in Wychford every Friday, I can try there.' He was often over that way in the course of his work.

On Wednesday evening Jill Lingard came out of York House, the Cannonbridge department store where she worked, to catch her bus. She stayed on the bus past her usual stop—she shared a rented terrace house, a few minutes' walk from Whitethorn Common, with two other working girls. She alighted by the council estate where her grandfather lived, she frequently dropped in on him in this way and he always made her welcome. He hadn't long got in from work himself when she knocked at his door; he gave her a cup of tea as they talked.

'Norman and I decided last night we're going to get

engaged on my birthday,' she told him as she drank her tea.

He looked anything but pleased. 'You know my opinion of that young man,' he said flatly. 'Up to no good when he was a lad. I wouldn't go bail for his honesty now.'

'You're not fair to him,' she protested. 'He's never in any kind of trouble these days.'

He thrust out his lips. 'He's got bad blood in him, his father was no good.'

'Tom Mansell thinks well of him,' she pointed out.

He gave a snorting laugh. 'That's because they're cut out of the same cloth.'

She gave him back a look as stubborn as his own. 'I'm going to marry Norman, you may as well make up your mind to it.' She smiled suddenly. 'Give him a chance, Granddad. For my sake.'

He made no response to that but demanded with an air of challenge, 'Where are you thinking of living if you marry him? You needn't imagine I'll have the pair of you here with me.'

She jumped up. 'We've no intention of asking you. We'll find somewhere to suit us.'

He looked up at her. 'You really are set on marrying him? He'll take some managing.'

She gave him a smile full of confidence. 'I wouldn't want a man that didn't take some managing.' She stooped to drop a kiss on his bald pate. 'We're not going to fall out about it, are we, Granddad?'

He reached out and touched her hand. 'That's the last thing I'd want.' He got to his feet, picked up her coat from the back of a chair. Something that had been bobbing about in his brain for the last few days surfaced again as he walked with her to the door.

'I intend tackling Mansell about more money,' he told her. 'The tradesmen have all had a rise but nothing's been said about me.'

She saw the familiar light of battle in his eye. 'Don't be too hasty,' she cautioned. 'It's probably just an oversight.

If you try laying down the law to Mansell you're liable to find yourself out on your ear.'

Shortly before ten next morning Harry Lingard, busy in his duties about the yard, spotted the unmistakable figure of Tom Mansell getting out of his car. Beside him, as usual, the equally unmistakable figure of his son, Stuart.

Harry at once abandoned what he was doing and set off smartly to intercept Mansell. A few yards away, Norman Griffin was standing by his van, running his eye down the list of materials he had to pick up from the builders' merchant, deliver out to various sites. He saw Harry stride purposefully up to Mansell, he caught the expression on Harry's face. Norman lifted the bonnet of his van, stooped to peer inside, a position which enabled him to cock an unobtrusive ear in Mansell's direction. Through the medley of sounds in the yard he could just about make out the gist of what Harry was saying. Silly old fool, he thought as he caught the drift, what does he imagine he can gain, tackling Mansell like that in the open yard, with other men about? The rawest apprentice lad could have told him all he'd be likely to get out of that would be a flea in the ear.

There could be no mistaking the cutting tones of Mansell's brief response, even if his actual words couldn't be distinguished. Mansell turned on his heel and went rapidly off towards the office, with Stuart tagging along. Harry remained where he was, his back to Norman. Judging by his stance, the angle of his head, the rebuff had by no means vanquished him.

Norman lowered the bonnet into place, climbed into his van and drove out of the yard. His route took him along Whitethorn Road. As he approached the common he saw, a little way ahead, Claire Holroyd standing alone at the bus stop, turning the pages of a book. She glanced up as he came to a halt beside her. He leaned across and opened the passenger door. 'Hello, there.' He gave her a cheerful smile. 'Hop in, I'll give you a lift into town.'

She hesitated. He picked up a duster from the dashboard

shelf, whisked it over the passenger seat with a flourish. 'Not a speck of dust, milady, clean as a whistle. Come on, hop in.'

She smiled suddenly, closed her book and stepped into the van.

In the hushed atmosphere of the Ladies' Coat Salon at York House, Claire stood before a long mirror, contemplating with an air of profound concentration the coat she had almost decided on. Jill Lingard, who was attending to her, stood near by without speaking; she knew better than to interrupt with some comment of her own when matters had reached this critical stage.

Claire turned this way and that, studying the slender, classic cut of the coat. Of supple, lightweight tweed, a subtle blend of soft greys and misty blues, with a touch of dark chestnut; suède-covered buttons in the same dark chestnut, an elegant suède trim edging the pockets.

She tilted her head in thought. The coat was undeniably expensive, but not, she finally judged, too expensive; she could just about get away with it. Edgar wasn't a man to throw his money around, nor to stand silently by while others threw it around on his behalf, but neither could he be described as close-fisted. Any purchase within reason and she would hear no complaint when he studied the monthly statement from their joint bank account.

She gave Jill a smiling nod of decision. 'I'll take it.'

'I'm sure you've made the right choice,' Jill assured her with total sincerity. It was always a pleasure to attend to Mrs Holroyd. She helped her off with the coat. 'Would you like us to deliver it?'

'Yes, please.' Claire stood pondering. 'A suède beret might be an idea for windy days, it might go well with the coat.'

'They've got some beautiful suède berets in the millinery department,' Jill told her. 'They've just come in. I'm sure you couldn't do better than one of those.'

A few minutes later, when Claire had gone off in search of

her beret and there was a temporary lull in the department, another assistant, a woman who had recently joined the staff, middle-aged, with a sharp, knowing face, came over to where Jill was replacing coats on a rail.

'I saw you serving Claire Holroyd,' she said. Claire Holroyd, Jill registered, not Mrs Holroyd. 'Do you know her?' Jill asked.

'I can't exactly say I know her,' the assistant answered with a movement of her shoulders. 'I worked with her at Hartley's a few years back.' Hartley's was a high-class establishment not far from York House, combining the functions of stationer, newsagent, bookstore and gift-shop. 'I suppose I knew her as well as anyone there—and that's not saying much. She was never one to stand around chatting, she was always reserved. She came to Hartley's straight from school, she worked there until her accident.'

'What accident was that?'

'She was in a car crash. Eight years ago now, that must be. She never went back to Hartley's after she was better, she got herself a job with the council, in the housing department.'

'She must have been really beautiful as a girl.' Jill felt not the faintest twinge of envy, securely content with her own ordinary share of looks; Norman thought her pretty and that was enough.

'The accident took the bloom off her all right,' the assistant said on a note of satisfaction. She leaned forward confidentially. 'I saw a piece in the local paper a couple of weeks back, about Claire's old boyfriend. He's back in Cannonbridge, got himself a senior job in Calthrop's, the estate agents, that's where he worked before. Ashworth, his name is, Robert Ashworth, he's a qualified surveyor.'

'Ashworth,' Jill repeated. 'My grandfather read me that piece out of the paper. He worked at Calthrop's till he retired, he's always interested in anything to do with the firm.'

'Claire was never actually engaged to Robert Ashworth,' the assistant enlarged. 'But we all took it for granted they'd

get married. Then she was in the car crash and that seemed
to be the end of it—don't ask me why, I never did know
the ins and outs of it. Ashworth left Cannonbridge and got
a job somewhere else. I heard he got married not long
afterwards—on the rebound, I shouldn't wonder. The
daughter of some businessman, so they said, pretty well-
heeled.' She slanted at Jill a look full of meaning. 'Robert
Ashworth's a good-looking man, a lot better looking than
Edgar Holroyd.' Her smile was laced with malice. 'I
wonder if Edgar knows Ashworth is back.'

A few minutes later Diane Holroyd drove into the York
House car park. Her own little car was in for a service, she
was temporarily using one of her father's vehicles. She got
out of the car and walked round towards the front of the
store. As she turned the corner of the building she saw
her sister-in-law come out through the swing doors. Claire
didn't see her, she set off in the opposite direction. Diane
walked slowly on, looking fixedly after the elegant figure
moving gracefully away into the distance.

At a quarter past twelve Claire left the public library. Her
face wore a look of satisfaction; she had managed to pick
up no fewer than four books on her college reading list.

The weather was fine, pleasantly warm. She strolled
without haste towards the bus stop. Never any rush to get
back to Fairbourne in the middle of the day, Edgar was
never at home for lunch during the week.

Ahead of her on the other side of the road lay the
imposing premises of Calthrop's, auctioneers and estate
agents. She glanced over at the frontage, ran her eye along
the windows, as she had done lately whenever she went by,
ever since the day towards the end of August when she had
come across the paragraph about Robert Ashworth in the
local paper.

She came to an abrupt halt, her heart thumping. She
stared across at the middle window on the first floor. A tall
man, thirty-five or so, stood with his head half turned away,

talking to someone behind him. He moved his head and she saw his face: Robert Ashworth, almost exactly as she remembered him. Her heart beat so fiercely she feared she might faint.

Robert glanced down, his eye lighted on her. He froze. She stood looking up at him, incapable of movement.

He leaned forward, smiled down at her, raised a hand in greeting. She felt a great rush of release. She smiled, waved back.

A young man carrying a sheaf of papers came up to Robert, spoke to him. Robert turned from the window, casting a final look in her direction.

On the bus home she sat lost in thought. The moment she closed the front door of Fairbourne behind her she dumped her things in the hall and went down to the basement, kept in immaculate order by her husband. She went to the shelves where he stacked old newspapers and magazines until he took them along to the recycling depot. It didn't take her long to find what she was looking for: the local weekly paper from the end of August.

She knew precisely where to find the item about Robert's appointment: half way down the third right-hand page. She gazed intently at Ashworth's image, sharp and clear for a newspaper photograph. She scanned the paragraph with close attention but it yielded nothing fresh, no forgotten detail. Only the same facts implacably confronting her: Ashworth was married with two young children, his family would be joining him later.

She restored the paper to the pile and went slowly back up the stairs. She changed her clothes, made herself a snack lunch before setting diligently about household chores. She was busy in the sitting-room when the phone rang. Her face lit up. She ran into the hall, snatched up the receiver, spoke her number.

'Claire?' asked a male voice at the other end.

CHAPTER 3

Summer gave way to autumn, the leaves turned gold. Dusk and dawn were veiled in mist, the pungent smoke of garden bonfires rose blue on the weekend air.

The Acorn dinner-dance marking the centenary of the club took place on the last Friday in October. A glittering occasion, much talked over before and after, fully written up and photographed for the local press.

On the evening of the second Thursday in November Harry Lingard left work and drove home in his little van. He liked to leave promptly, there was always some pressing chore or urgent piece of business awaiting him.

The bulk of his spare time during the latter part of every week was taken up delivering copies of the *Bazaar*, a local freesheet, long established; he had been one of the earliest recruits to the distribution team. His territory had grown over the years as distributors in adjoining districts fell by the wayside, and his round was currently the largest and certainly the best conducted; it earned him a very useful sum. He liked to vary the way in which he covered his territory, it helped to keep his interest alive. He prided himself on getting his deliveries finished by Saturday evening. Some distributors were still shouldering their satchels on Sunday morning; Harry considered that a slack way of going on.

The bundles of papers were dropped off at his house around two o'clock on Thursday afternoon, they were stacked on the bench in the front porch, which he left unlocked for the purpose. Before he set off on his first delivery he always glanced swiftly through the For Sale columns, in order to be the first, if possible, to snap up some bargain he could work on, re-sell privately or through the auction rooms. He had often struck lucky in this way.

At six-thirty on this nippy Thursday evening he was

ready to leave on his first foray, the official satchel—scarlet, with the *Bazaar* logo in black and white—slung over his shoulder. He never carried too heavy a load, always took time between trips, if he felt the need, to sit down in his kitchen for a hot drink or a snack. He took care to dress sensibly against the weather. This evening he wore woollen mittens and woollen cap nattily striped in brown and white; his feet were in black trainers, comfortably padded. The collar of his quilted grey jacket was turned up round his ears. In one lapel he sported an outsize red poppy—next Sunday was Remembrance Day, a notable point in Harry's year.

As he went out, locking the door behind him, he gave his customary good-neighbour glance over at the adjoining semi, checking all was in order. The house was in darkness, it had stood empty since the last tenants had left two weeks ago, to move to another town.

He was half way through his second trip when he ran into his granddaughter and her boyfriend on their way to a cinema. 'I've just been to tea at Norman's,' Jill told him. 'Mrs Griffin invited me. She went to a lot of trouble, she laid on a marvellous spread.' She eyed him teasingly. 'Isn't it about time you thought of inviting Norman to tea?'

Harry gave her a quelling look. Norman stood by in silence, his expression tinged with amusement. 'What about next Sunday?' Jill's tone was light but Harry saw by her eye that she meant business.

'Next Sunday's no good.' He couldn't repress a note of satisfaction. 'I'm going over to see Cyril Shearman in the afternoon, he'll be expecting me.' He had served in the army with Shearman, now a widower a few years older than Harry, no longer in good health; he lived in a retirement home in pleasant rural surroundings a few miles from Cannonbridge. Harry went over to see him every couple of months, he certainly wouldn't miss seeing him on Remembrance Sunday.

'No problem,' Jill batted back at once. 'We'll come to supper instead.' Her eyes sparkled with good-humoured determination. You'll accept Norman one day, her look told him, I'll make sure you do.

All at once he caved in. 'All right then,' he agreed. An engagement, after all, was very far from being the same thing as a marriage. Young women had been known to change their minds. In the meantime he had no intention of falling out with his only granddaughter over such a trifle as Sunday supper.

He plastered a smile on his face. 'Next Sunday it is. I'll see you both around seven-thirty.'

Remembrance Sunday dawned bright and clear, perfect weather for the annual parades. Harry would be marching to a special church service alongside other veterans, banners held proudly aloft, brass bands in stirring attendance.

He gave his shoes an extra shine, put on his best dark suit, a spotless white shirt freshly laundered by himself. He pinned his campaign medals to his chest, his poppy on one lapel, the gold regimental badge he always wore, on the other. On his little finger the gold signet ring with his entwined initials that his wife had given him the day they were married; on his wrist the gold watch bought for him two years ago on his seventieth birthday, engraved on the back with name and date, a joint present from Gareth and Jill.

When he was ready he surveyed himself with satisfaction in the long mirror of his wardrobe, then he let himself out of the house and set off for the rallying-point at a briskly military pace.

Tom Mansell's housekeeper had taken particular pains with today's lunch. Only the family, Mansell had told her, but a very special occasion. It wasn't till the coffee stage that Mansell rose to his feet with an air of ceremony.

'Thirteen years ago today,' he said, 'I took control of Dobie and Mansell's. I give you a toast.' He lifted his coffee-cup. He allowed nothing stronger than coffee in his house, he had been raised in a strictly teetotal household. 'To the next thirteen years!' The others echoed the toast, raised their cups, smiling.

Mansell remained on his feet. 'I give you another toast. To the new yard, in Wychford!' He saw the quick movement of all three heads, the look of surprise on the face of Diane and Stuart. But not on Lester's face. Lester's expression showed satisfaction, confirmation of something already guessed. Smart lad, Mansell thought with approval, no flies on Lester. 'We'll be starting the ball rolling any day now.' Mansell raised his cup again. 'To the future!'

Before setting off to see Cyril Shearman Harry checked that all was ready for supper. Traffic was light and he reached the home shortly after three. Shearman was, as always, pleased to see him, they sat in the almost deserted lounge, talking over old times. At half past four several residents came down from their rooms for tea and cake, dispensed from a trolley by a member of staff.

Shearman nodded over in the direction of one of the residents, an old woman with a weatherbeaten face, a countrified look, making her uncertain way into the lounge, leaning on a stick. 'That's Mrs Vaile,' Shearman told Harry. 'She came here a few weeks back from one of the company's other homes.' There were a number of homes under the same management, scattered over a wide area; residents could move, within reason, between one home and another. Mrs Vaile had sold her own house in the summer and had gone initially to a company home by the sea.

'She's been a widow for some years,' Shearman added. 'Her husband served in the army during the war.' He mentioned the name of Vaile's regiment which had fought more than once alongside their own.

Harry was immediately interested, he would like a word with Mrs Vaile. Shearman took him over to where she sat alone, drinking tea. She was pleased to see them. Harry sat down beside her and began to chat in a friendly fashion. He asked about her late husband, told her he would be delighted to do anything he could for her, as the widow of a man who had been—more or less—an old comrade-in-arms.

Before long she was telling him the saga of the last few difficult years, how she had at last decided to sell her house and move into a home. As she talked Harry grew even more interested. He began to ask questions; she answered freely. A gleam appeared in his eye. His questions became more inquisitorial, the gleam in his eye brighter.

Over supper Jill inquired how her grandfather had found Cyril Shearman.

'He's in pretty good spirits,' Harry told her. 'He introduced me to a new resident, I had a long talk with her.' He narrowed his eyes. 'A very interesting talk.'

'Oh?' Jill said idly. 'What was so interesting about it?'

Harry looked knowing. 'That's what Tom Mansell's going to find out.'

'Mansell?' Jill echoed. 'What has this old woman got to do with Tom Mansell?'

He didn't answer that. 'I'm going to tackle Mansell about it in the morning,' he declared with relish. 'I'll sort him out properly this time.'

Jill laughed. 'It's a wonder you haven't put the world to rights by now, you've been sorting folk out for long enough.'

He pushed his cup towards her for a refill. 'I'd better make some fresh tea,' she decided. 'This isn't too hot.' She went along to the kitchen.

'I've got Mansell well and truly by the tail this time,' Harry couldn't resist saying to Norman. 'He's not going to find it so easy to wriggle out of this one. I've had my suspicions once or twice before that there was something going on, a nice little band of brothers operating. I've a pretty good notion of the kind of tricks some of these johnnies get up to, given half a chance. But I could never get my teeth into anything solid.' He thrust out his lips. 'I've got hold of something good and solid this time and I'm not letting go.'

'What is it you fancy you're on to?' Norman asked with interest.

Harry tapped the side of his nose. 'Never you mind. I'm hardly likely to give you the details, you're Mansell's man.' He smiled grimly. 'Mansell still hasn't given me the rise I'm entitled to. We'll see how he likes what I've got to say tomorrow.'

'Is that what all this is about?' Norman asked in amusement. 'Some ploy to get your rise? You want to have a word with Lester Holroyd, he'll see you right. That's what you should have done in the first place instead of shouting the odds at Mansell. You could hardly expect him to take kindly to that. What boss would?'

Among Lester Holroyd's varied responsibilities was the general oversight of the yard office, though its day-to-day running lay in the capable hands of a middle-aged woman who had worked for Mansell for a number of years; she had the help of two part-timers, young married women.

On Monday morning Lester reached the office earlier than usual. He had woken well before the alarm was due to ring, his head buzzing with ideas churned up by his father-in-law's announcement at the end of Sunday lunch. He was sorting through the mail when Mansell drove into the yard with Stuart beside him. A minute or two later Mansell put his head round the office door.

'I want to catch Norman before he goes off out.' He broke off at the sound of an incoming vehicle and glanced over his shoulder. 'It's all right, that's Norman now.' He went off to where Norman was getting out of his van; Stuart followed. 'I want a word with you,' Mansell told Norman.

And I want a word with you, Norman answered in his mind.

'You're not on the carpet,' Mansell assured him with a grin. 'You're going to like what I've got to say unless I'm very much mistaken.'

I very much doubt you're going to like what I've got to say to you, Norman responded inside his head.

Mansell began to tell him about his plans for the new yard, the likelihood of a place in the new set-up for Norman, carrying some responsibility.

Over in the office Lester glanced out of the window and saw the trio standing by the van: Mansell smiling, talking, gesticulating; Norman looking pleased and stimulated, nodding his head; Stuart close by, not joining in but listening, observing.

As Lester watched he saw Harry Lingard's little van drive into the yard. Harry got out but he didn't go off about his duties, he remained where he was, his vehicle screening him from the other three. He stood looking intently across at them.

Lester went on watching. Mansell stopped talking, he clapped Norman on the arm in a gesture of friendly encouragement and turned to go. Norman's pleased expression vanished. He began to talk rapidly, with a serious look. Mansell's face changed. He stood arrested, half-turned away, frowning down at the ground; Stuart listened with keen interest.

Norman's flow ceased, Mansell turned to face him. He appeared to fire a series of questions, some of which Norman seemed to deal with at once, others he met with a movement of his shoulders or a slow shake of his head, as if signifying he didn't know the answer to that one.

The exchange ended. Men were moving about the yard. As Mansell went striding off with Stuart following, Harry Lingard stepped out from the shelter of his van to intercept them. Mansell halted, regarding Harry with a face of steel. Norman Griffin, on his way across the yard, glanced back and saw the two men in fierce altercation, with Stuart a silent onlooker. Norman halted for a moment, then continued on his way.

The office door opened and one of the female clerks came in. She greeted Lester and at once raised a query about an office matter. As Lester turned from the window to speak to her the phone rang. The day had begun in earnest, there was no more looking out of windows.

It was Jill Lingard's intention to call in on her grandfather on her way home from work on Thursday evening. In the event she left York House a little later than usual, missing the bus she normally caught. It was a raw evening, with a stiff breeze. She decided not to stand waiting in the cold for the next bus but to walk along to the stop by the college, where there was a shelter.

As she approached the college she saw a bus pull up at the other side of the road and passengers alight. Several crossed over towards the college; among them she spotted Mrs Holroyd carrying some books. She was wearing the grey-blue tweed coat Jill had sold her—and a suède beret, she noted with professional interest. I was right about the beret, Jill thought with satisfaction, it goes beautifully with the coat.

Mrs Holroyd saw her, they smiled, exchanged a word of greeting. How well she looks, Jill thought, better than she ever remembered seeing her. Under the street lights she seemed to wear a bloom of health and happiness.

When Jill arrived at her grandfather's she found him despatching a hasty meal before starting out on the first of his freesheet trips. 'I'm glad I caught you,' she told him. 'I won't delay you. I'm going over to Gareth's tomorrow evening, straight from work, I'm staying with them for a few days.' She was using up what was left of her annual leave. 'I rang Gareth and fixed it.' She was going by train, Gareth would run her back on Tuesday evening. 'He said he'd like to look in on you for an hour or so after he's dropped me,' she added. Gareth worked long hours, it was some time since Harry had seen him. 'He wants to know if you'll be in around eight o'clock on Tuesday.'

'I'll make it my business to be in,' Harry responded with energy. 'Tell him I'll be delighted to see him. Give my love to Anne and the children.'

She let herself out into the chill air. She wouldn't be

seeing Norman this evening; she was staying in to wash her hair, pack her bag, get an early night.

Friday evening was overcast and blustery, and though the rain held off it was cold enough to keep the strollers from the common.

Mrs Griffin had a good hot meal prepared for Norman, as she had every evening. By the time he had washed and changed she had it ready for him on the table in the kitchen, cosy from the warmth of the stove. She wore a housecoat, her hair was in rollers. She had just had a bath, and would be dolling herself up to go out as soon as she had cleared the table after Norman finished eating. Friday was one of her social club evenings; she went along to the club two or three evenings a week. She always went by bus but could usually rely on getting a lift home. She enjoyed every visit to the club but Friday nights were special, that was when they had the olde-tyme dancing. Tonight she must get there early, there was going to be a little ceremony before the dancing started, the presentation of a retirement gift to the club secretary.

Norman sat down before his piled-up plate and attacked it with a hearty appetite. His mother hovered about, cutting bread, pouring tea. She ran an eye over what he was wearing: his new trousers, good jacket, smartest shirt. 'You going out?' she asked.

'Might go along to the pub,' he said between mouthfuls. She gave a little nod. He liked a glass of beer with his mates, more to be sociable than anything else, no harm in that; she never ceased to be thankful he didn't drink the way his father had done.

By seven she was dressed, ready for the evening. She stuck her head round the door of the little workroom opening off the kitchen where Norman was fiddling with his old radios—they had been his hobby since schooldays. 'I thought you were going out,' she said.

He didn't look up. 'I've decided not to bother. Might as

well make use of the time while Jill's away, it's a chance to get on with this.'

'You should change out of your good clothes, ' she advised. When he made no response she let it go. She very rarely pressed a point with Norman, she had learned long ago that it didn't pay.

He glanced at his watch. 'You'll miss your bus,' he warned.

She was galvanized into motion. 'Right, then, I'm off. I'll be back around half-twelve or one.'

In the early hours of Saturday morning the force of the wind greatly increased. It blew strongly all day, driving clouds before it, tossing branches of trees on the common. Late on Saturday night it began to slacken in strength. By breakfast time on Sunday it had fallen calm again.

The day was bright and sunny. Householders emerged to wash their cars, tidy their gardens. In the ground-floor flat of a converted Victorian house on Whitethorn Road, Miss Tarrant, a middle-aged spinster, supervisor of the typing pool in a Cannonbridge firm, woke late: gone half past nine, she saw by the clock.

She got out of bed and drew back the curtains. She wouldn't bother with lunch today, she'd have a good breakfast and then get on with the hundred and one jobs awaiting her. She had recently bought the flat and was currently in the process of doing it up, furnishing it, tackling the garden.

In the kitchen a little later she discovered to her annoyance that she'd forgotten to buy bread yesterday. Fortunately the corner shop across the common was open on Sunday mornings, she could nip out and get a loaf.

She put on her coat and went out into the sparkling sunshine. She walked briskly up the road, crossed over on to the common. As she drew near Fairbourne she heard the sound of shears. She glanced in as she passed the front gate and saw Mr Holroyd at work a few feet away. She had some slight acquaintance with him in his official capacity; before she bought her flat she had been a council tenant.

She called out a friendly greeting. 'Much better weather today,' she added. He looked up, gave her a few words in reply.

She halted as a thought struck her. 'You wouldn't by any chance have finished with your copy of the *Bazaar*? Mine doesn't seem to have been delivered. I like to read the small ads, I'm still on the lookout for things for the flat.'

Edgar shook his head. 'I'm afraid I can't help you. My copy hasn't been delivered either.'

It occurred to her as she resumed her quick pace that she could ask at the corner shop, they might have a copy to spare.

A few yards ahead, young lads, eight or nine years old, were kicking a football around with more enthusiasm than skill. The ball suddenly came straight at her; if she hadn't jumped aside it would have struck her in the face. 'Watch what you're doing!' she called out sharply.

One of the lads came racing after the ball, throwing her a grin of apology as he darted by. A few moments later another random shot sent the ball soaring over the gate of the last house on this part of the common. Some of the boys snatched open the gate and ran in after the ball. They began to search about in the long grass bordering the drive, the drifts of dead leaves. One agile lad climbed nimbly up into a tall tree and directed his gaze over the ground below.

Miss Tarrant strode over to the gateway. She clicked her tongue at the sight of the youngsters ferreting about; they had no business in there at all, roaming over a private garden. She said as much in ringing tones.

'It's all right,' a lad assured her. 'There's no one at home, there never is this time of year. It's an old couple live there, they always go to Spain for the winter.'

She wasn't in the least mollified. 'That doesn't give you the right to trespass on their property.'

Another lad suddenly spied the football in a tangle of undergrowth and fell upon it with a cry of triumph.

'Come along!' Miss Tarrant ordered. 'Out of here, all of you!' They ran shouting and laughing out on to the common again. All except the lad up the tree. He was right at the top now, his feet securely lodged, glancing with lively interest.

Miss Tarrant marched in through the gate and positioned herself at the foot of the tree. 'You too,' she called up to him. 'Come along down. At once.'

He seemed not to hear. He craned forward, staring down into the shrubbery. She called up to him again, loudly and forcefully. He made no reply but suddenly began to descend the tree, scrambling swiftly down, dropping to the ground at her feet. He scarcely glanced at her but darted off at once towards the shrubbery. She set her jaw and went after him.

He came to a halt, stooped and peered under the drooping branches. Her gaze travelled after his, to a heap of bracken fronds. She uttered a gasping cry. A pair of legs was sticking out from the bracken, legs clad in dark trousers, the feet shod in black trainers. Her heart lurched in her chest, and she reached out to steady herself against a tree.

The lad swept aside the bracken, revealing the rest of the body, face down in the undergrowth, clad in a grey quilted jacket, a woollen cap striped in brown and white, darkly stained with blood.

CHAPTER 4

Mrs Griffin liked to dish up Sunday dinner promptly at one-thirty. At a quarter past twelve, Norman, who had spent the morning tinkering with his radios, washed and changed, ready for his usual pint of beer in the pub up the road.

The moment he walked in through the pub door he knew something was up, there was none of the customary laughter and badinage, only serious looks, hushed voices. 'What's going on?' he asked one of the regulars.

'Old Harry Lingard,' the man told him. 'They've found his body on Whitethorn Common.'

'His body?' Norman echoed with a look of stupefaction. 'You don't mean he's dead?'

'He's dead all right,' the man responded with energy. 'Back of his head bashed in. The common's crawling with police, they've got it all cordoned off.' A thought struck him. 'That girlfriend of yours, Harry's granddaughter, isn't she?'

'Yes, she is. She's not here just now, she's over at her brother's for the weekend. I'd better let the police know.' He left the pub at once. To reach the common he had to pass his own house again. He went inside for a moment to tell his mother the grim news and where he was bound; he had no idea how long he'd be.

She was thunderstruck. 'It'll be one of those muggers,' she declared with conviction as soon as she'd got her breath back. 'I can't believe it, I've known Harry all my life.' She began to cry.

He put an arm round her shoulders. 'I can't stop,' he told her. 'I've got to get along to the common.'

Police in gumboots and overalls were carrying out a fingertip search; scattered knots of onlookers watched from a permitted distance. The police photographers had finished their work, the body had gone to the mortuary. Pressmen from the local papers were in evidence; the local radio station had put out a newsflash.

The police doctor had put the time of death, at a rough estimate, at between six o'clock and midnight on Friday evening. The back of the skull had been shattered with a blunt instrument; minor scratches and abrasions to the face would seem to have been caused by the body being dragged by the feet, face down, over the last yard or two before being dumped under the trees.

The body was fully clothed but there was nothing in any of the pockets, no personal possessions of any kind on the body. There was no sign of any weapon, nor any sign of the scarlet satchel of freesheets Harry must surely have been carrying.

When Norman reached the common Detective Chief

Inspector Kelsey was talking to the coroner in the driveway of the property where the body had been discovered. The coroner, a local doctor of long experience, always made a point of viewing the body in the spot where it was found, if at all possible.

Norman spoke to a constable, saying he wished to speak to the officer in charge. He was directed to the driveway and stood waiting till the two men had finished their conversation. He saw the Chief Inspector register his presence. A big, solidly built man, Chief Inspector Kelsey, with massive shoulders. He had a head of thickly springing carroty hair, a freckled face dominated by a large, squashy nose.

At last the two men shook hands and the coroner went off to his car. Kelsey gave Norman an inquiring glance.

Norman introduced himself and explained about Jill and Gareth. Kelsey's shrewd green eyes ranged over him as he talked. A constable had already been despatched to Harry Lingard's house but had got no response there or at the adjoining semi. A neighbour further along had seen Harry leaving his house with his satchel of papers at around six-fifteen on Friday evening.

'Jill's not due back till Tuesday evening,' Norman told the Chief.

'We'll get over there and break the news,' the Chief said. But he had one or two matters to attend to first.

'All right if I come along?' Norman asked. 'Jill will be very upset, I'd like to be with her.'

'I don't see why not.' Kelsey consulted his watch. 'You can get off home now. Meet us at Harry Lingard's house at two-thirty sharp, you can ride with us.'

Five minutes before the appointed time Norman reached the house and stationed himself by the police car. Chief Inspector Kelsey, accompanied by Detective-Sergeant Lambert, was talking to the constable on guard. In the absence of any keys to the house the Chief had felt no necessity to force an entry; it was possible one of the two grandchildren might have a key. He had contented himself for the present with an external tour of the property.

Every door and window in the house had been carefully secured, the curtains were all closed; nowhere any sign of disturbance. Through the porch window the Chief could see copies of the *Bazaar* stacked in bundles on the bench.

The garage was locked, windows fastened; a small van was visible inside. The garden shed was not locked, though its windows were closed.

At two-thirty Kelsey strode out to the car. Norman was to ride in front beside the sergeant. The Chief took his seat in the rear where he immediately leaned back and closed his eyes, uttering not one syllable during the journey. It took three-quarters of an hour to reach Gareth Lingard's cottage which stood on the outskirts of a town; it had a sizeable piece of land attached.

An estate car was drawn up near the open front door when the police vehicle pulled up. A boy about four years old, wearing outdoor clothes, was jumping on and off the doorstep, counting his jumps in a clear treble. As Sergeant Lambert put his hand on the gate Gareth and his wife came out of the house, deep in conversation. Anne was leading a toddler by the hand; they were all dressed in outdoor clothes. They made to turn towards the estate car and caught sight of the trio at the gate. They halted; Gareth looked over at them with inquiry. He spotted Norman, his face took on a look of puzzlement.

The three men walked up the path. As the Chief was introducing himself Jill Lingard came out of the house to join the others. She gave a little cry of surprise at the sight of Norman. In the same moment her ears caught what the Chief was saying. Norman locked eyes with her but he said nothing, he made no move in her direction.

'I'm afraid we bring bad news,' Kelsey said gently, now including Jill in his gaze. 'Very bad news. I think it's best if we all go inside.'

'Yes, of course.' Gareth led the way into the sitting-room where Norman took up his position at Jill's side.

'It's about your grandfather, Mr Harold Lingard,'

Kelsey began. Jill gave a gasp and put a hand up to her face. Norman slid an arm around her shoulders.

'I'm very sorry to have to tell you he's dead,' Kelsey went on. Jill lowered her head and began to cry.

'Dead?' Gareth echoed in shocked astonishment. 'Has there been an accident?'

The Chief shook his head. He began to explain the circumstances in which Harry had been found. His bleak recital was punctuated by Jill's sobs, questions from Gareth. Anne sat in silence, her face full of concern and sympathy; the two children stared at the visitors.

Anne appeared to be a sensible and practical young woman. She produced a tray of tea and then busied herself packing Jill's suitcase. On the journey back to Cannonbridge Norman and Jill travelled with Gareth behind the police vehicle; their first stop was at the hospital mortuary. Gareth went inside with the two policemen to make the formal identification. When they came out again he looked white and shaken; he said nothing as he got back into the car. Norman offered to drive and Gareth made no resistance; Norman followed the police car to the council estate.

Gareth had no keys to his grandfather's house; neither he nor Jill had ever had any. But Jill knew of a key to the back door, kept in the garden shed. 'Granddad put it there for me,' she explained in unsteady tones, 'in case I ever needed it. I hardly ever used it.'

They went along to the shed and Jill indicated a pair of secateurs lying on a corner shelf. The Chief took a pen from his pocket and with the tip raised the end of the secateurs, revealing the key; he left it where it was. Both key and secateurs were of old, dull metal, far from smooth. Neither could be touched before being tested, although there was little hope of useful prints.

With Gareth's permission they broke a pane in the kitchen window to gain entry. Inside, all was scrupulously neat and tidy, the whole house spotlessly clean. Harry's private papers were kept in a bureau in the sitting-room but the bureau was locked. Gareth was able to supply the name of his grandfather's bank and the solicitor who had drawn up his will two years ago.

At the Chief's request Gareth and Jill set about compiling a list of what their grandfather might be expected to have on him. Watch, ring, regimental badge. Pigskin wallet —a present from Jill last Christmas. Zipped coin purse, oldish, of brown leather. Notebook, ballpoint pen, van keys, house keys—including the key to the bureau. A white handkerchief.

When the list was as complete as they could make it, Jill looked up at the Chief, her eyes bright with tears. 'Is that what Granddad's life was valued at?' she demanded fiercely. 'Is that what some thug thought it worth killing him for?'

CHAPTER 5

The Chief was at the police station early on Monday morning to assess the first results of the house-to-house inquiries before going along to the General Hospital where the post-mortem on Harry Lingard was shortly due to begin.

As always with a case of this nature there was no shortage of reports, once the news of the crime had been made public, of unsavoury-looking characters having recently been seen in the area. Vehicles, too; the public could always be relied on to recall strange vehicles parked in out-of-the-way spots, appearing abruptly, vanishing equally suddenly. None of these reports struck the Chief's practised eye as having any real significance, though all must be scrupulously followed up, however much valuable time and effort was wasted in the process.

One report did briefly arrest the Chief's attention, that of a householder, a young single mother living in a street off Whitethorn Road. She had got up during Friday night to attend to her crying infant. After she put the baby back in its cot she went down to the kitchen to make herself a hot drink. On her way downstairs she heard screeching sounds from the direction of the common, sufficiently loud and sudden to halt her on the stairs. She stood listening for a minute or so but there were no more screeches. Some freak of the wind, she told herself; it was certainly blowing strongly at the time, with fierce intermittent gusts. Or a fox, perhaps; they were not unknown at night around the common, they were capable of the most eerie, heart-stopping cries. She was able to give the time she had heard the sounds. When she entered the kitchen she had glanced up at the clock, a reliable timekeeper; it had shown twenty minutes past two.

It was when his eye fell upon this statement of the time that the Chief lost interest in the report. However variable the way in which Harry set about his round from one week to the next, it was scarcely conceivable that he could have been crossing the common at twenty past two in the morning. No other householder, the Chief noted, had reported hearing these screeching cries—but then, maybe, none of them had a two-month-old baby to get them out of bed at that time of night.

So far they hadn't come up with anyone who had actually spotted Harry putting a copy of the *Bazaar* through a letter-box that evening, nor had they discovered any householder on Harry's round who could tell them at what precise moment his own copy had dropped on to the mat.

The search of the common was not yet completed. It had yielded a variety of items; none appeared to have any connection with the murder. Nothing approximating to the blunt instrument they were seeking had so far turned up.

In one of the drawers of Harry's bureau, which had now been opened by a locksmith, they had found Harry's cheque-book and bank card but they had come across nothing that seemed to offer any clue to the crime.

Shortly after eleven the pathologist came out of the mortuary with Chief Inspector Kelsey; they stood talking in the corridor.

Harry Lingard had been in exceptionally good physical

condition for his age, he could well have been expected to live an active life into his late eighties.

Four savage blows had been dealt to the back of his head. The blows appeared to have been struck by a right-handed person, with both assailant and victim in an upright position; whether one or both were in motion at the time it was not possible to say. There had been little bleeding; the second blow had in all probability killed him. The assault had not required exceptional strength; it was not, for instance, beyond the power of a fit, strong female.

It wasn't possible to be more specific about the kind of blunt instrument used; some kind of heavy tool seemed most likely. Nor was it possible to fix the time of death with any certainty; the pathologist put it on Friday evening, between seven and midnight.

Gareth Lingard was not in a position to spend more time away from his business than was absolutely essential. He drove over to Cannonbridge in his lunch-hour to look in at the police station, learn the results of the post-mortem.

In the afternoon the Chief called in at Mansell's yard. Mansell was expecting them; Sergeant Lambert had phoned in the morning to make an appointment. The moment the police car drove in Mansell came out of the office with Stuart at his side. The Chief had some slight acquaintance with Mansell but he had never met Stuart. His father all over again, the Chief thought as the pair crossed the yard towards him.

'An appalling business,' Mansell said as they shook hands; he took them into the inner office. The Chief asked routine questions about the dead man and Mansell answered readily. Lingard had been an excellent worker, willing and obliging, unfailingly punctual, very honest. He had been well liked, had never been in any kind of trouble. Mansell knew of no personal or other difficulties. He seemed to take it for granted that Lingard had been the victim of a mugging.

His manner throughout was helpful and friendly, but

from time to time the Chief received a fleeting impression
of wariness and tension. Stuart was at no point called upon
to speak nor did he volunteer any observation; he held
himself alertly interested throughout.

The conversation didn't take long. As they were about
to leave, Lester Holroyd drove into the yard; he walked
across to the office, encountering the policemen in the doorway. There was a further brief exchange but Lester could
add nothing to what Mansell had told them.

Later in the day the local evening paper came out with
a four-page spread on the crime. Photographs of police
activities, interviews with residents of the council estate,
recounting Harry's many endeavours on their behalf.
Tributes from fellow members of the British Legion.

Mention was made of the fact that it was Harry's evidence which had been largely responsible on three separate
occasions over the past few years for the arrest and sentenc-
ing of local youths on charges of vandalism and thefts from
cars. What the paper didn't mention was that Harry had
reported yet another such case, lads breaking into cars, only
a matter of weeks back; he would have been giving evidence
when the case came up. The lads concerned were at present
out on bail.

A sizeable section of local opinion laid the murder firmly
at the door of some one or more of these tearaway youths,
either bent on revenge or maybe disturbed in the course
of committing some further misdemeanour. Possibly, such
opinion had it, there had been no serious intention of actually killing the old man, the wish had more probably been
merely to rough him up, teach him a lesson. Easy enough,
in the event, for someone to strike too hard, astonishing
himself—and any mates—by the violence of the aggression
sweeping over him.

But more general opinion in the local pubs inclined
towards a run-of-the-mill mugging that had got out of hand,
the victim being selected for ease in carrying out the robbery, with total indifference as to who that victim might be,

the perpetrators more than likely not from the locality at all.

It was on this last point that opinion most sharply divided, some firmly rejecting the possibility that local lads could be involved in such a brutal crime, others maintaining with equal vehemence that the choice of dumping-ground—a private garden with the owners absent—must surely argue a degree of local knowledge.

Both groups were united in believing more than one assailant must have been involved, probably with a vehicle of some sort nearby. How else account for the spiriting away of the satchel and freesheets? A lone attacker on foot, argued the know-alls, would scarcely set about lugging the body single-handed off the common and into the garden, and then attempt to make off under the street lights, weighed down with a heavy satchel, brilliantly coloured, specifically designed to be noticed.

Tuesday morning brought a conference and press briefing. At noon the Chief had an appointment with Harry Lingard's solicitor.

Harry's will was a straightforward document. After a number of bequests to charities he had actively supported, his estate was split down the middle between his two grandchildren. Apart from the house, Harry had owned stocks and shares, various other investments. 'A lot of folk are going to be surprised at the amount he leaves,' the solicitor said. 'He saved all his life, he was a shrewd investor.' Harry's wife had been the only child of a shopkeeper, she had inherited a substantial sum in her middle years; no mortgage had been needed when Harry came to buy his council house.

Gareth had been appointed joint executor with the solicitor. Both grandchildren knew the contents of the will; Harry had talked it over with them before the will was drawn up. To the best of the solicitor's knowledge Harry had always been on excellent terms with both grandchildren. As far as he knew, neither was in any financial difficulty.

The Chief pondered these points as he left the solicitor's office. Jill had reached Gareth's house around six-thirty on Friday evening. Anne was there with the children, Gareth came in from work shortly afterwards. They had spent the evening together in the house. Gareth's partner and his wife had come in for an hour or two after supper, arriving at about eight and leaving around ten-thirty. By eleven everyone had retired for the night.

Before returning to the station Kelsey called in at the bank and building society where Harry had held accounts. Both accounts showed substantial balances; there had been no unusual movement recently in either.

The afternoon saw an energetic round-up of every youth in the area who might be thought to have harboured a grudge against Harry Lingard. Clubs, discos and similar meeting-places were visited during the evening. Interviews took place in the police station, in the offices of clubs, in lads' homes, in the presence of parents where possible.

The effect of all this activity was to arouse a good deal of apprehension in a section of local society more usually remarkable for its carefree attitude to law and order. Petty crime might be an everyday staple but suspicion of murder was another kettle of fish altogether, one that had many of these characters quaking in their designer trainers.

Alibis for Friday evening were produced in the end for everyone—in some cases only after considerable red-faced shuffling about, understandable enough when it emerged that one pair had spent the evening rampaging over half the county in a succession of stolen cars; a second pair had improved the shining hours by nicking cigarettes and cash from a tobacconist's in another town; a third had amused themselves by breaking into an isolated dwelling some miles from Cannonbridge while the owners were out for the evening.

The youths currently on bail, against whom Harry would have given evidence, had operated as a gang of six, all living in the same area of Cannonbridge, a district with an unsavoury reputation, where the mere sight of a police car drawing up was normally enough to afflict every resident with dumbness, deafness, blindness and acute loss of memory.

Today, however, these afflictions were a good deal less severe and widespread. The fathers of some of the gang, themselves with records of one sort and another, were usually happy to turn a blind eye to whatever their sons got up to, no more in their indulgent eyes than might be expected from any lad of spirit. But on this occasion more than one of these citizens offered to beat the truth out of their offspring, given ten minutes without interference from the law.

It wasn't necessary to accept any of these obliging offers as the lads were able to account satisfactorily for the manner in which they had spent Friday evening. It appeared they had occupied themselves harmlessly for once. Two of the gang had taken part in a pub darts match at the other side of Cannonbridge, the rest had gone along to cheer them on. All six had remained in the pub till closing time and had then gone on with members of both teams to the nearby home of one of the captains where the team wives set about making coffee and sandwiches. There had been a party of sorts which broke up around one-thirty.

The inquest on Harold William Lingard took place at eleven on Wednesday morning. The proceedings were brief and formal, the inquest being adjourned with no date set for resumption; the body was released for burial. Few members of the public were present. Old hands knew initial proceedings were scarcely ever of much interest; it was resumed inquests that usually offered a better chance of eye-opening disclosures.

Among the few who did take their seats the Chief noticed a handsome, dark-haired young woman with a strong, passionate face. She came alone, sat alone, spoke to no one. She looked about with keen interest, listened intently, left the moment the proceedings ended. The Chief was certain he knew her face and after a minute or two it came to him that he had seen her once or twice with her father at functions in the town. She was Tom Mansell's daughter, Diane Holroyd, married to Lester Holroyd, Mansell's right-hand man.

When the Chief left the court house he found Gareth and Jill Lingard waiting for him at the foot of the steps. 'Something I remembered when I woke up this morning,' Gareth told him. Two or three years ago his grandfather had told him he kept a certain amount of ready cash in the house for his bits of dealing. 'He showed me where he kept it,' Gareth added. 'In a secret drawer of an old chest in his bedroom. He wanted me to know in case anything happened to him.' Gareth couldn't remember if Harry had mentioned a specific figure but his impression was that the sum might have been a few hundred pounds. 'I've no idea if he still kept money there,' he said, 'or how much it might be now. He never mentioned it again.'

'We'll get along there and take a look in the chest,' the Chief decided. Over his radio he arranged for a fingerprint officer to meet them at the house.

The kitchen window had now been repaired but this time they were able to make use of the backdoor key from the garden shed. The Chief had been right about the prints on the key and secateurs; such blurred traces as could be detected were too tiny to be of any use.

In Harry's bedroom Gareth showed them a Victorian chest of drawers, highly polished; he had never touched the chest since the day his grandfather had told him about the money and shown him how to open the drawer. The fingerprint officer set to work but could come upon no trace of prints anywhere on the gleaming surface. Following Gareth's instructions, he ran his fingers under a ledge above the top drawers, pressing at two points simultaneously to release the catch. The concealed drawer slid smoothly open.

Inside was a large old metal cashbox. And a money-belt made of canvas webbing. The cashbox was closed but not locked, although it was fitted with a lock holding a key; the metal surface showed a blur of fragmentary prints. The officer edged up the lid; the box was empty.

The money-belt had two webbing pockets furnished with large stud fasteners of some plastic material. Both pockets were open, both empty. The webbing offered no hope of prints but the studs showed blurred traces. The officer dealt with the prints on box, key and studs though there was little prospect of any useful result. Without being asked, Gareth volunteered in a matter-of-fact tone, 'You'll be needing fingerprints from Jill and me for elimination.' The offer was accepted and acted upon without comment.

Jill had known nothing of the secret drawer nor had she touched the chest in recent times. Gareth had never previously set eyes on the money-belt but he had once heard his grandfather mention it. That would be a year or two ago, one day when Gareth had expressed concern that his grandfather might be robbed if he carried sizeable amounts of money on him in the course of his deals. His grandfather had told him he needn't worry, he always wore a money-belt in such circumstances; he hadn't produced the belt to show Gareth nor had he indicated where it was usually kept.

Jill told the Chief she had known of the existence of the belt; Gareth had mentioned it to her, though she had forgotten about it until just now when she saw it in the drawer.

Had either Gareth or Jill ever mentioned the secret drawer or the money-belt to anyone else? Gareth answered at once, very positively: he was certain he had never spoken of either to anyone else, not even to his wife.

Jill didn't answer right away. When the Chief repeated his question she admitted, after further hesitation, that she had once mentioned the belt to Norman. There had been a case in the local paper a few months back, a youth convicted of handbag snatching. She had commented on the case to Norman, and it was then she had mentioned the money-belt.

'The backdoor key that was kept in the shed,' Kelsey went on. 'Did anyone else know of that?' He directed his question at Jill. Gareth hadn't known about the key.

Jill made no reply. Colour rose in her cheeks.

'Did you ever mention the key to Norman?' Kelsey pressed her.

She looked up at him with manifest unease. 'I can't remember mentioning it.'

'Was he with you on any occasion when you used the key?'

Again she hesitated. 'I don't think so,' she said at last, on the verge of tears.

'But you can't be sure?'

She didn't look at him, she shook her head in silence.

'What was your grandfather's attitude to Norman? Did he approve of your relationship?'

She pressed her hands together. 'Granddad was never fair to Norman,' she burst out suddenly. 'He never wanted me to have anything to do with him right from the start. Just because he got up to a bit of mischief years ago when he was a lad. And because his father wasn't up to much— as if Norman could be held responsible for that.'

Kelsey looked across at Gareth. 'Did your grandfather have anything more specific against Norman?'

Gareth glanced at Jill who stared defiantly back at him. 'I'm sorry,' he told her gently. 'I must tell the truth.' She set her lips in a mutinous line.

'Granddad did believe he had something more specific against Norman,' Gareth said in answer to the Chief. 'He spoke about it to Jill and me when she first started going out with Norman. The last year or two Norman was at school he had a part-time job, evenings, weekends, holidays, with a local dealer who does house clearances, goes to all the sales. When Norman left school the dealer took him on full time, helping out generally, going to sales with him and so on. One day at Calthrop's salerooms, when Granddad was working there, he noticed the dealer had a different lad with him. He asked what had happened to

Norman. The dealer told him he'd got rid of Norman, he was pretty sure he'd been helping himself to small items during house clearances. He had no positive proof, he wouldn't be bringing charges.' If Norman tried to get a job with any other dealer, he'd have a word, put the other man wise to his suspicions. But Norman hadn't looked for a job in the same field, he'd gone to Mansell's as a driver. The dealer had decided to say nothing, he felt there wouldn't be the same easy pickings with a builder.

Throughout this recital Jill had managed with some difficulty to keep silent. The moment Gareth had finished she sprang to Norman's defence. 'I told Norman what Granddad had said about him. I asked him if it was true. He said he'd never taken anything. I believe him. He's no thief.'

'Then why didn't he fight his dismissal?' the Chief wanted to know.

Her eyes flashed. 'What could he do? He was only a lad. He had no money, no one to fight for him, to advise him. And he wasn't actually sacked for stealing, he was just told he wouldn't be needed any more, though the dealer made it plain what he suspected. How could Norman actually prove he'd never taken anything? He decided to chalk it up to experience. He didn't go looking for a job with any other dealer, he never wanted to find himself in the same position again.'

'Did your grandfather have anything else against Norman?' Kelsey asked Gareth.

'I'm sorry,' Gareth said again to Jill before replying. 'Granddad thought Jill was keener on Norman than he was on her,' he told Kelsey. 'He thought it was Jill who was pushing things on, Norman just went along with it because of what he hoped to get out of it. Granddad said to me once, "Norman thinks Jill will come into money when I'm gone, he intends to get his hands on it if he can. Jill's too lovestruck now to see it but she'll wake up one day." He was sure Jill would never get as far as marrying Norman. She was certain to find him out before it got as far as that.'

Jill stood by in silence, with clenched jaw and burning cheeks.

'And you?' Kelsey asked Gareth. 'What's your opinion of Norman?'

Gareth moved his shoulders. 'He seems a decent enough guy to me. Granddad could be very intolerant and pig-headed. Once he got an idea into his head it was there for good. He'd never admit he could be wrong about anything. He'd got Norman down as a bad lot years ago and that was that, he could never go back on it.' He weighed his words. 'I'd trust Jill's judgement about Norman before Grand-dad's. I don't believe Jill's anybody's fool. I don't see why Norman shouldn't make her a good husband.'

Jill drew a little gasping breath. She flashed her brother a delighted smile of love and gratitude. He reached out and pressed her hand.

Her courage rose again. She looked at Kelsey with defiant challenge. 'You don't actually know there was any money in the drawer last Friday. Anyone could have taken it, days before.'

'Anyone?' Kelsey queried.

'It could have been someone who called at the house to do a bit of business, someone who'd been before, several times, maybe. If that person was always paid in cash, if Granddad always excused himself and went off to get the money, it wouldn't take a genius to work out he kept money in the house and whereabouts he kept it. That person could have got into the house, one way or another, when Grand-dad was out at work. Granddad wouldn't realize the money had gone, he wouldn't need to go to the drawer every day.'

They caught Norman as he came in from work in the evening. The Chief asked Mrs Griffin if he might speak to her son in private and she took herself off without protest. The Chief fired his first question at Norman without further ado. 'Did you know Harry Lingard kept a spare backdoor key in his garden shed?'

'Yes, I did know,' Norman answered without hesitation.

'Jill used it once when I was with her. She'd been over at Gareth's and I picked her up at the station when she got back. She had a cake Anne had baked for Harry, she called in with it on the way home. Harry was out and she used the key.' He cast his mind back. 'That would be three or four months ago.'

'Did you ever use the key yourself?'

He looked surprised. 'No, of course not. Why should I want to use it?'

The Chief didn't answer that. 'Did you know Harry kept quite a bit of cash in the house?'

'No, I didn't know, but I'm not surprised. He was always doing some deal or other.'

'You worked for a dealer yourself at one time?'

'That's right.'

'Ever come across a piece of furniture with a secret drawer?'

He smiled. 'I've seen quite a few of them. Old desks, writing tables, chests of drawers. It's the first thing anyone in the trade looks for, they're always hoping to find the family jewels or a pile of gold sovereigns.'

'You've tried such drawers yourself?'

He grinned. 'Sure, every time. I've never found anything. Except an old account book once, in a desk.'

'Do you know the chest of drawers in Harry Lingard's bedroom? Victorian piece, mahogany.'

He shook his head. 'Can't say I do. I was never in his bedroom.'

'You never glanced in? As you went past on your way to the bathroom, perhaps?'

Again he shook his head.

'Did you know the chest has a secret drawer?'

'No, I didn't.' Still easy, still patient. 'I told you, I didn't even know there was a chest.'

'Did you know Harry was in the habit of wearing a money-belt if he went out carrying more than a few pounds in cash?'

'Yes, I did know that. I'd forgotten about it but now you

mention it, I remember Jill telling me about it once.'

'Can you describe the belt?'

He shook his head. 'I've never seen it.'

'Do you know where it was kept?'

'No, I don't.'

'Do you know if Harry intended doing any deals last Friday evening?'

'No, I don't.'

'We found the money-belt in the house,' the Chief told him. 'In the secret drawer of the chest. The belt was empty.'

'Then he couldn't have been wearing it on Friday evening,' Norman responded at once.

Oh yes he could, Kelsey thought. A killer who knew about the chest could have removed the belt from the body, taken out the money, returned the empty belt to the drawer in the chest, entering the house by means of the keys found on Harry's body. He deposits the belt, takes any money he finds in the cashbox, closes the drawer again.

A savoury smell drifted enticingly from the oven. Norman's nostrils twitched. 'Is this going to take much longer?' he asked civilly enough. 'I'm starving.'

'We've just about done.' The Chief pushed back his chair. 'How did you spend last Friday evening?'

'I was here, in the house, all evening, mending my radios. It's a hobby of mine, doing up old radios. I had a chance to get on with it, Jill being away.' He nodded over at the door leading into the workroom. 'That's where I do it.'

'Was your mother in the house all evening?'

'No, she wasn't. She was out at her social club.' He went to the oven and glanced in at his dinner, switched the oven off.

Kelsey took the hint. 'We'll be off, then,' he said. 'And let you get on with it.'

CHAPTER 6

The funeral of Harold William Lingard was due to take place at eleven-thirty on Monday morning. Chief Inspector Kelsey woke early in a mood of despondency. The case seemed to be making no real progress. In all the phone calls from the general public, all the letters, all the visits to the police station, he had so far detected not one single shred of genuine knowledge of any hard fact of the crime on the part of anyone whatever.

A killing out of doors during the hours of darkness, with no witness, no weapon found, a lapse of time before the discovery of the body, was always one of the most difficult crimes to solve. And if it had been a lone mugger, if he kept his wits about him and his mouth shut, the crime would in all likelihood never be solved at all.

But the Chief was far from persuaded it had been a mugger—or muggers; it had seemed to him from the start there was more to it than that.

The funeral took place at a church near the council estate, the church Harry had attended all his life, the church his parents had attended before him. He was to be buried beside his parents, in the same grave as his wife.

The Chief had expected a good attendance but even so he was surprised at the size of the turn-out. Fellow-workers from Mansell's, from Calthrop's, *Bazaar* distributors from all over town. Representatives of local pressure groups Harry had supported, service welfare organizations he had been connected with. Residents from the council estate, clerks from the local authority departments Harry had battled against for so long, men and women who had been at school with him.

Pedestrians halted along the pavements to watch the slow passage of the hearse on its way to the church, followed by a line of cars. And a body of marching men, veterans, in their Sunday suits and brightly polished shoes, campaign medals and regimental badges proudly displayed.

The flag-draped coffin was borne into the church on the shoulders of six old comrades. There was a sea of flowers: wreaths, crosses, sheaves, posies, simple bunches. The Chief saw many a tear wiped away during the address, and later as a bugler sounded the Last Post over the grave. A steady stream of folk came up to speak to him afterwards, to wish godspeed to the investigation.

When it was all over and people were moving out of the churchyard the Chief noticed a man standing some little distance away, clearly waiting to speak to him; a white-haired man, spruce and well groomed, wearing a row of medals. As the Chief made his way towards him he caught a fleeting glimpse, in the throng of those leaving, of the handsome face of Diane Holroyd.

The old man came to meet him. Yes, he would be glad of a word. He introduced himself: Cyril Shearman, an old soldier, former comrade of Harry Lingard, living now in a retirement home a few miles away.

'I don't know if I should be bothering you with this,' he said apologetically, 'but I haven't been able to get it out of my head since I heard of Harry's death.'

He went on to tell the Chief about Harry's visit to the retirement home on Remembrance Sunday, his long chat with Mrs Vaile. 'Harry told me afterwards he wasn't at all happy about what Mrs Vaile told him about the sale of her house,' Shearman said. 'He believed she'd been swindled out of quite a bit of money. She was able to give him the names of one or two people involved in the sale, and Harry told me the names rang a bell with him. He'd had his suspicions about them once or twice before, things he'd heard. He was pretty sure there was some sort of ring operating.' He looked shrewdly at Kelsey. 'And he was pretty sure his own boss was mixed up in whatever was going on.'

'His boss?' Kelsey echoed.

'That's right. Tom Mansell. Harry told me he knew for

certain Mrs Vaile's property had ended up in Mansell's hands.' Mansell had a development scheduled for the site, planning permission had already been granted: the existing dwelling to be demolished, half-a-dozen houses to be erected on the land. 'Harry told me he had no intention of letting the matter rest, he was determined to see justice done for Mrs Vaile. One way or another, he was going to make sure she got every penny due to her.'

'Did he tell Mrs Vaile what he suspected? Or what he intended doing?'

'No, he was careful not to and he warned me to say nothing about it to her—or to anyone else, for that matter. He didn't want to worry her or get her hopes up too high. Time enough for her to know when she had to be brought into it.'

On his return from the funeral Cyril Shearman spoke to the matron of the retirement home and arranged that when the Chief Inspector and his sergeant called in that afternoon they would be shown into Matron's sitting-room where Shearman and Mrs Vaile would be taking tea with her. The police had no wish to alarm or distress Mrs Vaile, so she was to be told nothing of their visit beforehand. The call would ostensibly be in order to talk to Shearman about Harry Lingard; at an early stage Matron would take herself off.

All went as arranged. Mrs Vaile showed no reluctance to join in the conversation. 'I was very upset to hear what had happened to poor Mr Lingard,' she told the Chief. 'We had such a nice long chat.' It wasn't long before the Chief had steered her back to the substance of that chat, she was soon pouring out her whole tale again, pleased to find another such interested listener.

The dwelling she had sold stood on the edge of a village some distance from Cannonbridge, an old cottage of no great size but with a good parcel of land attached: paddock, garden, orchard; it had been in her husband's family for well over a hundred years.

After the death of her husband some years ago she had struggled along on her own until arthritis and deteriorating health made it impossible to continue. She had no children, no relatives, no near neighbours; she and her husband had never mixed in the village, had never been churchgoers. She had been forced at last to seek the help of the social services department. Her social worker was a competent woman who took immediate charge, came to see her with unfailing regularity and helpfulness. But the arthritis grew steadily worse and the social worker suggested she might think about going into a home; it was a relief in the end to agree.

The social worker had seen to everything, found the home for her, seen to the sale of the property, arranged for the disposal of her furniture and other belongings. The move into the retirement home had been an unqualified success, she felt better now than for a long time. She was delighted with the price the social worker had got her for the property, it seemed an enormous sum to her. She had feared no one would want to buy it at any price in its run-down state.

Jill Lingard had taken the rest of the day off after her grandfather's funeral. She was on her own in the terrace house, busy with domestic chores, when the Chief and Sergeant Lambert turned up on the doorstep. She seemed in equable spirits after the emotions of the morning.

The Chief asked if her grandfather had spoken to her about his talk with Mrs Vaile on Remembrance Sunday.

She didn't recall the name but she did remember her grandfather saying he'd had a long chat with an old lady at the home.

'Did he say anything to you about the sale of Mrs Vaile's cottage?' Kelsey asked.

She shook her head.

'Did he say anything about tackling Tom Mansell in the next day or two?'

Yes, she did remember him saying that but she couldn't recall what he had intended tackling Mansell about.

Did she know if Harry had in fact tackled Mansell about whatever it was?

Again she shook her head. 'I only saw Granddad once after that Sunday, when I called in for a moment on the Thursday evening. He wanted to get off on his round, so we didn't stay chatting.' A tear shone in her eye. 'You could try asking Norman. Granddad was talking to him that Sunday, while I was out in the kitchen.'

Norman hadn't taken the rest of the day off after the funeral but had changed his clothes and gone along to work. By the time the Chief and Lambert left the terrace house after talking to Jill, Norman was on his way home again at the end of the day. He arrived in his van as the two policemen got out of their car.

Mrs Griffin was out. The Chief didn't go into the house but stood by Norman's van, asking his questions. It didn't take long; Norman couldn't help them. Mrs Vaile's name meant nothing to him, he couldn't recall Harry mentioning it. He had only half listened to what Harry had said about his visit to the retirement home.

He did remember Harry saying he was going to tackle Mansell about something, he thought it was about a rise Harry believed was due to him. He had no idea if Harry had in fact spoken to Mansell about the rise or any other matter, he hadn't really talked to Harry again after that Sunday supper. Over the following week they'd exchanged no more than a passing word in the course of the day's work about the yard.

On Tuesday morning Lambert drove the Chief out to Mansell's yard again. 'You're lucky to catch me,' Mansell told them; he had been about to leave to keep an appointment with an architect.

The Chief asked if Harry Lingard had spoken to Mansell during the week before his death about a property sold in recent times by a Mrs Vaile and now about to be developed by Mansell's.

Mansell shook his head. Harry had never at any time mentioned the property.

How had Mansell acquired the property?

In the usual way. He had bought it from an estate agent he often dealt with.

Might the Chief ask what figure he had paid? There was an appreciable pause. Sergeant Lambert had a strong impression of Mansell's brain firing on all cylinders, though the expression on his face didn't alter. 'I'm afraid that comes under the heading of confidential business information,' Mansell answered at last, courteously enough. 'I'd have to be shown good reason before I felt obliged to answer.'

The Chief didn't press him. 'On Monday, November 12,' he said, 'the last Monday morning Harry was at work, did he approach you on any matter at all?'

Mansell thought back. 'Yes, he did. He wanted an increase in his hourly rate. He'd spoken to me about it before and I'd turned him down. I turned him down again, I thought he was well enough paid as it was.'

'Did he raise any other matter?'

'No, he didn't.' Mansell glanced pointedly at his watch and the Chief let him go.

Later in the day the Chief made time for a talk with an officer from the Fraud Squad who told him of a case up north some years ago where a property-buying ring had operated with considerable success over a long period before the fraud came to light. All the members of the ring had been well known to each other, bound by powerful ties of blood, marriage or long friendship, and a thirst for profit: a builder, estate agent, solicitor, social worker, plus a strategically placed clerk here and there.

The aim was to secure at prices far below their true value run-down properties with enough land for good development potential. The victims were always old people living alone, unsophisticated, vulnerable. No family or friends, in poor health, supervised by the social services, reaching the stage where they wouldn't be able to stay in their own homes much longer and the property their only real asset, having to be sold to provide the fees for the retirement or nursing home.

The social worker was always the linchpin. There was never any obvious link between members of the ring, various aspects of the transactions always being dealt with through different associated companies having no apparent connection with each other. The end result was a very satisfactory siphoning-off of profits all along the line.

The secret of the long-continued success of the ring lay in never being too greedy. Not too many deals, as few folk as possible in the know; never to select a property, however tempting, too close to where they'd operated before, in case some bright nosey-parker began to notice a pattern, started putting two and two together.

The ring had never had any need to worry about the planning side of things, there had never been any need to hand out sweeteners there—with all their attendant risks. Every development was well carried out, never any skimping on the quality of work or materials, never any breach of building regulations, never any fiddling of the grant system. Never anything, in short, likely to trigger off investigation or prejudice the next scheme in the pipeline.

'So what happened in the end to give the game away?' the Chief wanted to know.

'Human nature stuck its oar in,' the officer said. One of the lesser henchmen in the set-up started playing around, there was a divorce. He wasn't disposed to be over-generous towards his wife in the settlement and things got pretty acrimonious. The wife began alluding to sources of income he wasn't disclosing. The cat started slipping out of the bag and couldn't be stuffed back in again.

Something else came back to the officer: the victims had invariably been very grateful to the social worker for the help so unstintingly given. And they had always expressed themselves as more than pleased with the price they had received for their property.

'We'll have a quiet little tiptoe round,' the officer said as the Chief accompanied him to the door. 'If it turns out there's nothing in it, Mansell won't know we ever even heard his name.'

As the Chief came into the police station a couple of mornings later he was waylaid by a member of the murder investigation team. 'There's a guy I know,' he told the Chief, 'a regular in my local pub. He works at Mansell's, he's retiring tomorrow. He's been at Mansell's donkey's years, he started there when it was Dobie's, before Mansell's time. Can't say I care much for him, miserable sort of customer, a face that'd turn milk. Buckley, his name is. He was in the pub at the weekend, celebrating his sixty-fifth birthday, buying drinks for some of his mates from Mansell's.'

He hadn't been able to avoid overhearing some of their talk. It seemed Buckley didn't fancy coming to a sudden full stop as far as work was concerned. It had occurred to him that Harry Lingard's vacant job might suit him nicely for the next year or two. He had put the idea to Mansell, only to have it brusquely rejected, not a word offered in explanation.

'Can't say I blame Mansell,' the officer commented. 'I dare say Buckley's a good enough workman but I wouldn't be sorry to see the back of him myself, with that sour face of his, if I were in Mansell's shoes. Buckley seemed pretty fed up about it. I shouldn't think he's ever had much love for Mansell, by the sound of it, he still sees him as a Johnny-come-lately in the firm.' He gave the Chief an expressive glance. 'Now the Fraud Squad's coming into the picture, it might not hurt if they had a word with Buckley. He might have twigged a thing or two over the years, he might just be in the mood to talk.'

CHAPTER 7

Saturday, December 1 was Jill Lingard's twentieth birthday. No thought now of the party originally planned.

Shortly after breakfast Norman Griffin went round to the terrace house. 'We agreed we'd get engaged today,' he reminded Jill after giving her his kiss, his card and present.

She looked up at him with surprised protest. 'We can't now, surely? Not after what's happened. Not yet.'

'I don't see why not,' he maintained stubbornly. 'Your grandfather wouldn't want you to sit about weeping. He'd tell you to dry your eyes, get on with living.'

She had to acknowledge the truth of that. Norman went on pressing his case and she suddenly caved in. 'All right. We'll go ahead.'

He instantly dipped into his breast pocket and drew out a small box. 'You did say you'd rather have an old ring.' He sprang open the catch.

She was smiling now. 'I'd love any ring you gave me.'

He held the box out. The ring lay on its velvet bed. Gold; small garnets and tiny diamonds surrounding a larger garnet in a heart-shaped setting.

She gave a little gasp of pleasure. 'It's beautiful!' She threw her arms round his neck and kissed him.

He looked relieved and pleased. 'We can get it altered if it doesn't fit.' He took the ring from the box and slipped it on her finger; it fitted perfectly.

Her eyes shone. 'I love it! You couldn't have chosen better!' She smiled up at him, radiant. 'You're right about Granddad. Of course he'd have wanted us to go ahead.'

Her mood of reinvigorated optimism sent the pair of them off in the afternoon on a tour of the estate agents in search of run-down properties at rock-bottom prices. 'There's no great rush,' Norman tried to point out but once Jill had made up her mind she swept resolutely on. 'December's a good time to look at property,' she pronounced. 'You can see all the faults. We might come across a real bargain.' She was positive her grandfather's house wouldn't stay on the market long. With its pleasant situation, excellent state of repair, larger than average garden, all the improvements Harry had made, it was sure to fetch a good price.

By the time the last estate agent's office closed she had a list of half a dozen properties to consider. They could make a quick preliminary survey of the lot tomorrow afternoon, to size up neighbourhood, position, access, exterior condition. Then, if any seemed at all suitable, they could make an appointment to view.

The properties on Jill's list were widely scattered. They no longer carried sale boards, the agents knowing only too well that where properties had long stood empty, such boards merely served to invite a variety of offences, from vandalism and squatting to outright gutting of the premises.

On Sunday afternoon Norman and Jill began their tour by driving out to the farthest property, a few miles from Cannonbridge, then working their way inwards. Jill was dressed for the foray in an old pair of jeans and a superannuated jacket.

Dusk was falling as they came out through the gateway of the fifth property. It wasn't up to much but then none of the other four had been up to much either. Each had some major defect that decisively ruled it out. They got back into the van and Norman headed for home, where his mother would have a substantial tea ready for them.

'There's still the house in Tolladine Road,' Jill reminded him as they approached Whitethorn Common; Tolladine Road ran along the north side of the common.

Norman had by now had more than enough of the fruitless expedition. 'That house will be no different from the rest,' he prophesied. 'And it isn't as if you were ever really interested in it, you only put it on your list to shut the agent up. Let's scrub it and go home. I'm starving.'

But Jill's nature didn't incline her to quit any endeavour

before it was finished. The house was on her list, it ought to be seen. True, she had shaken her head when the agent had first mentioned the Tolladine Road property, she had wanted something on the outer fringes of town. And there seemed to be considerable doubt about the property being on the market at all. But the agent had been persistent and she had noted down the address.

'Won't do any harm to take a look,' she said persuasively. After the disappointments of the afternoon she was ready to be less finicky in her requirements.

'We won't be able to see anything in this light,' Norman warned. It was almost dark now.

She dug her heels in. 'We'll be able to see well enough to decide if it's worth coming back in daylight.' She'd come prepared with a torch, it had a good strong beam.

Norman gave up arguing and sat in silence till they pulled up outside the dwelling.

Overgrown trees and shrubs rioted about the front garden, drooping branches obscured the gateway. The garden was bounded on the right by an alleyway; on the left stood an old chapel belonging to some obscure sect. The chapel had long fallen into disuse, the wall nearest the house sported a rash of graffiti sprayings.

Across the road a row of lock-up shops stood dark and silent. 'It's certainly quiet enough round here, this time on a Sunday,' Jill commented as they got out of the van. 'I dare say it's livelier during the week when the shops are open.'

Norman held aside the overhanging branches and opened the gate; the gravel path was full of weeds. Together they set off on a torchlit tour of the garden. It had run completely wild but was larger than Jill had expected. And it was wonderfully private.

'This is a total waste of time,' Norman declared as they turned towards the house. 'We're not even sure the place is genuinely up for sale.' It had belonged to an eccentric old woman. On her death it had passed to her younger brother, equally eccentric, a well-to-do scholarly recluse living in the wilds of East Anglia. He had at first instructed the agent to sell the property but had changed his mind shortly afterwards and withdrawn it from the market; it was possible he might decide to live in it himself one day. He had repeated this irritating on-off performance on two subsequent occasions. He had been in touch with the agent again only last week, the house was currently back on the market—but for how long? 'I do really believe now,' the agent had assured Jill, 'that if someone were to put in a firm offer, he'd accept it. I believe he's reached the stage where he'd be glad to have the matter decided for him.'

'I'm pretty sure we could get this place for a very reasonable figure,' Jill said as they approached the front of the house. 'The agent would move heaven and earth to push the sale through.' Her share of her grandfather's estate would be worth a good deal more than she had ever imagined; along with Gareth she had been astonished to learn of all the investments Harry had amassed.

Norman wasn't to be cajoled. 'The whole place is probably riddled with dry rot,' he surmised gloomily. 'Cost a fortune to put right.'

The house, like the garden, was larger than Jill had expected. She did her best to peer up at the roof from various vantage-points; from what she could make out in the deepening darkness it appeared pretty sound.

'Do come along,' Norman urged as she continued her scrutiny, working her way along the gravel path round the house, trying windows. 'Mum's expecting us.'

Jill was by now round at the rear. One of the window sashes moved without difficulty under her hands. 'I can get in here,' she called out to him. 'I'm going to take a look inside.'

He uttered a groan. 'You'll have us arrested,' he said with heat as he went round to stop her. 'It's trespassing — or worse.'

She raised the sash. 'You might give me a hand,' she rebuked him.

But he would have nothing to do with such capers. 'You don't know what you could be getting into,' he warned.

'Rotten floorboards. Rats, mice, cockroaches.' Even that didn't shake her. He turned on his heel. 'I'm going back to the van,' he flung over his shoulder. 'You're on your own.' That ought to fetch her.

But it didn't. She went up on to the sill, let herself carefully down inside, testing the floorboards before trusting herself to them.

The bright glow of her torch revealed a fireplace, a door. She made her way towards the door, emerging into a hallway. She tried a light switch, without result.

A door opposite gave into another room, similar to the first. She returned to the hall, progressed along a passage, found a kitchen on her left, another room opposite. She contemplated the staircase, played her torch over the treads. She mounted slowly, cautiously, up to a landing with three bedrooms opening off it. Further along, a bathroom.

A short, narrow flight of stairs took her warily up to the attic. She sniffed the air but could detect no hint of dry rot. Nor could she discern any sign of leaks from the roof. She smiled in the darkness. The house had undoubted possibilities.

She made her way slowly down the stairs again, into the hall. In the light of her torch she spotted a door she had missed earlier. She turned the handle, disclosing a flight of stone steps disappearing into Stygian blackness. Cellars, no doubt. She spied a stout handrail and began to descend.

At the foot of the steps was a flagged area with two doors leading off. The door on the left gave into a good, dry, stone-flagged cellar amply provided with storage shelves and cupboards.

She opened the door on the right. Another cellar. Her torch moved over the walls. More shelves and cupboards. The circle of light travelled on across the floor. Stone flags, again. The beam probed the corners, came to rest on something. She advanced gingerly towards it, peering down.

She halted abruptly, letting out a horrified gasp. She was looking down at a pair of legs. A woman's legs, slender and shapely, the narrow feet encased in flat-heeled shoes. She stared down, rigid with fright, her heart thumping wildly.

She sent the beam on, over the prostrate form. It was clad in a tweed coat, grey-blue. She began to tremble violently. A hand stuck out of a sleeve, the delicate wrist and fingers bare of watch or rings.

The limbs were sprawled in a graceless parody of sleep. The head was turned to one side, a suède beret crammed down over golden-chestnut curls. She had a partial view of a face, the eyes closed. A face she knew, a face she had seen many times.

CHAPTER 8

Sunday evening was crisp and clear. Edgar Holroyd strode briskly along under the street lamps and rounded the bend into Tolladine Road. He slackened his pace at the sight that met his eyes: vans and cars drawn up outside one of the houses, a uniformed constable stationed at each end of the line of vehicles. A busy to and fro of men, some of them uniformed police, entering and leaving the property, brightly illumined inside and out by the aid of a portable generator. At the other side of the road onlookers crowded the shop doorways, took up half the width of the pavement for several yards.

Edgar stood rigid for a moment, then he approached a policeman, an officer he knew slightly, to ask what was going on. The constable gave him an odd look. He seemed surprised, even startled, to see him. After a brief pause he said, 'I think it would be best if you spoke to the Chief Inspector.' Edgar gave him a glance of puzzlement but the constable offered no explanation. 'If you'd come along into the house,' he said.

They went up the path to the front door where another constable was posted. 'If you'd wait here,' the first officer said to Edgar, 'I'll be back in a moment.' He paused to murmur something to the second man who nodded in reply; the first officer went into the house. The second man—an officer unknown to Edgar—gave him a long, searching look but said nothing.

After a brief interval the first officer returned and asked Edgar to step inside. He led the way into a room where a trestle-table and folding chairs had been set up.

Two men in civilian clothes stood inside the open door. Edgar recognized the larger of the two from his recent photographs in the local paper: Detective Chief Inspector Kelsey. The Chief Inspector directed a nod at the constable who immediately returned to his duties outside.

'Mr Edgar Holroyd?' the Chief Inspector asked.

Edgar acknowledged his identity. The Chief introduced himself and Detective-Sergeant Lambert. The Chief asked Edgar to sit down and the two policemen took their seats facing him across the trestle-table.

'We went along to Fairbourne earlier,' the Chief Inspector said, 'but there was no one at home.'

'I've been out walking,' Edgar explained. 'I take a walk most evenings.' He paused. 'Is this something to do with the housing department? I know this property has stood empty for some time.'

The Chief shook his head. 'It's nothing to do with the housing department.' He gave Edgar a long look. 'I'm afraid we have bad news for you. Very bad news.'

Edgar frowned. 'What kind of bad news?'

'The worst kind, I'm afraid,' the Chief said heavily. 'It's about your wife.'

'My wife?' Edgar jerked up in his chair. 'What's it got to do with my wife? She's away, staying with her aunt.'

The Chief shook his head. 'I'm afraid you're wrong. She's not at her aunt's. The fact is, the body of a woman has been found here, in the cellar of this house. We have reason to believe it's the body of your wife.'

The blood drained from Edgar's face. 'It can't be Claire,' he said in a shaking voice. 'She's been over at her aunt's for a couple of weeks.'

The Chief stood up. 'The body is still here,' he said. 'If you'll come with us . . .'

Edgar got to his feet without a word. He remained where he was, staring down with a poleaxed air. The Chief halted on the threshold and looked back at him. 'Better get it over with,' he advised gently. 'Best to know, one way or the other.'

Edgar forced himself into motion. He followed them out into the hallway, down the steps, into the brilliantly lit cellar. Several men were at work; they glanced up briefly. A silence fell over the room as they realized from his look, his gait, who the third member of the trio must be.

They crossed the cellar to the corner where the body lay. Edgar didn't glance about but kept his gaze fixed and level, staring straight ahead like a blind man. It was some moments after they had all halted before he at last lowered his head and looked down. The Chief stood watching him.

His face was ashen. He gave a sobbing gasp, a brief nod, staggered slightly. He put out a hand and steadied himself against the wall.

The Chief asked him formally if he identified the body as that of his wife. In a low, trembling voice he answered that he did.

The pathologist who carried out the post-mortem examination on the body of Claire Margaret Holroyd, age 28, was the same man who had performed a similar service two weeks earlier in the case of Harold William Lingard.

Shortly before noon on Monday morning Chief Inspector Kelsey followed the pathologist out of the mortuary. The thin sunshine of early December cast a pale yellow light through the corridor windows as they stood talking.

Two savage blows had been struck to the back of Claire's head. The first blow had killed her, smashing in the skull. There had been scarcely any bleeding; what little there was had been taken up in the abundant curls of her hair. The body was fully clothed, there were no signs of any sexual assault. No sign, either, of any struggle; she would appear to have been taken totally by surprise.

At the time the blows were struck she had not been wearing the suède beret; that had been pulled down over her hair after she was dead. The attack had not demanded excessive strength, it was not, for instance, beyond the power of an ordinarily strong, fit woman, particularly one in the grip of frenzy.

Both blows had been struck from a position above and behind the victim, lending extra force to the assault. The difference in position might suggest that the assailant had been upright, the victim seated, kneeling or crouching. Or the victim could have been on a lower level than the attacker, as, for example, on a staircase or on sloping land. It might even simply be that the assailant was considerably taller than the victim.

Both blows would appear to have been delivered with the same weapon, by the same right-handed person. The nature of the injuries suggested they could have been inflicted by the rounded knob of a heavy hammer of the ball-peen type.

As to the time of death, it was impossible to offer more than a very rough guess. The pathologist would estimate that the body had lain in the cellar between two and three weeks. Claire would appear to have died some four hours after she had last eaten.

Three questions at once sprang to the Chief's mind. Had Claire been killed on the same evening as Harry Lingard? Could both murders have been committed by the same person? Could the same weapon have been used?

The pathologist did his best to answer. Yes, the medical evidence did permit the possibility that Claire had been killed on the same evening as Harry Lingard. Nor did anything in the findings rule out the possibility that both murders could have been committed by the same person. But in response to the third question he shook his head: the same weapon had not been used in both cases.

Not even, the Chief pressed him, if the ball-peen hammer

had been up-ended in the first murder, the blows to Harry's skull being inflicted with the handle? No, definitely not, he was assured; such a handle would not have been heavy enough to produce the injuries.

In neither case did the blows suggest they had been struck by more than one person. Though that didn't mean, the Chief reflected, that another person—or persons— might not have been present, actively involved in the planning and commission of the crimes, the dumping of the bodies.

'Claire Holroyd was a very fit young woman,' the pathologist added. 'No sign of any disease.'

One other fact the post-mortem had revealed: Claire had been pregnant. At the time of her death the pregnancy had been of some four or five weeks' duration.

Before going over to Fairbourne to give Edgar Holroyd the results of the post-mortem the Chief called in at the police station. He spent the next half-hour closeted with officers from the forensic teams at Fairbourne and the house in Tolladine Road.

It was clear that wherever Claire Holroyd had been killed, it was certainly not in the cellar—nor, for that matter, in any other room—of the house in Tolladine Road. Her body had merely been dumped there after death. The choice of that particular house for the dumping would seem to argue some degree of local knowledge as the house sported no sale boards.

The window by which Jill Lingard had gained entry showed marks suggesting it had recently been opened by means of a blade slipped between the sashes.

Adhering to the surface of Claire's tweed coat were a number of extraneous fibres from two different sources: wool fibres, light blue in colour, and cotton fibres in a shade of buttercup yellow.

The interior of the house in Tolladine Road was totally bare of furnishings of any kind. They had been over Edgar Holroyd's house and car but had been unable to find any curtain, carpet, rug, upholstery or any other item that might have been the source of either fibre. They had in fact discovered nothing in Fairbourne of any real significance.

CHAPTER 9

While waiting for the Chief Inspector's visit, Edgar Holroyd was attempting to keep himself occupied in his basement workshop. No thought of lunch crossed his mind; scarcely anything had passed his lips since he had stood in the cellar of the house in Tolladine Road yesterday evening.

At the sound of Sergeant Lambert's ring at the bell he came dragging up the stairs to open the door. His face was haggard. He made no move to show the two men into the sitting-room but stood dumbly in the hall, gazing into the Chief's face with an utterly lost, stranded look, as if barely hanging on to the outermost fringes of everyday life. The Chief suggested they might all go inside and sit down. 'Oh . . . yes,' Edgar agreed in an abstracted fashion. He remained motionless.

The Chief took charge of the situation. He crossed the hall and opened the door of a room on the right. 'All right if we go in here?' he asked.

'Oh . . . yes,' Edgar said again. He jerked himself into motion.

'Have you seen your doctor?' the Chief asked when they were all finally seated.

Edgar shook his head.

'I think perhaps you should,' the Chief advised. 'You've had a tremendous shock.'

Edgar shook his head again. 'I'll be all right.' He looked as if he might at any moment break down completely.

The Chief gave him the results of the post-mortem in as gentle and undramatic a fashion as the grim facts would allow. Edgar listened with his head bowed and his eyes closed, his hands clasped before him.

At the mention of his wife's pregnancy his head shot up. He stared at the Chief, then he dropped his head again into his hands.

'Did you know she was pregnant?' the Chief asked.

Edgar could only shake his head. The Chief gave him time to recover. 'She couldn't have known herself,' Edgar said at last in unsteady tones. 'It was what she wanted more than anything. What we both wanted.'

The Chief regarded him. According to his statement Edgar had last seen his wife on the morning of Friday, November 16, when he left for work; she had appeared in every way as usual. Nothing out of the ordinary had recently happened in their lives, there had been no disagreement of any kind between them. They got on well together; in the four years of their marriage there had never been any quarrel. They were both quiet and self-contained, with interests of their own.

He had told Claire earlier that he wouldn't be home that Friday evening till around ten or ten-fifteen, as he had to attend a council meeting—this happened from time to time. Claire didn't mind, she never minded. It was in any case one of her evenings at the College of Further Education. She had no need to bother about a meal for him, he would get himself a snack before the meeting as he always did.

He had spent the day at work as usual. At five-thirty he had left the office and walked to a nearby sandwich bar. He had gone there alone, had eaten alone, but he had seen and spoken to a couple of female clerks from the office who were also eating there.

He had left the sandwich bar at around six-fifteen for the meeting, which was due to start at six-thirty and normally ended soon after nine. Coffee and sandwiches were then always served and people stood around, talking.

But that Friday evening the meeting ended a good deal earlier than usual, amid a certain amount of uproar. Some highly controversial cut-back proposals figured on the agenda; demonstrators from action groups staged noisy protests; there was much lively argument and some ill-feeling in the debate. Edgar had been present throughout.

In the end the meeting couldn't continue. At about seven-thirty it was adjourned to allow time for tempers to cool, less provocative measures to be worked out. There was no standing about talking, no coffee and sandwiches. Edgar drove straight home. He had supplied the Chief with the names of the two female clerks in the sandwich bar as well as several council officials who could vouch for his presence throughout the meeting. The Chief had already known of the disrupted council proceedings which had been fully reported.

Edgar had reached home at about a quarter to eight. He wasn't expecting Claire back from her class till getting on for eight-thirty. He went upstairs to change his clothes, then along to the kitchen to make himself some coffee.

Shortly after eight, while he was still in the kitchen, the phone rang in the hall. It was the class lecturer from the college, asking to speak to Claire. Edgar said surely she had been at his class and was told she hadn't attended that evening. The lecturer was arranging a theatre visit in connection with the course and Claire had earlier expressed interest. He had to know definitely in the next day or two if Claire would be going, he had to book seats. Edgar promised to pass on the message. He was not in the slightest degree worried when he replaced the phone. He imagined Claire had decided to skip her class and go to the cinema or theatre instead, as she had done more than once before. He had no interest in such entertainments himself and she never minded going alone.

He returned to the kitchen, reflecting that she would probably not be home now till ten or half past. He finished his coffee and went down to his basement workshop.

Just before ten he went upstairs to watch the news on TV. The instant he switched on the sitting-room light he saw the envelope propped up against the clock on the mantelpiece. He knew at once what would be inside; he had found more than one such envelope in the last four years. It would be a brief note from Claire to say she was off to stay with her Aunt May—Mrs May Finch, Claire's only close relative, her mother's sister, a widow living in a cottage in a village some miles away.

His own acquaintance with Mrs Finch was slight, though amicable enough on both sides. He had met her on two or three occasions before his marriage and had thought her a sensible, good-hearted woman. The wedding had taken place very quietly, in the Cannonbridge register office, at Claire's express wish. Mrs Finch had not been present, there had been nothing in the way of a reception.

Claire had gone off to her aunt's in this way on a number of previous occasions, leaving home without warning while he was out at work, returning equally unheralded days or weeks later—again, while he was out of the house. He would come in from work one evening and there she would be, as if she had never been away.

There was no phone in Mrs Finch's cottage. In the note Claire had left the first time she had gone, she had said she would be grateful if he would make no attempt to get in touch with her. She needed time to be on her own, she would be back in a week or two. He had forced himself to accept this, though not without many misgivings and much anxiety; they had been married only a few months.

But after ten days she had indeed returned. She had offered no further explanation, certainly no apology for any distress she had caused. In fact she had made no reference whatever to her absence, behaving in her customary calm and pleasant way. She had taken up her ordinary life again cheerfully enough, things had continued much as before. He had felt it would be churlish to force a discussion on her when she had made it so plain it would be unwelcome.

He couldn't say how Claire had travelled to her aunt's on these occasions, she had never told him. Claire didn't own a car, she had never learned to drive. She could have got there by train or bus, or she might have used a taxi. Six months after her first such departure he had come home again one evening to find the same thing had happened again. He was a good deal less agitated this time; she had stayed away for two weeks. There was then an interval of a whole year before her third departure, which had lasted the best part of three weeks. By then he was inured to it, it had scarcely troubled him at all; he had come to accept that that was the way Claire was, the way it seemed likely she would continue to be. There had been one or two further departures, the last being some eight or nine months ago, when she had stayed away a little over two weeks. None of these departures had ever appeared planned, she always seemed to take off very much on the spur of the moment, he had never seen any warning signs. And she had invariably left a few minor matters unattended to.

Although she always appeared poised and self-possessed her nature inclined her to bottle things up. He believed that was the root cause of these abrupt departures. When a certain degree of tension had built up inside her she sought to discharge it by removing herself from everyday life, running back to where she had been a carefree child.

When, therefore, he had found Claire's note on the evening of Friday, November 16, he had read it all with philosophic acceptance, certainly without distress. During the weekend he remembered the phone call from the lecturer so he rang the college on the Monday morning, leaving a message for the lecturer to say Claire would not be going on the theatre trip. He had also informed the office that Claire wouldn't be attending any classes for the next week or two, she had gone to stay with a relative.

No, he couldn't produce the note Claire had left. He hadn't kept it, there had been no reason to, he had never kept any of the notes she had left. Nor could he shed any light on when Claire might last have eaten. He had no idea at what time she had left the house that day; it might have been shortly after he left for work in the morning. He could tell them nothing of his wife's weekday eating pattern, he was never at home then.

This long and detailed statement squared well enough with the very much briefer statement Edgar had made to the officer from the house-to-house team who had called at

Fairbourne on the Sunday Harry Lingard's body had been found. The Chief had looked out that earlier statement; in it Edgar had said he had heard nothing unusual or suspicious in the neighbourhood of the common during the evening or night of November 16. He had attended a council meeting, had got home at a quarter to eight, had seen nothing of Harry on his rounds as he drove home, he had noticed nothing unusual on the common. He had remained in the house for the rest of the evening, had gone to bed at his usual time, around eleven. There had been nothing to disturb him during the night.

The officer had asked if anyone else lived at Fairbourne and was told Edgar's wife lived there. Had she heard anything? He was told she hadn't been at home that evening, she was staying with her aunt. Edgar had made no mention to the officer of finding Claire's note, or the circumstances of her departure, but then, the Chief reflected, in the same circumstances he would himself have said nothing about it to a police officer.

Edgar sat in remote silence with his head bowed as the Chief regarded him. Checks were currently going forward to verify the time Edgar had reached his office that Friday morning, the way in which he had spent the rest of the day. Inquiries were also under way among taxi-drivers, busmen, railway staff, in an attempt to discover any sighting of Claire that Friday.

There had been no bag or grip of any kind in the cellar at Tolladine Road, no jewellery or other item of value on the body; the pockets of Claire's coat were empty. Edgar had done his best to describe for them such valuable items as she might have been wearing or carrying. Her chequebook and bank card—she owned no credit cards. A ring of keys; maybe a hundred pounds or two in notes. Gold wristwatch, wedding ring, engagement ring—a diamond solitaire. She might have been wearing additional rings but he couldn't be certain which; she wore other rings as fancy took her. She might also have worn a pin, a brooch or bracelet. Earrings, possibly; a gold neck chain—she had several. She hadn't taken her jewel-box with her, she never did.

At the Chief's request Edgar had looked through the box to ascertain if any particular piece he remembered might be missing. But he hadn't known exactly what she had owned. And he had still been in a state of shock, his brain wasn't working with total clarity.

There were one or two further points the Chief now wished to raise. He began by asking if Claire had had any kind of job in recent times.

Edgar made a strong effort to rouse himself. He told the Chief Claire had never had a full-time job since they were married but she had done occasional relief work in the office at Mansell's. He explained that his younger brother Lester, who worked for Mansell's, had oversight of the office. 'One of the female clerks was away ill and they couldn't find a suitable replacement. Lester asked Claire if she could possibly step in for a week or two, he made a great favour of it.' He cast his mind back. 'That would be about eighteen months ago. Claire found she enjoyed it, she went quite a few times after that, when they were stuck for someone. It might be for two or three days, or a week or two, sometimes longer. The last time was for several weeks, that was back in the spring. She finished around May or June.'

'Why did she stop going?'

'She told me she wasn't enjoying it any more, they were taking her very much for granted, expecting her to fill in whenever it suited them. I think it was the last long stint that did it, the novelty had worn off by then.' He gave the ghost of a smile. 'They'd made a big fuss of her the first time or two, then all that fell away. It was just an ordinary job of work, solid slogging, not particularly interesting to her. She had no need to go out to work. If it was occupation she wanted, then she'd prefer to go to classes or do some charity work.'

'Did anyone at Mansell's try to get her to change her mind after she stopped going?'

'Tom Mansell phoned her here, asking her to reconsider.

I know he phoned at least twice because I happened to be in the house on two occasions when he rang. But she wouldn't be talked into going back.'

The Chief asked what work Claire had done before her marriage.

'She went to Hartley's after she left school,' Edgar told him. 'She was there for some years. Then she took a job with the local council, in the housing department where I work—that's how we met. She was there two or three years, until we got married.' He stared down at his hands. 'She was very domesticated. She enjoyed having a home of her own, she even liked housework.' He drew a ragged breath. 'And we were always hoping to start a family.' He fell silent, then he added, 'She talked recently of going in for more serious study, taking a course that might lead somewhere. I thought it a very good idea.'

The Chief asked if Edgar knew of any close women friends Claire might have had.

'She wasn't the kind to have close women friends,' Edgar told him. 'She was an only child, she didn't even have cousins her own age. She knew a good many women, of course, one way and another, but I can't think any of them were at all close.'

'What about your brother's wife?' the Chief asked. 'Was Claire friendly with her?'

Edgar shook his head. 'I can't say she was. Diane's father is Tom Mansell, the builder.' He fell silent again, looking infinitely weary. 'I was against the marriage. I thought Lester was too young to tie himself down.' He grimaced. 'That got me off to a bad start with Diane. When I got married myself, a year after Lester, Diane wasn't in the mood to be very friendly towards any wife of mine, whoever she might be. But I don't think Diane and Claire would have hit it off in any case, they had nothing much in common, very different temperaments.' After Claire told Lester she was no longer willing to act as a fill-in at Mansell's office, the lack of warmth between the two households had turned into a decided coolness. Contact grew even less frequent, eventually ceasing altogether.

The Chief turned to the matter of Claire's finances. Had she owned anything substantial? Property, shares, and the like? Had she made a will?

Edgar shook his head in reply to both questions. 'She didn't even have a separate bank account,' he told them. 'We had a joint account.' She had always been sensible in her spending. She had come from a very modest background; to the best of his knowledge all she had ever inherited had been a few pieces of old jewellery from her godmother. Claire had never made a will. Apart from personal belongings she had had nothing to leave.

Lastly, the Chief asked if Claire had kept a diary.

Only a little pocket diary, he was told, to note down appointments and so forth. It would probably have been in her shoulder-bag.

When the Chief got up to leave, Edgar suddenly said, 'Surely the two murders must be in some way connected?'

'That's a very open question at this stage,' the Chief responded.

Edgar's tone grew agitated. 'Both killed in the same sort of way, at roughly the same time—they must be connected!'

'It's far too early to come to any firm conclusion,' the Chief said patiently.

Edgar began to pace the room. 'Claire was killed because she saw something. I'm sure of it! Something to do with Harry Lingard's murder.' His face was ravaged. 'She happened to be in the wrong place at the wrong time.'

'It could just as easily have been the other way round,' the Chief pointed out. 'Harry Lingard could have chanced to see something of Claire's murder. He could have been the one who happened to find himself in the wrong place at the wrong time.'

CHAPTER 10

Mrs Finch's cottage stood on the outskirts of a village half an hour's drive from Cannonbridge. Twilight was descending as Lambert pulled up by the gate. Dogs set up a fierce barking round the back as the two policemen walked up the path.

Mrs Finch had just come in after a day spent caring for a sick friend. She went to quieten the dogs before opening the door to the Sergeant's ring. She gave the two men a smiling look of inquiry. She was a small, slight woman in her sixties, still pretty, a face of great kindness.

The Chief told her who he was. She jumped at once to the conclusion that he had called to ask for directions or because his car had broken down. Her smiling look began to fade as he gently disabused her of these notions. He asked if they might come in, he was the bearer of bad news. She stepped back at once in anxious silence, holding the door wide for them to enter. She took them into a sitting-room gleaming with polish, bright with flowers. Her eyes searched their faces.

'It's Claire, isn't it?' she asked as they sat down, her voice barely a whisper. 'Something's happened to her.'

'I'm afraid so,' Kelsey said. She pressed her hands together.

The Chief broke the news as gently as he could. She asked at once if Claire had been the victim of a sex attack and was told there was no sign of it; that seemed to afford her some slight relief. She asked if it had been robbery and was told it was a possibility. The Chief let her have her cry, and despatched Sergeant Lambert along to the kitchen to make tea.

'I heard about the old man who was killed on the common,' Mrs Finch said when she was somewhat recovered. 'They said he'd been robbed. Do you think it could have been the same person—or more than one person—that killed Claire? Robbed her and then killed her?'

The Chief could only tell her: 'At this stage it's impossible to say.'

She seemed steadier now, so he asked if she felt up to answering questions. She gave a quick little nod, she was only too anxious to help in any way she could.

She had last seen Claire back in the spring. She had arrived on the doorstep without warning, as usual; she had stayed more than two weeks. She had come all the way by taxi that time, though at other times she had come by bus or train.

There had never been any contact with Edgar during these visits of Claire's, that was how Claire had wanted it. According to Claire, Edgar never complained about these absences, never subjected her to questioning, he was always kind and understanding.

Had Mrs Finch any idea what could have caused these fits of despondency?

'Claire was always one to take things hard,' Mrs Finch told him, 'even as a small child. If she had a kitten or puppy die on her she would grieve over it for weeks. It was a terrible blow to her when she lost her father, she was only seven at the time. She was always a quiet child but she got even quieter after that, she seemed to go right into herself. Her mother died ten years later and she took that every bit as hard, more so, if anything.

'When she used to turn up here on my doorstep I never asked her what had brought her over. She was never one to talk freely about anything personal. The way I see it, things used to get too much for her every so often. It was her nature as much as anything, I think she would have been the same whatever kind of life she lived. Her way of dealing with it was to run away till she felt better. I expect it was a better way than dosing herself with pills, the way some folk would. She'd mooch about here, very quiet, and then, quite suddenly, one day it would be over. She'd jump out of bed as bright as a button and tell me, "I'll be off home today." And that would be that—till the next time.'

She stood up and went to a drawer, took out an album of photographs to show the Chief: Claire as a chubby baby, as a plain little girl, an awkward adolescent. 'She was a very shy child,' Mrs Finch told Kelsey. 'Anyone would have laughed if you'd said she'd turn out a beauty. But that's what did happen when she was sixteen.' She turned another page and there was Claire, now a lovely young girl. 'It was like a miracle to her, something she'd never dreamed could happen. She took such care of herself from then on, as if she was afraid it might be snatched away if she didn't value it. Her shyness went, she blossomed out, though she was never free and easy, she always had a quiet manner. She took such care of her clothes, too, kept them immaculate, she always looked as if she'd stepped out of a bandbox.'

'Did she have many boyfriends?' Kelsey asked.

She shook her head. 'She only ever had the one serious boyfriend before she married Edgar, that was when she was working at Hartley's. Ashworth, his name was, Robert Ashworth. He was quite a bit older than she was, very good-looking. He worked at Calthrop's, the estate agents, he was taking his exams to be a surveyor. He had to do a lot of studying, he used to go to evening classes.' She sighed. 'I liked him a lot. He was a hard worker, very keen to get on. He was very fond of Claire but he was never one to take liberties, never kept her out late. I always knew I could trust him to look after her, she'd never come to any harm with him. They were never actually engaged but I took it for granted they'd get married, they seemed so settled and steady. I'm sure Claire thought so, too.' She was silent for a moment. 'Till the accident, that is. That changed everything.'

'The accident?' Kelsey queried.

She nodded, 'She was in a car crash when she was just turned twenty. One of the girls at Hartley's had got engaged to a businessman, very well off. They were giving an engagement party, a dance with a buffet, over at the other side of the county, where he lived, it was at one of those big country houses turned into a hotel, very posh sort of place. Pretty well all the Hartley staff were invited. Claire was told she could bring Robert along.'

But when she told Robert he said he was sorry, he wouldn't be able to go. He had an important exam coming up at that time, he had two papers on the day of the party, two more the day after. He'd have to get an early night in between, to do himself justice. He'd told her about the exam some time before but she'd forgotten the exact date. It was the first time he'd ever refused to go along with what she wanted, she was sure he'd change his mind; she accepted the invitation for both of them.

But he didn't change his mind. When she realized he really wouldn't be going she decided she'd go anyway. 'There was a young lad working at Hartley's, a nice boy, only eighteen. He'd had a crush on Claire from the day he'd started work at Hartley's, though he was never a nuisance to her.' The lad had recently bought an old car and Claire asked if she could go along with him to the party. He was overjoyed, he couldn't believe his luck.

On the way to the party a storm blew up. It began to rain heavily, the road ran with water. The lad wasn't an experienced driver, he didn't really know the car or the road. They came to a steep downhill stretch, he skidded on a bend. He was killed in the crash.

The car wasn't fitted with seat-belts and Claire's head went through the windscreen. She suffered broken ribs, a great deal of bruising—and multiple cuts to her face. She was in hospital for some time. Later, over the next year or two, she had plastic surgery for the scarring. There was no compensation for her injuries, the lad hadn't been comprehensively insured. The plastic surgery had been very successful but by the time Claire had done with the operations the fine bloom of her youthful beauty had gone for ever.

Mrs Finch turned another page in the album. 'That's the last photograph I've got of Claire.' Smiling in the garden, radiantly lovely. 'It was taken just before her twentieth birthday. She had such beautiful skin before the accident, like a magnolia. She never liked having her photo taken after the accident.'

Claire's old job at Hartley's had been kept open for her while she was in hospital but when she came out, while she was waiting for the operations, she couldn't bring herself to go back to work in a place where she'd be so much in the public eye. Her old shyness came flooding back, compounded by crippling self-consciousness because of the scars. She couldn't face the curiosity and pity that would replace the admiring glances she had been used to.

'But she had to work somewhere,' Mrs Finch said. 'She got herself a job with the council in the housing department. She had no direct contact with the public. That's where she met Edgar. He was very good to her. She had to have a lot of time off for plastic surgery but he fixed all that, so she needn't have any worries about her job.

'She'd been thinking about learning to drive before the accident, but afterwards it took her all her time to sit in a car at all, she was absolutely terrified. She got over that, of course, but she never wanted to learn to drive again. Edgar always drove her to the supermarket one evening a week for the bulk of the shopping.'

Claire had never once seen Robert Ashworth again after the accident. 'He was devastated when he heard what had happened. He kept going round to the hospital, trying to see Claire, but she would never see him. He came over here more than once to see if I could suggest anything he could do to get her to change her mind. But it was no good. He was heartbroken about it all.' She gave a long sigh. 'She never did change her mind. She wouldn't discuss it with me. She never spoke Robert's name to me again.'

When Robert was finally forced to accept that it was all over he applied for a job elsewhere; he'd passed his exams, passed them well. Mrs Finch had never heard of him again.

'Claire's fits of depression,' she said. 'I put a lot of it down to the accident, the way it changed her whole life. It was a very big mouthful for her to swallow, I don't know that she ever managed to swallow it all.' Tears shone in her eyes. 'And there was another thing: the fact that it was taking her so long to get pregnant.

'She never really talked about it to me but I know she minded a lot. She'd skate round the subject sometimes, she'd ask me about her mother and grandmother, how long they'd been married before they had children. Both those women married young and they were both turned thirty before they had a child—I could see Claire was comforting herself with that. She persuaded herself it ran in the family, she'd be sure to fall pregnant in another year or two. I wasn't so sure myself, I thought she should talk to her doctor about it, but she wouldn't hear of it. She said there'd be all sorts of tests and questions, not just for her, for Edgar too, she couldn't put him through that.' She looked at Kelsey. 'Edgar's a very private sort of person. She was sure the trouble was all on her side, she was banking on it being all right in a couple of years.'

When the Chief gently disclosed that Claire had been in the early stages of pregnancy at the time of her death, Mrs Finch could no longer maintain her brave front but collapsed into grief-stricken weeping. When at last she dried her tears the Chief added that it was possible Claire had not been aware that she was pregnant. Edgar had known nothing of it and the Chief hadn't yet spoken to Claire's doctor.

'It seems so dreadfully cruel,' Mrs Finch said with infinite sadness. 'To die just when she was getting her dearest wish, maybe not even knowing it. And poor Edgar, too. To lose the child as well as Claire. How delighted they would both have been to have a child at last.'

CHAPTER 11

Claire Holroyd had been a patient on the list of a small medical practice on Whitethorn Road; her husband was on the books of a larger practice near the council offices. The

Chief arranged to call on Claire's doctor before surgery on Tuesday morning.

The doctor told him Mrs Holroyd had joined his list some four years ago, shortly after her marriage. She was a healthy young woman and had consulted him on only two occasions, on minor matters. He knew nothing of her pregnancy, she had never consulted him for problems of infertility, had never mentioned bouts of depression. She could well not have realized she was pregnant but it was equally possible she had known of it: she could have bought a test kit. 'The best of them can give an accurate result, even at that early stage,' the doctor added.

The Chief sat in brooding silence as Lambert drove him back to the police station. Claire had been indisputably alive when Edgar left for work at eight-thirty that Friday morning, she had been seen later in the morning by the milkman and the postman. She had visited a local shop at around eleven; two women had seen her walking away from the shop in the direction of Fairbourne at about a quarter past eleven; that was the last sighting the police had of her.

Edgar's account of how he had spent that Friday had now been thoroughly checked and stood up in every particular. He had been at work from 8.45, was accounted for throughout the day, including the whole of the lunch-hour. Nor had inquiry revealed any weak point in his account of that evening, right up until the time he arrived home. But among the many questions bobbing about in the Chief's brain one was currently paramount: was Claire out of the house, as Edgar had stated, when he arrived home that evening at a quarter to eight?

Later in the morning the Chief went along to the College of Further Education. Claire's brutal end had created a tremendous stir, much talk and speculation. One of the office clerks clearly recalled Claire's husband phoning on the Monday morning to say she wouldn't be going on the theatre trip, wouldn't be attending classes for the next week or two, she'd gone to stay with a relative.

The lecturer in charge of the Friday-evening drama class Claire should have attended wouldn't be in college until five-thirty; the Chief said he would return then. In the meantime the Principal would have a list made out of the names and addresses of all students—and lecturers—in the three classes of which Claire had been a member.

As the Chief got back to his office after a snack lunch in the canteen a message came through from the desk sergeant: a woman had just come in, asking to speak to the Chief Inspector.

A constable brought her along to the Chief's office a few minutes later. She was a smartly dressed woman of seventy or so, with a briskly competent manner. A spinster, a retired shop manageress, devoting her time now to voluntary work for local charities. She didn't live in the Whitethorn area but she had heard from friends who did live there the kind of questions the house-to-house teams were asking; she believed she might be able to help. She had been collecting in the Whitethorn area for one of her charities that Friday afternoon, she had seen and spoken to Mrs Holroyd at around five-fifteen.

The Chief sat up. 'You're certain of the time?' he asked.

She gave a decisive nod. 'Quite certain. I've been over it in my mind. It was getting dark, the street lamps were on, the lights were on in the houses.' And she had looked at her watch when Mrs Holroyd had spoken of being in a hurry. She couldn't recall having seen anyone about the common that evening, the weather was cold and blustery. She produced for the Chief's inspection the pocket notebook in which she kept a scrupulous record of her collection rounds.

She had had some acquaintance with Mrs Holroyd from her charity work. That Friday afternoon she had taken the opportunity to ask Mrs Holroyd if she would like to lend a hand at a Christmas charity fair she was helping to organize. She closed her eyes in an effort to recall, at the Chief's request, the exact exchange that had taken place.

'I said: "If you've got a minute to spare, I could come

in now and tell you what it would entail." Mrs Holroyd
said: "Please don't think me rude but I haven't got time
just at the moment, I have a bus to catch, I must get ready.
Could I get in touch with you about it later?"'

'Are you sure she said "later"?' the Chief pressed her.
'Could she perhaps have said, "in the next day or two"?'

She frowned in concentration. 'I'm pretty sure she said
"later". I told her that would be fine, there was no great
hurry, the fair wasn't till the middle of December.'

'Did she seem at all agitated? Or depressed?'

She shook her head at once. 'Far from it. She was always
pleasant and polite but I particularly noticed how well and
happy she seemed.'

'Did she mention the exact time of the bus she was catching? Or where it was going?' Inquiries were still going forward, so far without result, in an attempt to discover if
Claire had boarded any bus or train that Friday, had made
use of any taxi.

She shook her head again. 'She didn't say.'

'Did she say she had to meet someone? Or that someone
was expecting her?'

Once more she shook her head.

'Did she have her coat on?'

She thought back. She couldn't recall exactly what Mrs
Holroyd had been wearing but she was sure it wasn't outdoor clothes.

When she didn't hear from Mrs Holroyd she made no
attempt to contact her again about the fair; if Mrs Holroyd
wasn't interested in helping she wouldn't want to press her.

The Chief was thoughtful after the woman had left. It
seemed now he was in a position to answer the question
bobbing about in his brain. Yes, it would appear that Claire
had been out of the house that Friday evening when her
husband returned from his meeting at a quarter to eight.

At five-twenty the Chief left the station for the college. He
spoke separately to all three lecturers in charge of the
evening classes Claire had been attending. Their reports

were all pretty much the same: Claire had been an interested, intelligent student, quiet in manner, pleasant and
courteous. Her attendance record was about average.

None of the three knew of any close relationship between
Claire and any other student or member of staff, nor had
any of the three had any acquaintance with Claire other
than the normal relationship between tutor and student.
The last class Claire had attended had been on the Thursday evening, November 15, from six till eight; there had
been nothing in any way unusual in her appearance or
behaviour.

The lecturer in charge of the Friday drama class clearly
recalled his phone call to Fairbourne after the class had
ended. He confirmed in all particulars Edgar's account of
their conversation.

Wednesday morning was busy with a conference and
briefings. In the afternoon the Chief paid a visit to
Hartley's. The manager hadn't known Claire, he had been
at the branch less than twelve months; he had been brought
in to carry out a programme of rationalization, in the course
of which the size of the staff had been much reduced. There
was no longer anyone at the store who had worked with
Claire but the manager was able to give the Chief the name
of a female assistant who had worked at Hartley's throughout Claire's time and was currently employed at York
House.

Trade at York House was slackening off when the Chief
and Lambert went in through the swing doors in the late
afternoon. The Chief was able to speak to the female assistant alone in the manager's office; she was a middle-aged
woman with a sharply knowing face.

She wouldn't go so far as to say she had been a friend of
Claire's, Claire had made no close friends at Hartley's,
though always pleasant enough. The woman's manner as
she spoke of Claire wore at first an appropriate overlay of
muted sorrow but as the Chief let her run on her manner

grew livelier, she began to speak more freely, traces of envy and malice started to surface.

'Claire thought a lot of herself in a quiet way,' she said with a movement of her head. 'She thought herself a cut above the common ruck. What was she, after all? Only an ordinary village girl.' She compressed her lips. 'Men that came into the shop always looked at her. I could see she liked that well enough, though she always made out she didn't notice.'

She leaned forward. 'It wasn't always grown men, either. There was a lad used to be forever hanging about, no more than a schoolboy. Saturdays, school holidays, he was never away from Hartley's, making out he was looking at birthday cards and paperbacks, gazing at her like a lovesick calf. She could have choked him off as easy as that.' She snapped her fingers. 'But she never did.'

She gave the Chief a smile charged with significance. 'Do you know who that lad was? Lester Holroyd, that's who. Brother of Edgar Holroyd, the man her ladyship married in the end. Funny the way things turn out.' She settled back in her chair. 'We all expected her to marry Robert Ashworth.' She slanted a look at the Chief. 'I expect you've heard all about him by now. You'll know he's back here in Cannonbridge, working at Calthrop's again, only this time of course he's a lot further up the ladder. He's been back here since August.'

She gave the Chief another meaningful smile. 'He got married no time at all after he and Claire broke up. Makes you wonder what sort of marriage it's turned out. They don't all prosper, not when folk go rushing into them on the rebound.' She seemed all at once to catch the tone of her own observations and fell abruptly silent. When she resumed her voice was once more discreetly subdued.

'I had a lift to work this morning from a woman in the footwear department here. She said Claire ordered some boots a while back and they came in a couple of weeks ago. She sent Claire a card to let her know.' She paused to give due weight to her next utterance. 'Edgar Holroyd came in to collect the boots.' At the Chief's request she took herself off, full of importance, to summon the footwear assistant. The store was on the point of closing when the assistant came along to the office a few minutes later.

She explained that Mrs Holroyd took a very narrow fitting, it was always necessary to order specially for her. She had paid the usual deposit for the boots—an expensive pair, high fashion, in first-quality suède—at the time the order was put in, early in November. On November 21 the assistant posted a card to say the boots had arrived. The following Saturday morning, November 24, Mr Holroyd called in to pay the amount outstanding and pick up the boots.

She hadn't been too happy about letting them go. They were very close-fitting, very elegant. Mrs Holroyd had always come in herself to pick up the order, make sure of the fit, she had always been most particular about that. But Mr Holroyd had explained that his wife had gone away for a break, he couldn't say exactly when she'd be back. He thought he'd better take the boots, he was sure it would be all right. 'So I let them go,' the assistant said. 'I couldn't really do otherwise.'

As the two policemen left the store Sergeant Lambert caught sight of a face he recognized in the steady stream of men and women pouring out through the staff exit. 'There's Jill Lingard,' he told the Chief.

'Nip across and catch her,' the Chief instructed. 'We'll run her home.' Lambert came back with her a minute or two later, she seemed pleased at not having to join a bus queue. On the way across the car park the Chief asked how she was feeling, if she had recovered from the shock of her discovery on Sunday evening.

'I'm getting over it,' she told him. She had been shaky and tearful, unfit for work, all day Monday, but when she woke on Tuesday after a good night's sleep she had been relieved to find she was well enough to go back to her duties. It had been the best thing for her, it had helped to take her mind off what had happened. That was something Norman had made her see after her grandfather's death, that it's best to get on with normal living as soon as possible, they should go ahead and get engaged, the way they'd agreed. As they halted by the car she smiled and held out her left hand. 'Would you like to see my ring?' she asked the Chief. 'It's Victorian,' she added with pride and pleasure. 'Norman knows I prefer old jewellery.'

The Chief took her hand and gazed down at the ring: garnets and diamonds set in a heart shape, the stones too small to have any great value. 'Very pretty,' he told her. 'Do you know where Norman got it?'

'Wychford,' she answered promptly. 'At the antiques market. He didn't have to pay over the odds for it, he got it for a lot less than if he'd bought it in a shop.'

After dropping Jill the Chief consulted his watch. Too late now to phone Calthrop's to get Ashworth's address. But Lambert knew a girl who worked in Calthrop's office, he rang her flat, catching her as she came in. Yes, she knew Ashworth's local address, he was renting one of the furnished properties on Calthrop's books, a very nice old cottage in a village a few miles from Cannonbridge. He lived there during the week, returning at weekends to his home a hundred miles away. He would be selling his own house, looking for one locally for his family.

Lambert drove the Chief straight over to the cottage which stood in a secluded spot down a lane some distance from the centre of the village; lights shone out from the dwelling as they approached.

Ashworth answered the door to them; an undeniably handsome man, tall and broad-shouldered. He hadn't been in long, he was making himself a meal. He abandoned his preparations and took them into the sitting-room. He had been horrified to hear of Claire's death and was still clearly distressed at what had happened.

The Chief told him he had spoken to Mrs Finch, he knew about Ashworth's old relationship with Claire, her accident, the way things had ended between them. Ashworth expressed relief at that; he would have found it painful to have to go over it all for them himself at this moment. He seemed to share the common view that Claire had been killed by whoever had killed Harry Lingard, in the course of some mugging attack that had gone wrong.

He answered questions readily. After the breach with Claire there had always remained a sore point in his mind about the way things had ended, but during the eight years he had been away from Cannonbridge he had never had contact of any kind with her, had never made any attempt to get in touch with her again, fully accepting that that was what she wanted. When he returned to the town a few months ago he had no intention of seeking any contact with her. He had heard of her marriage. He was happily married himself, with two children.

But one morning in town, not long after his return, he had chanced to see her and it was plain she had seen him. He realized this was likely to keep on happening, it couldn't be avoided. He had phoned her later that same day to suggest a meeting. It would be better to deal head-on with the situation right away, dispose once and for all of possible awkwardness in any future encounters.

She had in no way misunderstood his purpose in phoning, she agreed immediately it would be a good idea. They arranged to meet for lunch a few days later—that would be around the third week in September. He picked her up in the town and they drove out to a country pub. The meeting had accomplished all he had hoped for. It had resolved the past for both of them, given them both some kind of absolution from mistakes and misunderstandings, sent them back to their separate lives with the slate wiped clean.

'It was all very civilized and friendly,' he said. Claire had struck him as having plenty of interests, a very positive attitude towards the future. She had told him she was thinking of taking an Open University course. One of the university tutors had visited the college to give a talk. Claire had spoken to the tutor afterwards, he had been very encouraging. She felt she had a whole new area of life opening up.

Afterwards he had driven her back into town. There was no suggestion on either side of any further meeting. He had never spoken to her again. The only time he had so much as seen her was at the Acorn dinner-dance a few weeks later. She had been there with her husband. 'I thought she looked very beautiful,' he added with great sadness. He had smiled across at her but had received in reply only a fleeting nod; it was clear she had no wish for him to approach the two of them. He had respected that wish, he believed he understood; she would probably have felt awkward, introducing him to Edgar, and she certainly wouldn't have relished the notion of chance onlookers who knew their story watching the encounter with interest and curiosity. He had never afterwards so much as glimpsed her in the street.

CHAPTER 12

The inquest on Claire Margaret Holroyd was set down for eleven o'clock on Thursday morning. Shortly after ten a uniformed constable from the team that had dealt with house-to-house inquiries after the death of Harry Lingard came along to Chief Inspector Kelsey's office, wishing to speak to him.

The constable was currently engaged in making return calls on households where it was deemed necessary. One such call yesterday evening was to a Mrs Locke, an elderly widow living close to the council estate where Harry Lingard had lived. Mrs Locke had a lodger, a steady young man of twenty in regular work; he had been fully cleared on the constable's first visit.

But this lodger had a friend—or, more correctly, a casual acquaintance met at a disco—of about the same age. He had spun a hard-luck story and the lodger had persuaded Mrs Locke to let him stay at the house for a few days around the middle of November. He had left Mrs Locke's on the morning of Saturday, November 17; neither Mrs Locke nor her lodger knew his home address or precisely where he was bound when he left the house. He had told them he would be back again before long. Mrs Locke had thought him a decent enough lad, she had told him she could always find him a bed if he was stuck another time. There was no reason to believe he had been in any way involved in Harry Lingard's death but a return visit must be made in every such instance. When the constable called again yesterday evening Mrs Locke told him the lad hadn't so far shown up or got in touch.

But the reason the constable wished now to speak to the Chief had nothing to do with the vanishing young man, it had to do with Mrs Locke. At the end of the constable's visit yesterday evening she had spoken to him with some distress about the second murder, the discovery of Claire Holroyd's body. 'It turns out,' the constable said, 'Mrs Locke worked for the Holroyd family for years, she knew them all well. I thought I'd mention it in case you felt it might be worth having a word with her.'

Five minutes later Sergeant Lambert found himself snatched from his desk and despatched to Mrs Locke's. The morning was wet and blowy, raw blasts assailed him as he got out of the car and ran up the front steps to press the doorbell.

When he told Mrs Locke who he was her lined face broke into a smile. 'I'm glad you've called,' she declared. 'It'll save me a trip to the police station.' She peered out at the boisterous morning. 'Come in, come in,' she bade him. 'You look as if you could do with a good hot cup of tea.' Lambert offered no resistance. She ushered him into a warm kitchen, bustled about with kettle and teapot, produced a tin of her own dark gingerbread, sticky and delicious.

'We had a postcard this morning from the young man the constable was asking about,' she told Lambert. 'He's coming back here on Monday for a few days. I'll see he calls in at the station—I'll go along with him myself to make sure.' Now that that was satisfactorily out of the way she began without prompting to talk about the murder of Claire Holroyd. 'Her poor husband,' she said. 'It must be terrible for him. I did wonder if I should call round to see how he is, if there's anything I can do, but then I thought better not, it might seem like an intrusion.' She needed no encouragement to launch into a nostalgic account of her long connection with the Holroyd family.

She had gone to work at Fairbourne—for Edgar's grand-mother—as a general domestic, as soon as she left school. She had worked there, on and off, full-time or part-time, through all the years of her growing-up, her marriage, the birth of her children, her widowhood, until a few years ago when she had finally decided to call it a day. 'Edgar had just got married,' she said. 'His wife was sure she'd be able to manage without help, so I didn't feel I'd be leaving them in the lurch.'

Edgar had always treated her with every consideration. 'A real gentleman,' she pronounced him. 'Takes after his father. Now Lester, he takes after his mother's side. Lovely-looking woman, she was, she died the day after Lester was born. She wasn't a young woman by that time, and she'd never been strong. Her poor husband took it very hard, though he never talked about it. Folk that didn't know him might think he hadn't cared for her, but I knew different. Still waters, that's the type he was. Edgar's just the same.

'I did my share of mothering Lester—I'd got to be cook-housekeeper by then. Edgar could hardly take it in his mother was dead, he'd been that fond of her. He was always a sensitive boy, very serious, always thoughtful and helpful. He'd often give me a hand round the house, he got to be quite useful. After their father died, Edgar brought Lester up himself, he thought the world of that boy, always nursed him when he was ill, as good as any woman. I always fancied he saw it as a kind of trust from his mother, to look after the baby she'd died bringing into the world.

'Lester's a very different nature from Edgar, always high-spirited and adventurous. And he knew how to get his own way, he could charm the birds off the trees when he'd a mind to. He always had a quick temper, quickly up and quickly over. Now Edgar, I never once knew him to lose his temper, he was like his father in that. Very fond of exercise, Edgar, that's another way he took after his father. He went right through school as fit as a flea, never once missed a day through illness. Lester was a strong, sturdy little lad but he took pretty near every childish ailment you could mention—not that he took any of them badly.' The clock on the mantelshelf struck the half-hour. Lambert pushed back his chair. Time to be off, back to the station, the Chief would shortly be thinking about getting along to the inquest.

Mrs Locke didn't interrupt her flow as she walked with him to the front door. 'I was ever so pleased when Edgar got married. I'd thought for sure he'd stay single all his days, he never had a ladyfriend before, to my certain knowledge.' She shook her head sorrowfully. 'And now this dreadful thing to happen. I doubt he'll ever get over it.'

The court proceedings were as brief and formal as in the case of Harry Lingard. Edgar Holroyd looked pale and strained when he arrived at the court-house, even more pale and strained when he left. On the way out the Chief told him he would be glad of another word; they followed Edgar's estate car back to Fairbourne. 'Would there be any objection to my going back to work tomorrow?' Edgar asked the Chief as he let them into the house. 'I find it very difficult being here by myself all day. No one comes near me, I can understand well enough. They don't know what to say.'

'What about your brother and sister-in-law?' Kelsey put in. 'Have they been in touch?'

Edgar shook his head. 'I saw Diane at the inquest just now but she was gone before I had a chance to speak to her. I hadn't seen her since the Acorn dinner-dance, when she was there with Lester. Neither of them came near Claire or me all evening.' He was silent for a moment. 'They're young, it must be difficult for them to know how to handle the situation.'

He put up a hand and pressed his forehead. 'I do my best to keep occupied but I can't stop going over it all in my mind, trying to work out what could have happened, who could have done it.' His face was haggard. 'It's wearing me out.' He had seen his doctor, he had been prescribed pills for day and night. 'But that's not the answer,' he said with distaste. 'All they do is make me feel like a zombie. I'd be better if I could get back to work.'

'We've no objection,' the Chief assured him.

'That's good,' Edgar exclaimed with marked relief.

The Chief brought up the matter of the boots Claire had ordered at York House. Yes, Edgar remembered them. He took the Chief upstairs to the spacious front bedroom. The room had a deserted look, the twin beds had been stripped, the tops of the dressing-table and chest of drawers were bare. Not a single personal oddment was anywhere in evidence. No trace now of perfume, only the mingled scents of air freshener, polish, household cleaner.

Edgar saw the Chief's ranging glance. 'I've moved into the room across the landing,' he said flatly. He went to a cupboard and took out a large plastic carrier bag bearing the name of York House. Inside was a cardboard box; inside that, wrapped in layers of tissue paper, a pair of elegant boots in fine suède, a subtle shade of light brown. On top of the boots was a folded receipt dated November 24.

'I thought it best to pick them up,' Edgar said as he restored the boots to the box, the box to the bag. He was about to replace the bag in the cupboard when it appeared to hit him that there was now no need for that, Claire would never be coming home again, would never go to the cupboard to take out the boots, her eyes bright with pleasure.

He stood frozen, holding the bag, looking utterly stricken. Then he rallied himself, set the bag down on the floor without a word and led the way out of the room and downstairs again.

The Chief asked if there had been any similar matters Edgar had had to attend to, matters Claire had forgotten or overlooked.

Edgar was steadier now. Yes, there was the hairdresser, he had rung the salon on the Saturday morning to cancel Claire's next appointment. And he had looked out her library books and returned them. He had learned those two lessons the first time Claire had taken herself off; there had been a hairdresser's bill to pay for a missed appointment, library fines on overdue books.

The Chief turned to another matter. He asked if Claire had owned a garnet ring.

'Yes, she did,' Edgar replied at once. 'Her godmother left her some pieces of Victorian jewellery, one of them was a garnet ring, set with little diamonds and garnets in a heart shape. No great value but very pretty.'

'Would you mind looking through her jewel box to see if the ring is there?' the Chief asked.

Edgar left the room and came back with the box. He set it down on a table, lifted out the trays, subjected the contents to scrutiny. 'It doesn't seem to be here,' he said at last. 'She must have been wearing it.' A thought seemed to strike him with the force of a blow. He flashed a distraught look at the Chief. 'Why are you asking about the ring? How did you know she had a garnet ring? Have you found it?'

The Chief raised a calming hand. 'Take it easy. You're going much too fast.' Edgar drew a deep breath, tried to steady himself.

'Perhaps you could sketch the ring for us,' the Chief suggested.

Edgar was ready to try. He went to a drawer and took out a pen and paper, he set about his task with concentration. When he had finished he surveyed his efforts. 'I don't think that's too far out,' he said as he handed over the drawing. The Chief studied it; a very workmanlike sketch.

There could be little doubt; it was either the ring Jill Lingard had shown him or its identical twin. Again he changed tack. 'One other thing: are you acquainted with a Mr Robert Ashworth?'

Edgar showed no surprise. 'I've never met him but I know who he is. Claire was very friendly with him years ago, when she worked at Hartley's.'

'Are you aware that Ashworth recently returned to Cannonbridge?'

Edgar nodded. 'I saw a paragraph about it in the local paper.'

'Did you mention the paragraph to your wife?'

'Certainly not!' Edgar said with a return of energy. 'Ashworth belonged to the past. Claire had put all that behind her. It was Claire who broke off the relationship, not Ashworth.'

'Did you know your wife met Ashworth for lunch not long after he came back to Cannonbridge?'

Edgar gaped at him. 'That's not true!' he declared with force. 'I don't know where you got such a tale.'

'We got it from Robert Ashworth,' the Chief informed him. 'Yesterday evening.' Edgar made no reply. 'Your wife made no mention to you of any meeting?' the Chief pursued. Edgar shook his head in silence. 'According to Ashworth,' the Chief added, 'there was just the one meeting. It was by way of laying the past to rest.'

That seemed to bring a measure of comfort to Edgar. 'In the circumstances,' he said heavily, 'I suppose it was the sensible thing to do.' He looked at the Chief. 'And not telling me about it, I think I can understand that. Claire wouldn't want to upset me in any way.'

CHAPTER 13

Late on Thursday afternoon the Chief decided to call on
Buckley, the newly retired Mansell worker. The Chief had
had another word with the Fraud Squad; it seemed that
Buckley had readily supplied some useful pointers.

Buckley lived in a semi-detached house on a mixed development put up by Mansell five years ago. Solidly built
dwellings, the area pleasantly landscaped, shaded by ma-
ture trees, the whole estate attractive to the eye.

Buckley was lounging unshaven on a sofa in the sitting-
room, smoking, eating crisps, drinking beer, watching a
soap opera on TV. His wife was in the kitchen preparing
the evening meal. She clicked her tongue in irritation at the
sound of Sergeant Lambert's ring on the bell. She darted
out of the kitchen and snatched open the front door. The
Chief gave her a swiftly assessing glance: rising sixty, smart
and well groomed in her fashion, a chronically discontented
expression, forehead seamed with lines.

He didn't explain who they were, he had a strong feeling
it might prove counter-productive; he merely asked if her
husband was in. She raked the pair of them with her sharp
little lizard eyes. The Chief gazed blandly back. She gave
a curt nod, wheeled about and went at a rush along the
passage. She threw open a door, stuck her head inside and
flung three words into the room: 'Someone for you.' She
about turned and whisked back to her kitchen, leaving the
callers to make their own way into the sitting-room.

The Chief played no games with Buckley but told him at
once who they were. Buckley displayed no irritation at the
intrusion, he appeared to relish the prospect of a chat,
though his enthusiasm didn't propel him to his feet. He
snuffed out his soap opera by means of the remote control
switch and waved his visitors into armchairs. He wasted no
time on social graces, didn't offer them any of his store of

goodies though his own consumption continued unchecked.

'I've had a couple of your Fraud Squad lot round here,' he announced with an air of mingled importance and self-congratulation. 'I expect you know about that.' He tapped the side of his nose with a forefinger, assumed a theatrical expression of low cunning—to indicate, presumably, that he could be relied on to keep his trap shut.

'That isn't what I'm here about,' Kelsey said. He asked if Buckley knew of any recent confrontation between Harry Lingard and Tom Mansell over the purchase of a property for development.

Yes, Buckley did know of such a confrontation. He hadn't witnessed it himself but he had heard talk about it from men who had. It had taken place in the yard, first thing on the Monday morning before Harry's death. He didn't know which particular property was involved. It seemed that Harry had some personal interest in the matter, some connection with the vendor; he hadn't been too happy about the price paid. He had got short shrift from Mansell.

'Norman Griffin,' the Chief said. 'What do you make of him?'

'Boss's man,' Buckley replied at once with a sour grimace. 'Mansell's opening another yard over in Wychford, Lester Holroyd's to be in charge of it. I hear Master Norman's getting a leg up as well when the yard opens. It certainly pays to crawl.'

'You've not got a very high opinion of Norman,' the Chief observed.

Buckley snorted. 'He doesn't need my good opinion, he's got a good enough opinion of himself. Fancies himself a real ladies' man.'

'Is that so?'

Buckley cocked an eye at the Chief. 'Mrs Holroyd, her that was murdered, whenever she did a turn in the office Norman was always hanging about, giving her the eye every chance he got. You can ask any of the men, they all used to pull his leg about her.'

'Did she notice?'

He gave another snort. 'She'd have had to be blind not to notice. Lester Holroyd had to speak to Norman about it a couple of times.'

'Did Mrs Holroyd take it as a joke? Or was she offended?'

Buckley's eyes glinted. 'The lads always had it she fancied Norman.'

'Do you know if there was ever anything between them?'

'Can't say I actually know of anything,' Buckley answered with regret. 'She was always very much the lady.' He pulled down the corners of his mouth. 'But that type's not above fancying a bit of rough when it comes down to it. And for sure Norman would have been in there, given half a chance.'

On their way to the Griffins' cottage they called in at the police station to pick up a driver. As they entered the road leading to the cottage Lambert spied Norman's van turning into the driveway. When they followed him in a couple of minutes later the van was drawn up by the garage and Norman was opening the garage doors. He remained where he was, looking across at them in silence, his face expressing nothing. The Chief got out and went over to him. 'No need to put your van away just yet,' he said. He offered no explanation and Norman didn't ask for any. 'We'd better go into the house,' the Chief added.

Norman led the way in through the back door, into the kitchen. An appetizing smell hung on the air; a single place had been laid at the table. There was no sign of Mrs Griffin but an old envelope propped up against the sugar basin bore a message to say she was baby-sitting for a neighbour, she wouldn't be back till nine. Norman would find his dinner in the oven. 'You can eat while we talk,' Kelsey said but Norman shook his head, he would wait till they'd gone. He didn't offer to make tea. He drank a cup of cold water from the tap and took his seat opposite them at the table. The Chief wasted no time. 'You knew Claire Holroyd,' he began.

'We all knew her at the yard,' Norman said flatly.

'You fancied her,' the Chief said. A statement, not a question.

Norman didn't deny it. 'She was a very good-looking woman. I dare say every man in the yard fancied her.'

'Maybe so, but Lester Holroyd didn't feel obliged to speak to every man in the yard about it.'

A spark of anger flashed in Norman's eye. 'That didn't mean anything. Lester only said it as a joke.'

The Chief let that go. 'The engagement ring you gave Jill Lingard—where did you get it?'

Norman was very alert now. 'I bought it in the antiques market in Wychford.'

'When did you buy it?'

'I can tell you that exactly. Three weeks before Jill's birthday. On a Friday, the market's always on a Friday.' He went to a wall calendar and ran a finger down the columns. 'November 9, that would be.'

'How much did you pay for the ring?'

'Two hundred pounds.' He couldn't tell them the name of the stallholder but he was sure he could find the stall again, sure he could recognize the man.

'How did you pay for it?' the Chief wanted to know.

'I paid in cash,' Norman told him.

'Where did you get the cash?'

'I drew it out of the building society at dinner-time the day before. You can take a look at my passbook.' He went rapidly from the room, returning a minute or two later. He slapped the open passbook down on the table in front of the Chief, stabbed a finger at an entry. 'Withdrawal. £200 cash. November 8.'

'How did you know you'd find a ring for the exact amount you drew out?'

'I didn't know. It was pure chance. I had over a hundred in cash on me before I went to the building society. I was prepared to go to two-fifty for a ring.'

'All that entry proves,' the Chief said blandly, 'is that you drew out two hundred pounds, you could have spent it on anything, paying bills, buying clothes.' He looked through the passbook before handing it back, there was no record in recent weeks of any cash sum having been paid in. He asked if Norman had any other account, bank, building society, post office, and was told no. 'Now,' the Chief said briskly, like a man who has disposed of inessentials, 'let's get down to the nitty-gritty. You never bought that ring at any antiques market.' Norman sat very still, his eyes wary. 'That ring belonged to Claire Holroyd,' Kelsey said.

Norman suddenly broke into speech, almost before the Chief had finished. 'All right, so I did get it from Claire. I bought it off her for two hundred pounds.'

'Is that so?' Kelsey said on a note of strong scepticism. 'You'd better tell us about it.'

Norman plunged into his tale. 'I was in Cannonbridge town centre one dinner-time. I can tell you the date: November 7. I was looking in a jeweller's window, at the engagement rings. Claire came up behind me. She asked me if I was thinking of getting engaged, she said it in a friendly, jokey way. I told her yes, I was, I was trying to get an idea of prices, what the shops were asking for new rings, but it wasn't a new ring I was after, Jill would much rather have an old ring, she liked Victorian jewellery.

'Claire said maybe she could help me. She had a Victorian ring she was thinking of selling, she had it from her godmother. She wanted the money to buy a special Christmas present for her husband. I asked if I could see the ring. She said sure. She was just on her way to catch her bus home. I had the van parked round the corner, I said I'd give her a lift.

'As soon as I saw the ring I knew it was exactly what Jill wanted. We agreed the price. Claire said she'd like it in cash. I drew the money out of the building society next day, November 8, as it shows in the passbook. I went straight along to Fairbourne with the money. A couple of weeks later I took the ring into a jeweller's in Cannonbridge, making out I was thinking of selling it. I was offered two-fifty for it on the spot, so I was well satisfied with my bargain.'

'The notes you gave Claire, what were they? Tens? Twenties? Fifties? Did you notice if they were old or new?'

'I did notice, they were new, in sequence, twenty-pound notes. I remember being pleased they were new, Claire was the sort of person you'd rather not pay in dirty old notes.'

'You handed over the money, she gave you the ring, and that was the end of it?'

'Yes, except she said she'd like the deal kept just between the two of us, she'd rather I didn't even tell Jill. I said OK.'

'Any objection if we take a look round while we're here?'

'None at all, I've nothing to hide.' He didn't follow them round but stayed in the kitchen to eat his meal. He had just about finished when the two policemen came back into the kitchen after a fruitless search.

'We'd like to take a look at your van,' the Chief told him. Norman offered no objection, he followed them outside. The Chief made straight for the police car and spoke to the driver who got out and went across to Norman's van; he opened the door and got into the driving seat. The keys were still in the ignition, he switched on.

'You're never taking the van away?' Norman cried in tones of outrage. 'I thought you were going to look at it here.'

'Job for Forensic,' Kelsey said. The driver reversed the van to drive out. 'I need it to get to work,' Norman protested. 'I've got to have it back by tonight.'

The Chief shook his head. 'That won't be possible. Can't say how long they'll keep it, depends what they find.' The driver moved off, out, away. As the Chief walked towards his car he was halted by Norman's voice. 'If Claire was having it off with anyone from Mansell's it certainly wasn't me. I wasn't the only one at the yard that fancied her.'

The Chief swung round. Norman looked as if he could say more but was weighing the wisdom of going further.

'So who else fancied her?' the Chief pressed him.

Still Norman hesitated. The Chief had a fleeting but distinct impression that he was contemplating more than one name, but when he did speak he uttered the name of only one man: 'Lester Holroyd.' An instant later he looked as if he was already regretting opening his mouth.

'Go on,' Kelsey urged. 'You can't stop now.' Norman hesitated again, eyeing the Chief. At last he appeared to make up his mind. 'It was one afternoon, back in the summer. I was driving out to a site a few miles out of Cannonbridge. There was a traffic diversion, I had to take another road. That took me past a property Tom Mansell had bought a month or two before, an old farmhouse with quite a bit of land. He was going to turn the house into flats, put up starter homes on the land. I thought I'd stop and take a look.

'I left the van by the gate and had a walk round. I came across a car parked round the back, Lester Holroyd's car. I thought nothing of it, he'd just be taking another look at the property. Then I heard a woman laughing inside the house, it stopped me in my tracks. The woman said something, then there was a man's voice. I couldn't make out what they were saying but I thought I knew both those voices. The woman laughed again, she said something else, then the man's voice again. I was quite sure then. It was Claire Holroyd. And the man was Lester.'

'How did that make you feel? Jealous?'

'No,' Norman replied calmly, 'it did not make me feel jealous. It made me feel very keen to remove myself from the property in double-quick time and make no noise about it, either. I was back in my van and off down the road in a flash.'

'Did you say anything about it afterwards to anyone? Anyone at all?'

He gave a forceful shake of his head. 'I most certainly did not. I know when to keep my mouth shut.'

'You're opening it now,' the Chief observed.

'I've no intention of letting myself be stitched up for something I know nothing about,' Norman said with heat. 'I had a taste of that when I was a lad, too young to be able to do anything about it. As sure as hell I'm not letting it happen a second time.'

Jill Lingard was washing her hair when the police car pulled up outside the little terrace dwelling. One of the girls who shared the house showed the two policemen into the living-room and went off to fetch Jill who came along a minute or two later with her head swathed in a towel.

The Chief took her back to last Sunday afternoon. Was it Jill or Norman who had first suggested looking at the house in Tolladine Road?

'I suggested it,' Jill replied at once. 'Norman never wanted to look at it, not even after we got there. He was positive all along it wouldn't suit us.'

'Why was he so sure?' the Chief asked. 'It doesn't seem at all a bad house to me.'

'I thought it was pretty good,' she agreed. 'I don't really know why he was so against it. I thought at the time he was being unreasonable. He said it was sure to be full of dry rot, but it wasn't. I think maybe he'd got it into his head it was bound to be in a bad state if it had stood empty so long, so he just wrote it off, wouldn't even consider it.'

'Had he been in the house himself at any time before last Sunday?'

She looked surprised. 'No, of course not, he'd have said if he had.' She put up her hands to adjust her slipping towel and he saw her fingers were bare.

'You're not wearing your ring,' he said.

She smiled. 'I haven't lost it, if that's what you're thinking. I took it off to wash my hair.'

'I'm afraid I must ask you to let us have the ring—just for the present.'

She was astounded. 'Let you have my ring? What on earth for?'

'It's possible it may have some connection with the case.'

She stared at him in open-mouthed bewilderment, then her expression changed to one of dawning horror. 'You think it belonged to Mrs Holroyd.' Her face was contorted. 'You think—' She broke off with a shuddering breath.

'If you could fetch the ring,' the Chief said gently. 'We'll take good care of it.' She burst into tears and ran from the room. Her feet pounded up the stairs. A few moments later they came pounding down again. She ran into the room and threw the ring at him. 'If it was hers, if it was taken off . . .' She was sobbing and gasping. 'I don't want it back again. Ever.'

CHAPTER 14

'Lester Holroyd's place,' the Chief instructed Lambert as they got back into the car. They found Lester at home, finishing his supper. 'My wife's out at work,' he told them. 'She's a trained nurse.' He mentioned a factory on the industrial estate. 'She works the second shift, two till ten.'

'Has she been on the second shift long?' the Chief asked.

'Since June.' Lester's face took on a look of distress. 'This is a terrible business about Claire, I find it difficult to take in. You know she did relief work sometimes at the yard?'

'Yes, we do know. It's about one of Mansell's men we'd like to ask you now. Norman Griffin. Were you ever aware of any relationship between Norman and Claire?'

Lester didn't appear surprised. 'Nothing of any consequence,' he replied with a movement of his shoulders. 'I think Norman may have been a bit smitten, nothing serious.'

'Did you ever have occasion to speak to him about it?'

'I may have said something once, nothing heavy. He was hanging round the office, if I remember. I asked him if he'd nothing better to do.'

'Did you ever notice anyone else at the yard paying attention to Claire?'

He shook his head. 'She never encouraged anything like that.'

The Chief changed tack. 'Have you and your wife been in touch with your brother since Claire's body was found?'

There was an uncomfortable silence before Lester answered. 'No, we haven't.'

'May I ask why not?'

Lester shifted in his chair. 'Neither of us could think what to do or say. We hadn't been in touch with either of them for some time, the two women never got on. Diane thought it would seem hypocritical to go round now after being unfriendly to Claire while she was alive.'

'How did you get on with Claire when she worked in the office?'

'Well enough. She was a good worker, very accurate. She was always very quiet, she never stood about chatting. I didn't see all that much of her. I'm out of the office a good deal.'

'Did you see anything of her outside the office?'

'No. As I told you, we hadn't seen anything of either of them for some time.'

'What I'm asking you,' the Chief enunciated slowly and clearly, 'is this: did you, on your own, see anything of Claire, on her own, outside the office?'

Lester frowned. 'Just what are you suggesting?'

'I'm suggesting nothing. I'm putting a plain, straightforward question. Did you see anything of Claire outside the office?'

'And I'll give you a plain, straightforward answer,' Lester retorted. 'No, I did not.'

The Chief pressed on, undeterred. 'Did you ever arrange to meet Claire, drive her out to some quiet spot? Some secluded property on the firm's books, perhaps, not yet ready for work to start on it?'

'I most certainly never did anything of the kind,' Lester returned angrily. 'It's monstrous to suggest such a thing.'

'Perhaps you have some other lady friend—or more than one lady friend—you're in the habit of driving out to empty properties on the firm's books?'

'I have no such lady friends,' Lester declared with increasing warmth.

'So if someone tells me your car was seen parked on one

of the firm's sites one afternoon, parked round the back of the house out of sight, and that person heard voices inside the house—'

'So that's what all this is about!' Lester broke in with a broad smile. 'That's easily accounted for. I'd be over at the site, whichever one it was, checking something or other. I always have a pocket radio with me when I'm out, I like to keep up with the sports results.' He sat back in his chair. 'That's what your snooper heard.'

'So you never fancied Claire? Never at all?'

'I wouldn't go so far as to say that. I had a crush on her years ago when I was a lad, still at school—when she was working at Hartley's.' He smiled slightly. 'It didn't last long, they never did. I must have had a crush on a dozen females before I left school. I don't suppose Claire even noticed me, just one more spotty schoolboy. She certainly never mentioned it after we met, years later, when she got to know Edgar.'

'Wasn't it you that asked her if she would do relief work for Mansell's?'

'Yes, but only because Mansell asked me to ring her and suggest it.'

'One more thing,' the Chief went on. 'Just a matter of routine. Could we have a note of your movements for the evening of Friday, November 16?'

If he expected Lester to erupt into protest he was disappointed. After a short pause to cast his mind back Lester answered readily. The evening had been much as usual. He had got in from work around six-thirty, had a meal, read the paper, watched TV. At around a quarter past eight he left the house, got into his car and made a tour of various sites belonging to the firm, arriving home again shortly before ten. Diane had got in from the factory at her usual time, around ten-fifteen; she was tired and went straight to bed. He had stayed up for another hour or so, watching TV. They had spent a quiet weekend, Diane hadn't felt well. He had suggested she took a day or two off work but she insisted she was recovered by Monday morning and went to work as usual.

'Do you often drive round the sites in the evening?' Kelsey asked.

'Yes, I do,' Lester told him. He found it a useful aid to security, particularly on a Friday and Saturday when the risk of depredations by drunken louts was at its highest; he enjoyed the drive round. He didn't go out every evening, nor did he visit every site on every run, but he never left any site unvisited for long. His times of setting out and returning varied according to the weather, his inclination, what programmes were on TV.

'Did you meet anyone you knew while you were out that evening?' the Chief asked. 'Did you speak to anyone?'

Again Lester cast his mind back. 'Yes, as a matter of fact I did.' He had encountered two men he knew, encountered them separately, several miles apart. The first encounter was with a bricklayer, currently employed by the firm, who had been walking to his local pub in a village close to Cannonbridge. Lester had slowed the car, had stuck his head out and exchanged a few joking remarks. 'That would be not long after nine,' he guessed.

The second encounter was with a former employee of the firm, living in a village some distance from Cannonbridge. Lester had come across him as he walked back to his car after checking a site; it could have been around nine-thirty. The man was taking his evening constitutional, he was in the habit of stopping by that particular site to check progress, keep an eye out for thieves and vandals; even though he had been retired a couple of years he still took an interest in the firm's activities. Lester had come across him more than once on his checking runs; he had stopped and spoken to the man for a few minutes that Friday evening, as he had done on previous occasions.

He gave the Chief the names of both men. He couldn't offhand supply their addresses but he would phone the addresses through to the station first thing in the morning, as soon as he got to work.

Shortly after the offices of the Cannonbridge weekly newspaper came to life on Friday morning the Chief went along
to look at the back number carrying a report and colour
photographs of the Acorn dinner-dance. He was also shown
a further batch of colour photographs, taken during the
evening but not used in the paper.

In the ordinary way the Chief would have been present
at the dinner-dance himself; it was one of the local events
he felt obliged to attend although not the kind of evening
he much enjoyed. A divorced man, with little of a social life
nowadays, it was always a tricky business finding a suitable
partner for such a function. He had never been more than
a barely adequate performer on the dance-floor; he no
longer drank or smoked. Chronic indigestion ensured
that any but the most modest sampling of the rich fare
invariably provided would be well and truly paid for afterwards.

This year he had been away for the second half of
October, using up the last of his annual leave. He had
bought two tickets for the dinner-dance, given them away,
made a donation to the Acorn fund and then taken himself
off with a clear conscience for two weeks of coarse fishing
on the Wye.

He studied the paper, then the batch of photographs. He
spotted Robert Ashworth right away, in a group of men in
earnest conversation by the bar. Lester Holroyd and Stuart
Mansell, looking very matey, chatting and laughing on their
way out of the dining-room. Edgar Holroyd, standing alone,
watching the dancing, his face empty of expression.

Diane Holroyd was easy to pick out. She appeared
in several photographs, eye-catching in low-cut, figure-
hugging scarlet, clearly in high spirits. Her sister-in-law
took more finding. He came upon Claire at last in two
photographs; in both she was at Edgar's side. She was
dressed with understated elegance in a softly draped gown
in a delicate shade of blue-grey. She looked very beautiful
but somewhat remote as if not much enjoying the evening.

Tom Mansell looked out of many photographs. In the forefront of a jovial group of men, being slapped on the back. Saying a few words at the donation ceremony, pleasure and satisfaction plainly discernible under a veil of would-be modesty. Seated at the dining-table with Diane beside him, smiling and chatting. On his feet, still at the dinner-table, raising his glass in a toast.

Kelsey picked up the final photograph. Tom Mansell again. On the dance-floor this time for some dreamy number, lights turned low; a slow waltz, perhaps, near the end of the evening. His partner held in a close embrace, her eyes shut. His son Stuart standing on the edge of the floor, gazing across at the slowly circling pair: his father with an absorbed look on his face, and his father's partner, Claire Holroyd.

CHAPTER 15

Diane Holroyd was busy with household chores when Sergeant Lambert pressed the doorbell at half past nine. She answered the ring almost before the sound had died away; she didn't need to be told who they were. The Chief asked if they might step inside, there were one or two questions he would like to ask, he would try not to keep her long. 'Don't worry about that, I'm in no rush,' she assured him as she showed them into the sitting-room. Her manner was breezily confident, she exuded the same air of raw energy as her father. She sat them down, whisked out of the room, returning swiftly with a tray of coffee.

The Chief began by asking about her relationship with Claire. She made no secret of the fact that they had never taken to each other, she readily admitted it was her own attitude that had prevented herself and Lester getting in touch with Edgar after the discovery of Claire's body. She was very sorry Claire was dead, very sorry she had died in such a horrific way, but she had never liked her and she couldn't suddenly start acting as if she had; she had felt herself at a total loss in the appalling situation.

The Chief took her back to Friday, November 16. She told him she had left for work at her usual time, shortly before two. 'At the end of your shift,' Kelsey asked, 'did you leave the factory at your usual time?'

She shook her head. 'No, I didn't. I left early that Friday.'

'Why was that?'

'I had a migraine, I get them sometimes. I cleared it with the manager that I could go off—he rang a relief nurse and she came in to take over.'

'What time would that be?'

'I left around six-thirty.'

'Did you phone your husband to tell him you were leaving work early?'

She looked surprised. 'No, I didn't, it wouldn't cross my mind.'

'What time did you get home?'

'Around my usual time, ten-fifteen.'

'Ten-fifteen?' the Chief echoed in astonishment. 'What were you doing between six-thirty and ten-fifteen?'

'I was at a friend's flat. As soon as I left the factory and got into the car I knew I was in no state to drive home. A girl I know lives not far from the factory. Melanie Scaife, her name is, she's a nurse at the General Hospital. I went along to her flat to lie down till the worst of the migraine was over. I knew she wouldn't be in, she'd be on duty, but I know where she keeps a key. I let myself in and lay down on the sofa in the living-room. I went straight off to sleep. When I woke up my head was much better. I made myself some strong coffee; that helped a lot. I knew I'd be all right for driving home.'

'Was your husband in when you got home?'

'Yes, he'd not long got in from his security round.'

'Did you mention the migraine?'

She shook her head. 'No point in boring him with all that. All I wanted was to get off to bed.'

'Did you leave Melanie a note saying you'd been in the flat?'

Again she shook her head. 'No need to. I often pop in there when I'm shopping in town, if I want a cup of coffee or to put my feet up for five minutes. Melanie thinks nothing of it, she's got other friends who do the same. She's pretty easy-going.'

Later in the morning the Chief had a report from the officer despatched to verify Norman Griffin's statement that he had shown the garnet ring to a Cannonbridge jeweller. The jeweller had verified Norman's statement, he recognized the ring as soon as the officer produced it. He clearly recalled Norman's visit—Norman hadn't given his name but the jeweller supplied a pretty accurate description of him. What had particularly imprinted the incident on his memory was the fact that some fifteen minutes after Norman had left his shop a customer had come in looking for an anniversary present for his wife. He had indicated the kind of gift likely to please her and the jeweller had immediately thought that the garnet ring—if only he still had it to sell—would have been the very thing. He had in fact sold the customer a Victorian pearl and turquoise brooch; he produced a ledger showing the entry; the date chimed in with what Norman had told them. The Chief sat contemplating that date: November 23. One week after someone had seen fit to smash in the back of Claire Holroyd's skull.

The Chief was about to leave the station again, bound for the factory where Diane Holroyd worked, when a uniformed constable came along to his office. He had just finished a spell of traffic duty in the centre of Cannonbridge, in the course of which he had had occasion to speak to a woman driver, a Mrs Rudd, for a minor traffic violation. Mrs Rudd hadn't received his observations at all well. She had demanded to know why he was wasting his time and the taxpayer's money harassing female motorists when he would be much better occupied chasing after real criminals such as those involved in the recent murders. To her certain knowledge there were folk swanning around as large as life who had had more to do with Claire Holroyd than they were probably letting on.

It was neither the time nor the place for the constable to start questioning the woman but he had made a note of her address. She had been on her way to work, she wouldn't be home till turned six. 'May be nothing in it,' the constable added. 'She's a stroppy type, she could just have been talking off the top of her head.'

The Chief's call at the factory took very little time, he was able to speak to the manager right away. Yes, Diane had left work early that Friday because of a migraine, she had gone off duty at six-thirty.

The two policemen went next to the basement flat occupied by Diane's friend, Melanie Scaife. Repeated rings on the doorbell produced no response but a woman going by stopped to say she had just spoken to Melanie in the corner shop. 'She'll be along any moment,' she assured them. 'She was just getting something for her lunch.'

A few minutes later a young woman came hurrying up the street, clutching a carrier bag of shopping. 'You wanting to see me?' she queried as she darted in through the gate. The Chief told her who he was, explained he would like a word with her, he wouldn't keep her long. She was much intrigued. 'Come on inside,' she invited cheerfully. 'Make yourselves at home.' She urged them before her into the kitchen. 'You won't mind if I press on,' she said. 'Mustn't be late on the ward.' She immediately set Sergeant Lambert to making coffee while she busied herself assembling with speed and dexterity an appetizing lunch from the contents of her carrier bag. 'Fire away,' she instructed the Chief as she worked.

Did she know a Mrs Diane Holroyd? Yes, she did. 'She's not in any trouble, is she?' She paused briefly in her salad washing. The Chief reassured her. He merely wished to establish Diane's whereabouts on a particular evening, it might have some bearing on a case.

'It's not those murders, is it?' she asked with sharp

curiosity. He acknowledged that it was. 'You're never telling me Diane had something to do with them?' She laughed outright.

'No, I'm not telling you that,' the Chief returned patiently. 'We're simply trying to build up a picture of a whole evening. It involves knowing the whereabouts of a great many folk—including those related by marriage to one of the victims, as Diane was. It certainly doesn't mean we think every one of them was in some way connected with the murders.'

'Yes, I see that,' she conceded briskly. She offered them a share in her lunch which they politely declined. She offered them coffee which they accepted. She sat down at the table and began to eat, swiftly and neatly.

'Do you happen to know where Diane spent the evening of Friday, November 16?' Kelsey asked as he drank his coffee.

She looked up, astonished. 'How on earth would I be expected to know that? I haven't seen Diane since I got back from my holidays at the beginning of September.' She frowned. 'She didn't tell you she spent the evening with me?'

'She told us she left work early that day with a migraine. She wasn't fit to drive home so she let herself in here, went to sleep on the sofa, drove home around ten.'

Melanie seemed perfectly satisfied with that. 'If that's what she said, then that's what she did. Diane's not a liar. She often pops in here.'

Kelsey studied her. 'Did she phone you this morning to tell you to expect a visit from the police? And to tell you what she'd told us?'

She gave him back an unwavering gaze. 'No, she did not phone me this morning, I haven't spoken to her for weeks.' She paused, then added with deliberate emphasis, 'For your information, Chief Inspector, I'm not a liar either.'

Shortly after six the Chief had the results of the tests carried out on Norman Griffin's van. All negative; nothing to

associate the vehicle in the slightest degree with either murder. The Chief gave orders for the van to be returned to
Norman forthwith.

He glanced at his watch. The stroppy female driver
should be at home by now. Better give her time to get her
supper down before they called or she'd more than likely
be stroppier than ever.

The address Mrs Rudd had given took them to an undistin-
guished semi in a stretch of ribbon development leading
out of Cannonbridge. The door was opened to them by a
respectable-looking man in his fifties. Yes, his wife was in.
He clearly had no idea why the police should wish to speak
to her but he admitted them courteously, without delay or
questioning. He took them into a sitting-room where his
wife had just sat down to watch TV after a busy day. A
neat little hen-sparrow of a woman, not best pleased to be
deprived of a favourite programme, though she didn't resist
when her husband firmly switched off the set.

She at once concluded the police visit was in connection
with her negligent driving that morning. She began to com-
plain loudly: her offence had been trivial, it surely didn't
warrant the attention of a Detective Chief Inspector. 'It's
nothing whatever to do with that,' the Chief explained
patiently. That took the wind out of her sails. 'I understand,' the Chief went on, 'you gave the constable the
impression this morning that you might be in possession of
some facts about Claire Holroyd that haven't so far come
out.'

She looked vastly uncomfortable. Her husband turned
and bent a look upon her; a steely quality had entered his
gaze. 'It was the constable,' Mrs Rudd said defensively.
'He got my goat, the way he spoke to me.'

'Either you know something concrete or you do not know
something concrete,' her husband put in with the air of an
examining magistrate. 'You can't play games with something as serious as this.' His wife's expression turned sulky.

The Chief briefly pondered the wisdom of asking Rudd

to retire from the room but decided reluctantly against it. He had a shrewd notion the request would merely precipitate a lengthy and unfruitful wrangle about the rights of citizens in general and of husbands in particular, in the course of which anything his wife might have had to tell them would be lost in floods of tears. 'Do you know something?' he asked Mrs Rudd with great courtesy. 'We'd be glad to hear it if you do.'

Her expression brightened. Without glancing at her husband she launched into rapid speech. 'It was not long after I'd been made redundant—I used to work for the council, in the planning department, I was made redundant at the end of June, so that would make it, say, early June that I'm talking about. I was at home, out of work. I was upstairs one afternoon, in the front bedroom, it would be around half past two. I happened to look out of the window and I saw a bus coming up the road. There's a stop across the way, a few yards along. I stood there, watching the bus pull up, the folk getting on and off, I'd no particular reason for watching. After the bus moved off again and the folk had gone, there was one person left, a woman.'

She began to relax, pleased to find herself the centre of interest, three men listening intently to her recital. She warmed to her tale. 'The woman started walking up and down. I was looking at her clothes, I thought how nicely dressed she was. Then she got nearer and I looked at her face. I knew right away who she was.' She paused for greater effort. 'It was Claire Holroyd. I couldn't mistake her, I often saw her when I was with the council, the office where I worked was right next door to hers when she worked in the housing department a few years back.'

'Were you a friend of hers at that time?'

She shook her head. 'She wouldn't even know I existed. I used to notice her because she was so good-looking, always so smartly dressed. Anyway, to get back to that afternoon, she walked up and down for a few minutes and then this car came along. I could see she was expecting it.

As soon as she saw it she stopped walking and stood on the edge of the pavement, smiling at the driver. She was more or less opposite here when the car stopped. The driver had the door open the moment he pulled up and she hopped straight in. He said something to her, then he got out and lifted the bonnet. He fiddled about under it, then he got back in again and they went off.' She waved a hand. 'Out that way, towards the hills.'

'Did you recognize the car?'

She shook her head. 'But I recognized the driver all right. I saw his face as plain as plain when he was tinkering with the engine.' She leaned forward. 'It was Claire Holroyd's brother-in-law. Lester Holroyd.'

'You're sure of that?'

'Absolutely. He often came into the planning department on business from Mansell's.'

'What's wrong about giving his sister-in-law a lift?' Rudd put in with stern reproof. 'You're surely not trying to make something out of that.'

She thrust out her lips. 'It looked a lot more than that to me.'

'Is that the sum total of it?' Kelsey asked her. 'You saw Claire get into Lester's car on this one occasion in broad daylight?'

'Oh no!' she responded with lively pleasure. 'There was more to it than that. I saw her get into his car at the same spot three or four times after that.'

'He could have been giving her a lift every time,' her husband insisted. She ignored him. 'I won't deny I was plain curious,' she admitted to Kelsey. 'She'd always seemed so quiet and reserved, so touch-me-not. Any day I happened to think of it around that time in the afternoon I'd pop upstairs and take a look out of the window when the bus was due.'

'Was it always the same day of the week when you saw them?'

'No, it was different days of the week but always the same time.'

'These three or four occasions that you saw them, over what period of time would that be?'

'Over about a month, that's all it could have been. This job I've got now, I started it the first week in August. The pair of them could have gone on meeting after that, it's just I wasn't at home in the afternoon any more to see them. I forgot all about it when I started working again but it came back into my head after I heard about her body being found.' She made a deprecating gesture. 'I'm not really suggesting Lester could have had anything to do with her murder. He always struck me as a very nice young man, a very decent sort. I don't suppose there was anything in it, or if there was, it was only a bit of harmless flirtation. It was just this morning, the policeman ticking me off like that in front of everybody, it suddenly came popping out.' She smiled sheepishly. 'To tell the truth, I surprised myself when I came out with it.'

Kelsey turned to her husband. 'Did your wife mention any of this to you at the time?'

Rudd gave a forceful shake of his head. 'She certainly did not, she'd know better than to come running to me with that kind of tale—standing at windows, spying on folk, making something out of nothing. That sort of silly, idle gossip's a very good way to go about ruining perfectly ordinary, decent lives.'

Back at the police station the Chief began to nurse the hope that he might be able to get off home at a reasonable hour for once. But he had reckoned without the officer engaged in checking Lester Holroyd's statement that he'd spoken to two men during his security round that Friday evening. The officer came along to make his report as the Chief was leaving his office; he turned back inside to hear what the officer had to say.

He had called on both men in their homes; both were very willing to answer questions. But neither man could properly substantiate what Lester had said. Certainly the bricklayer recalled Lester going by in his car one evening as he walked along to his local pub. Lester had indeed slowed his car and stuck his head out, they had exchanged a few joking words before Lester drove off again. Yes, the time would have been shortly after nine. And yes again, he had definitely understood Lester was in the middle of one of his security runs—it was common knowledge in the yard that Lester made such runs regularly, he was very hot on security.

But the bricklayer could by no means definitely place the encounter on the evening of November 16. He wasn't at all sure of the date but if forced to it he would have put it a week or even two weeks earlier.

'And the other man?' Kelsey asked. 'The retired worker.'

There again, the man confirmed that he had come across Lester in the vicinity of one of Mansell's sites during his regular evening stroll. Nor did he have any quarrel with the time Lester had given—around nine-thirty. He walked up there regularly around that time of evening and Lester regularly included the site in his round. As often as not when they met, Lester would be on foot, on his way to or from his car; they usually stopped for a word. But he had come across Lester in that area at around that time on at least half a dozen occasions over the last couple of months. He couldn't possibly say now if one of these encounters had taken place on November 16.

As the door closed behind the departing officer the Chief looked at his watch, all thought of getting off home now totally evaporated. If he left right away he stood a chance of catching Lester in. And Lester was in, he had eaten his supper and was reading the newspaper. The Chief gave him the gist of the officer's report. 'What it amounts to,' he pointed out, 'is that you have no evidence of any value to prove you were out on a security run that evening.'

'That doesn't alter the fact that I was out on a run,' Lester returned stubbornly.

The Chief let that go. 'Did you ever meet Claire in the afternoon?' he asked. 'Did you drive her off somewhere quiet?'

Lester eyed him with irritation. 'We're back to that again, are we? I thought we'd dealt with that. I'm no womanizer. Even if I were, my brother's wife would surely be the last female I'd think of tangling with.'

Maybe so, Kelsey thought. And then again, maybe not. The relationship could have been the very thing to lend a particularly piquant flavour to the association, plus the fact that Claire was a very different type, physically and temperamentally, from Lester's wife. And a swipe at a father-figure of an elder brother thrown in for added spice. But all the Chief said aloud was: 'Claire was a very good-looking woman, the girl you'd had a crush on as a lad—a pretty potent combination.' By way of reply Lester merely uttered a sound of disgust. 'Do I take it that indicates repudiation?' the Chief pressed him.

Lester flashed him an icy look. 'You take it right.' He lit a cigarette, drew in a lungful of smoke.

'Then if Claire was seen getting into your car and driving off with you around two-thirty in the afternoon, where would the two of you be going?'

Lester answered at once. 'I should imagine I came across her, wherever it was, and stopped to give her a lift home.'

'You were seen driving off in an opposite direction from Fairbourne. You drove out towards the hills.'

Lester frowned. 'I suppose it could have been some time when she was doing relief work at the office. She might have asked if I'd give her a lift to some place she wanted to go. Maybe she knew I'd be going out in that direction anyway, on business.'

'And if she was seen getting into your car at precisely the same spot, at precisely the same time, on a number of occasions? Surely then you'd expect to remember where it was you were taking her?' There was an appreciable pause. Lester drew deeply on his cigarette. 'Seen by a pretty good witness,' the Chief enlarged. 'Someone well able to recognize the pair of you.'

Lester took another long drag on his cigarette. 'All right,' he said suddenly. 'So we were having a little fling. That's

all it was, you couldn't even call it a flirtation. I took her
out for a run once or twice.' He didn't appear unduly dis-
concerted. 'It didn't last long, there was never anything in
it. We were neither of us fools, we saw where it could lead,
we decided to pull out before it got properly started.' He
stubbed out his cigarette with force. 'That was the reason
Claire stopped doing relief work at the office. We both
decided it would be best if she left. The only time I even
saw her after she stopped working at the office was at the
Acorn do. I never spoke to her again, not even on the
phone.'

'How did Tom Mansell take it when Claire stopped doing
relief work?' the Chief wanted to know.

Lester grimaced. 'He wasn't best pleased. He kept asking
if I knew why she wouldn't come any more, if something
had happened to upset her, could I suggest anything that
might make her change her mind, and so on. I just told
him I thought she'd had enough of the job, the novelty had
worn off.'

'Does your wife know about this flirtation that never was?
Does she know that was why Claire stopped working at the
office?'

Lester's face expressed lively alarm. 'Good God, no! And
she mustn't find out!'

CHAPTER 16

Tom Mansell and his son were up early on Saturday morning. A couple of contracts were nudging completion dates,
there would be no free Saturday mornings for a while. By
the time light was breaking they were ready to leave for the
yard. As they came out of the back door and walked across
to the garage Mansell heard the sound of a vehicle. He
glanced over his shoulder and saw the police car turning in.
He let out an exasperated breath and strode off to where the
car was pulling up.

The Chief could scarcely fail to read Mansell's expression. 'We won't keep you long,' he promised. Mansell turned without a word and led the way into the house. 'We'd appreciate a word with your son first,' Kelsey said when they reached the sitting-room. Mansell gave a nod and left the room. The Chief wasted no time but asked Stuart for an account of his movements on the evening of Friday, November 16.

'That was the night of the big fight,' Stuart said at once. He had gone up to his room after supper, around seven-thirty. He had spent some time studying—he attended the Cannonbridge College of Further Education as a day release student. He had then played some music tapes. Just before eleven he went down to the sitting-room to watch the fight; his father was there, they watched together. Stuart went to bed shortly after midnight, leaving his father still up.

Kelsey asked if he knew where his father had spent the earlier part of the evening. 'I remember he went along to his study after supper,' Stuart told him. 'I didn't see him again till I went down for the boxing.'

'Would you have heard if he'd driven away from the house during that time?'

'Not if I was listening to music.'

'When you joined him for the boxing, did he say anything about having been out?'

Stuart shook his head. 'We started talking about the fight right away.'

Kelsey changed tack. 'You knew Claire Holroyd?'

'Only very slightly, through her working at the office.'

'Did you fancy her?'

Stuart looked surprised. 'I never thought about her in that way, she was a lot older than me.'

'It's not unheard of for young men to fancy women ten years older than themselves.'

'I'm sure you're right,' Stuart said courteously, 'but I don't happen to be one of them.'

The Chief considered him for some moments, then he

said: 'We won't keep you any longer. Would you ask your father to come in?' Mansell came along at once. The Chief began by asking for an account of his movements that Friday evening. Like his son, Mansell was able to recall the evening by the big fight. He had gone to his study after supper. At around a quarter to ten he had left the house for a breath of air, as he did most evenings. He had stayed out for about an hour, he couldn't remember encountering anyone he knew. When he got back he went along to the sitting-room, switched on the TV. The sporting pundits were in the studio, airing their views before the fight. Stuart came along just before the match started. Afterwards Stuart went up to bed. He had stayed up till around one, as he often did, watching TV.

Had he spoken to his housekeeper in the course of the evening?

He shook his head. He couldn't say if she had gone out that evening or not. She often went out in the evening, she had several friends locally, she took an active part in village life.

The Chief changed course. 'How well did you know Claire Holroyd?'

'Not very well,' Mansell told him. 'Only through her working at the office.'

'Was it you who suggested she might be asked to fill in?'

'Yes, it was. We were stuck at the time. I knew she had worked for the council and for Hartley's before that.'

'Why didn't you ask her yourself?'

'Lester runs the office, it was up to him whether he took up my suggestion or not.'

'Did you fancy her?'

The muscles stiffened along Mansell's jaw. His brilliant sapphire-blue eyes darted arrows at the Chief. 'I'm not in the business of running after married women,' he answered brusquely. 'I'm not interested in games of that sort. I never have been.'

Once again the Chief changed course. He asked about the firm's vehicles, which of them were regularly used by himself, Stuart, Diane, Lester. Mansell told him both he and Lester were currently driving estate cars as their every-day vehicles; Stuart drove a small coupé. He gave details of make, year, colour. All three vehicles were on the firm's books. In addition, they all three made use of other vehicles belonging to the firm as occasion arose. Diane drove at present a small saloon car which she owned herself, not on the firm's books. She would borrow one of the firm's vehicles if her own car was off the road for any reason or if she needed a larger or more robust vehicle for a particular purpose. He couldn't offhand recall if he had himself made use of one of the firm's other vehicles over that Friday or Saturday, nor could he say if any of the other three had done so. No record was kept of such borrowings, they were always very short-term, very informal.

The Chief thanked him for his assistance, there was no need to keep him or Stuart any longer. But he would be glad of a word with the housekeeper before leaving. 'Right, then,' Mansell said with energy. 'We'll be on our way. I'll send the housekeeper along.' She came into the room a minute or two later; her manner was friendly and relaxed. Kelsey asked her to take her mind back to November 16. She was able to recall the day without difficulty as the Women's Institute had held a rummage sale the following afternoon and she had been busy lending a hand on both the Friday and Saturday. She had gone along to the village hall on the Friday afternoon and again after supper that evening, helping to set up stalls and price articles for sale. When she left the house after clearing the supper things she believed Stuart was upstairs in his room and Mr Mansell was in his study.

After she had finished at the hall she went back with some friends to their house nearby for coffee and sandwiches. The husband drove her home around eleven-thirty and she went straight to bed. She didn't see either Stuart or Mr Mansell but she heard the sound of the television as she went by the sitting-room. She assumed they were both in there, watch-ing the boxing match they had talked about. During the time it took her to get into bed and fall asleep she had heard no sound of any vehicle arriving or departing.

Sunday morning in the middle of a double murder investigation was little different from any other day of the week as far as the Chief was concerned. The time-consuming process of verifying every last detail was going steadily forward. Edgar Holroyd had indeed phoned the hairdresser shortly after the salon opened on the morning of Saturday, November 17, to cancel Claire's next appointment; he had told the girl his wife had gone to stay with a relative. There had still been no sighting of Claire on any bus, train or taxi that Friday.

Shortly after ten a man called in at the police station, asking to speak to the Chief Inspector. He was smartly dressed, with an urbane manner, the owner of a high-class jeweller's in a town several miles away. He had chanced to catch an item on last night's regional news concerning the progress of the murder investigation. For the first time he had seen, clearly displayed on the screen, a photograph of Claire Holroyd. He was at once positive she was the woman who had come into his shop at the end of September— September 28, to be precise, he had checked the date in his ledger.

She had chosen an item from his stock, giving him to understand it was intended for a Christmas present. She had paid a cash deposit and asked him to put the gift aside, she would pay the balance when she returned to collect it in a couple of months. She had never returned and he had no means of getting in touch with her. In the ordinary way he always took a customer's name and address when an article was laid aside but when he asked for the woman's name she showed marked reluctance to give it, saying she couldn't see it was at all necessary. He explained he must record the transaction and so must attach a name to it. She then told him her name was Mrs Finch. He didn't go on to ask for her address and phone number as he normally would, he felt sure that would provoke further resistance and might end in his losing the sale.

He produced from his pocket a small parcel which he unwrapped, disclosing a jeweller's box. He clicked it open, held it out for the Chief's inspection. Inside was a pair of men's gold cufflinks; an elegant classic design, a high standard of workmanship. 'They're our top-quality links,' the jeweller told him on a note of professional pride. 'One hundred and eighty-five pounds.'

The day was crisp and sunny as Lambert drove the Chief along to Fairbourne. The common was back to its normal Sunday-morning self again: people exercising dogs, children playing, old folk chatting. Edgar Holroyd was in his workshop, restoring a gilt picture frame. He seemed steadier and calmer, he took them into the sitting-room and waited for the Chief to say what was on his mind.

The Chief began by asking if he wore cufflinks. Edgar's face showed surprise but he answered without comment. Yes, he regularly wore them, he had several pairs, including some belonging to his father and grandfather, which he still wore. Kelsey told him of the jeweller's visit, the deposit Claire had paid. As Edgar listened something of his calm began to dissolve. 'I'd like to have the links,' he said unsteadily when the Chief had finished. 'They would have been Claire's last present to me.'

The Chief went on to ask if anyone had rung Fairbourne asking to speak to Claire between November 16 and the discovery of her body on December 2. Edgar tried to remember. Yes, he told them after some moments, there had been some calls; five or six, he thought, both male and female callers. He hadn't asked any caller for a name. His impression now was that the callers had been classmates or fellow charity-workers. He hadn't taken any messages, he had merely told every caller Claire was away, staying with a relative, he wasn't sure when she'd be back—as he had done every other time Claire had gone to May Finch's.

Had he recognized the voice of any male caller? He shook

his head. 'I don't know any of the students or charity
workers.'

'Would you recognize Norman Griffin's voice?' the Chief
wanted to know.

Again he shook his head. 'I didn't even know he existed
until . . .' He fell silent. Until the evening Norman drove
Jill Lingard to view the house in Tolladine Road, Sergeant
Lambert supplied in his mind.

'You'd have recognized Tom Mansell's voice,' the Chief
said; a statement, not a question. Edgar nodded.

'What about Robert Ashworth?'

Once more Edgar shook his head. 'I wouldn't know his
voice. I've never spoken to him, never met him.'

But for sure you'd have recognized the voice of your
own brother, Sergeant Lambert said to himself. If the same
thought also crossed the Chief's mind, he didn't voice it
now.

CHAPTER 17

In the middle of Monday morning the Chief Inspector had
a visit from Buckley, the recently retired Mansell employee.
Buckley came strolling into the station with an air of vast
self-importance. 'I don't know if what I've come to say is
of any interest,' he told the Chief. 'I thought I'd pass it on
for what it's worth.' He lit a cigarette and settled himself
back in his chair. 'The moment you left Mansell's place
last Saturday morning, Mansell was on the blower whistling Lester Holroyd back from the yard. Norman Griffin as
well—Norman was getting into his van to drive out of the
yard when Lester cam running out of the office to stop him.
Mansell got Diane over from her house, and of course
Stuart was already on the premises. Then they all sat down
round the table and there was some sort of pow-wow, an
almighty kerfuffle from what I hear.'

He cocked a knowing eye at the Chief. 'You're going to

ask me how come I know all this, not being a fly on the wall.' He drew on his cigarette. 'I got it all in the pub on Saturday night. When Norman got back to the yard from Mansell's place on Saturday morning, he sounded off about it to one of his mates. I heard this mate gabbing about it to another Mansell man in the pub. The pair of them had no idea what the pow-wow was about, Norman wasn't daft enough to spill all the beans. But they'd have known something was up even if Norman hadn't opened his mouth at all, because Mansell never got to the yard on Saturday morning till gone ten—absolutely unheard of when there's contracts pushing the deadline.'

'You've no idea why Mansell called them all together?' Kelsey asked.

Buckley reluctantly admitted that was so but his self-importance soon found another outlet. 'I had to smile,' he said with relish, 'when I heard you'd taken Norman's van in to have it gone over.' He leaned forward. 'I'll bet a pound to a penny you thought the van you took was the one Norman had been driving all along.' He sat back again, savouring his moment. 'I can tell you quite definitely it wasn't.' He couldn't refrain from smiling with pleasure at the abrupt change in the Chief's expression. 'The first time I ever laid eyes on the van you took,' Buckley went on with deep satisfaction, 'was on the Monday morning, two weeks before I retired.' He screwed up his eyes. 'November 19, that would be. It was near enough a dead ringer for the van Norman had been driving before. The only way I spotted the difference was by the number plate.'

'Did you say anything about it to Norman?'

He shook his head. 'I thought nothing of it at the time.'

'Do you know what happened to the van Norman was driving before?'

'It was still in the yard when I finished at Mansell's. It wasn't anyone's regular van, it was in general use.' He was soon off again, proffering his gobbets of rumour and gossip, larded with an occasional fact. The Chief listened with what

patience he could muster; it was some little time before
Buckley had him pricking up his ears again.

'Diane used to give Norman the eye, years ago, when
Norman first started working for Mansell. The pair of them
wouldn't be much more than kids at the time. Diane was
always popping into the yard on one excuse or another.'
He closed one eye. 'You can bet your bottom dollar Norman
would have had a fling with her if he'd thought he could
get away with it.'

'It never came to anything?' Kelsey asked.

Buckley grimaced. 'Not likely. Norman wasn't a complete fool. He knew the minute Mansell got wind of anything like that he'd have had him out through the gate so
fast his feet wouldn't have touched the ground. His precious
daughter and one of his own workmen! Mansell would have
had a blue fit. Diane's always been able to run rings round
her father but she couldn't have got away with that one.
Mansell always spoiled her, he spoiled Stuart too, to an
extent, but Diane more so than Stuart. Diane and Stuart
have always been as thick as thieves. She's still the big
sister, he's still the kid brother, always at her beck and
call.' He moved his shoulders. 'Probably goes back to their
mother running off the way she did, that must have thrown
the two kids together.'

'When was this?' Kelsey put in sharply. 'That Mansell's
wife ran off?'

'Couldn't say for sure. It was before he came over this
way and went in with Dobie. I only know what I heard in
the trade, that she ran off with some foreigner.'

Buckley looked very cosy and comfortable as if he could
happily have sat there all day confabbing with the Chief,
two weighty men of affairs putting their heads together. But
the Chief had a good many other fish demanding to be
fried. As he steered Buckley out into the corridor he asked
if he could put him on to any female clerk who had worked
in Mansell's office in recent times but had now left.

Buckley didn't have to ponder. Yes, there was a young
married woman living in his own neighbourhood. She had

left Mansell's some eight months ago, a few weeks before her baby was due. She hadn't got another job, she was at home, looking after the baby.

The Chief reckoned the best chance of catching at home a young woman with a baby was around lunch-time, so at twenty minutes to one he presented himself on the doorstep of Mansell's former clerk. She was indeed at home, she didn't appear to mind being snatched from her chores. Yes, she had worked at Mansell's, she had been there for four years. She had been horrified to learn of the two murders, she would willingly do anything she could to help the police. She took the two men into the kitchen, to keep an eye on her pans as they talked.

Yes, she had known both Harry Lingard and Claire Holroyd, though she hadn't been closely acquainted with either. Some folk had considered Harry an officious little so-and-so but she had always believed his heart was in the right place, even if he did sometimes go over the top. She wasn't aware that he had ever aroused any real enmity at work.

During her own time at Mansell's Claire had worked a number of relief stints. She had found Claire hardworking and efficient, quiet in manner, reserved and self-contained, though always pleasant.

Had she ever been aware of anything going on between Claire and Lester Holroyd?

She looked surprised. No, she had never been aware of anything. 'Lester never struck me as a ladies' man,' she commented. 'He's no office Romeo, he always behaved very properly.'

'What about Tom Mansell?' Kelsey asked. 'Did he show any interest in Claire?'

She looked even more surprised. 'Good heavens, no! Mansell's not that type at all—not from anything I ever saw or heard. Work and family, that's Tom Mansell, nothing else. Though perhaps I should put it the other way round, family and work. If push came to shove I believe he'd put his family before anything else.'

Had she been aware of strong feeling towards Claire on the part of anyone at Mansell's?

No, she hadn't. 'The men always knew when Claire was around, of course, you'd see the heads turn if she crossed the yard. There was a bit of leg-pulling used to go on with one or two of them, but never anything serious, not that I ever knew of. Just what you get anywhere there are men working near a good-looking woman.' She stopped suddenly.

'You've remembered something,' Kelsey said.

She made a dismissive gesture. 'It was nothing.'

'What was it?' he pressed.

'I wouldn't want you to make anything out of it,' she insisted. 'It was one afternoon back in the spring. Tom Mansell had gone into town for a dental appointment, so Stuart wasn't with him for once. We were very busy in the office. I noticed Stuart hanging around outside but I didn't have time to go out to ask him if he wanted anything. Then someone rang with a complicated query and I had to go into the back office to look up the records. As I was coming out again I saw Stuart come into the front office. He darted up to where Claire was sitting and dropped a little parcel on the desk. It was done up in gift wrapping, with a ribbon rosette. He said, "Many happy returns!" He was grinning all over his face. Then he looked up and saw me, he went bright red and ran off out again. I had to carry on with my phone call, it was some time before I finished. When I put the phone down I looked across at Claire. She was getting on with her work as usual, head down, hard at it. There was no sign of the little parcel.'

'Did you find out what was in it?'

She shook her head. 'I've no idea. I must admit I was curious but I didn't like to come right out and ask her, I didn't want to seem nosey. She was never the sort you could be free and easy with in that way. Anyway, when she was getting her coat to go home I couldn't help saying: "You're not forgetting your present, are you?" She didn't answer. She just gave me a cool little look as much as to say: "I don't care for vulgar curiosity." She could be very uppity when she wanted. I heard they used to call her the Ice Queen when she worked at Hartley's.'

'Was it her birthday that day?'

'I've no idea. She'd said nothing about it to me. I didn't like to ask her, I didn't fancy getting squashed again.'

The two policemen reached the Griffins' cottage just ahead of Norman at the end of his working day. He was driving the van Forensic had examined; the Chief went up to him as he got out. 'Who owns this vehicle?' Kelsey demanded.

'The firm does,' Norman responded. 'The same as anything else I drive. I don't own any vehicle, I never have.'

'How long has the firm owned it?'

'Just over three weeks. It was bought November 17.'

'You're very sure of the date.'

'I ought to be, it was me did the buying.'

'Where did you buy it?'

'At a car auction.' He named the town where the auction was held. The side door of the cottage suddenly opened, revealing Mrs Griffin. She took a step or two outside, her face full of anxious inquiry. 'It's all right,' Norman called across to her. 'I won't be long.' She went reluctantly back inside.

The Chief fired another question. 'On whose instructions did you buy this van?'

'On Tom Mansell's,' Norman told him. 'I got back to the yard just before knocking-off time on the Friday afternoon. Mansell was looking out for me.'

'That would be Friday, November 16?' Kelsey put in.

'That's right. Mansell said he'd been out in one of the other vans earlier in the day and it had played him up. It wasn't the first time but he'd make sure it was the last. He'd had it put into shape during the afternoon, enough to be able to put it up for sale. I was to take it to the auction next morning, bring back another in its place, make sure it was a good one. On no account was I to get one of the same make as the dud, he'd never have one of that make in the yard again. He gave me the log book and a thousand pounds in notes to cover any difference. I left my usual van in the yard and drove the duff one home. I took it to the auction next morning, sold it and bought this one. I had to give another six-fifty on top of what the duff one made. I gave Mansell back the three-fifty on the Monday morning.'

Not a lot of point at this stage, the Chief reflected, trying to chase up the van Norman had sold, it could have been through another couple of auctions since then, could be at the other end of the country by now, or out of the country altogether. But, useless or not, the attempt must still be made.

'Was it on Mansell's instructions you bought a van the dead spit of the one you'd been driving yourself?' Kelsey asked.

'No, it wasn't,' Norman said. 'Mansell left the choice up to me as long as it wasn't the same make as the dud. It was just the luck of the draw, I didn't set out to buy one the same as I'd been driving, though I'd always been very satisfied with that one. I went with an open mind, to get the best bargain I could. I saw this one, it seemed in very good nick. I got it for what I thought was a very fair price.' He slapped the side of the van. 'I did right, too. First-class buy. Not a thing wrong with her, right as rain.'

'Had you ever been to a car auction for Mansell before?'

He nodded. 'I've bought one or two vehicles for him.' He made a dismissive gesture. 'Can't blame me for the dud van, though; it wasn't me bought that one.'

'This van you bought, that you've got now, when did you start driving it as your regular van?'

'Right away. When I showed it to Mansell on the Monday morning he said, "You seem pretty pleased with it, you'd better keep it." That suited me fine.'

'Why didn't you tell us all this when we took the other van away?'

Norman gave the Chief a challenging look tinged with

amusement. 'If you'd bothered to ask one single, sensible question about the van, I'd have told you what I've told you now. But you just informed me you were taking it. No by-your-leave, not a word of apology for any inconvenience. OK, if that was the way you wanted to play it. But it didn't exactly put me in the mood for volunteering information.'

'Right,' the Chief said briskly. 'As you're so keen on sensible questions we'll try one or two out on you now. This last Saturday morning Mansell called you out from the yard, over to his place. What was that in aid of?'

'It wasn't just me,' Norman said. 'He got Lester Holroyd out of the yard as well. Lester gave me a lift there and back.'

'Did Lester know why you were both being summoned?'

Norman shook his head. 'He had no more idea than I had. When we got over to the house Mansell came running out and pulled us in. He shoved me into a room by myself and told me not to budge. He pushed Lester into another room. Stuart and Diane were already in there. I was left twiddling my thumbs for a good fifteen minutes. Then Mansell came marching in and plonked himself down beside me. He had sparks flashing out of his eyes. He said: "I'll ask you what I've asked the others, together and separately: What the hell's been going on? If anyone's been up to anything behind my back I want to know about it now, every last syllable of it."

'I told him I hadn't been up to anything and I didn't know that any of the others had been up to anything. I hadn't the foggiest notion what he was talking about. He said: "I'm talking about goddamned murder detectives quizzing me from morning till night. That's the last thing I need right now, goddamned policemen sticking their noses into my business."

'He asked me if I knew anything about what had happened to Harry Lingard and Claire, anything at all? I said I'd no idea, which is the truth. He went on about that for a bit. Had I been mixed up in any of it in any way at all? Had I any suspicions? If I had, I'd better open my mouth and tell him there and then. I told him I knew nothing at all, which I don't. He calmed down a bit and that was that.

'On the way back to the yard I said to Lester: "What was all that about?" But he just shook his head and said: "God alone knows." Lester seemed pretty shaken. I went straight out on a job when we got back to the yard. I gather Mansell came in later and it was business as usual.'

'Would you consider yourself a good friend of Diane Holroyd?' Kelsey asked.

'I should hope so,' Norman replied at once.

'If she ever asked you to do something for her, would you be willing to help her?'

'I should hope so,' he said again.

'Did she get in touch with you that Friday evening, November 16? Did she ask you to help her?'

Norman shook his head with energy. 'No, she did not.'

'Did Stuart get in touch with you that evening? To ask for your help?'

Again he shook his head. 'No, he did not.' He looked levelly at the Chief. 'Whatever all these questions are in aid of, you're very definitely barking up the wrong tree as far as I'm concerned. No one at all got in touch with me that Friday evening, for any reason at all. I never spoke to a living soul after my mother went out to her club.'

Before they left, the Chief went into the house to have a word with Mrs Griffin. He tackled her in the kitchen when Norman had gone upstairs for a wash. He asked her only one question: Did Norman ever wear cufflinks?

She looked at him in astonishment. 'Cufflinks?' she echoed, as if she couldn't credit she'd heard aright. 'Norman?' She burst out laughing. 'You must be joking. Cufflinks are hardly Norman's style.'

CHAPTER 18

It wasn't till well on into the afternoon on Tuesday that Kelsey managed to get away from the police station and headed for the town Tom Mansell had left when he moved to Cannonbridge. The firm that had employed Mansell was able to supply his address during the time he had worked for them. The address took the Chief to a pleasant dwelling in a quiet suburb. The woman who answered the door knew nothing of any Mansells, she had lived in the house only five years, but she directed them to an old lady along the road who had lived all her life in the neighbourhood.

The old lady was happy to talk to the Chief. Yes, she remembered the Mansells well, a fine-looking couple with two handsome children. Laura Mansell's maiden name had been Peplow, the Peplows had attended the same church as herself. She didn't really know the details of how or why the couple had split up. There had clearly been some sort of family upheaval and then Mrs Mansell was gone; Mansell had remained in the house with the two children. A couple of years later the house was sold and Mansell went elsewhere to live, taking his children with him; she didn't know where they had gone.

'But I can tell you where you can find Mrs Mansell's sister,' the old lady added. 'Her name's still Peplow, she never married. She works in the baker's shop where I buy my bread. She lives in the flat over the shop now, she moved there after her mother died a few years ago.'

The interior of the baker's shop was warm and bright, full of enticing smells. Three female assistants were busy serving. The Chief approached the oldest of the three, a middle-aged woman with a gentle face and sweet smile; he identified himself discreetly and asked if her name was Peplow. Yes, it was. He assured her he wasn't the bearer of bad news, he would appreciate it if he might have a word with her somewhere more private. She spoke to one of the other assistants and then took the two men through a curtained doorway into a passage.

The Chief explained that she might be able to give them some information that could prove helpful in connection with a case he was working on; he gave her a brief outline, just sufficient to put her in the picture. He would like to know a little more about her sister, Laura Mansell.

Yes, Miss Peplow would be willing to help in any way she could. 'But you can see how it is,' she added. 'I can't simply walk out and leave the others to it.' The shop would be closing in half an hour. If they could wait till then they might do worse than pass the interval in the café attached to the bakery.

Half an hour later she came in search of them and took them up to her snug little flat. The Chief's eye rested on a group of framed photographs ranged along a shelf in the living-room; Miss Peplow followed his gaze, she picked up one of the photographs. 'These are my parents,' she told the Chief. Her mother had the same gentle face as herself, her father was a handsome man with a strong cast of countenance—and a marked resemblance to his granddaughter, Diane Holroyd.

Miss Peplow replaced the photograph and picked up another. 'My sister Laura,' she said, gazing fondly down at it. 'She was a few years younger than me, there were just the two of us.' She handed him the photograph. 'That was taken just before she married Tom Mansell.' Kelsey looked down at the smiling, lively face. The same vigorous good looks as her father—and her daughter Diane. 'Laura was barely eighteen when she married,' Miss Peplow said as she sat them down. 'Far too young. Tom Mansell was only a few years older but he was so confident and masterful he swept her off her feet. He was a striking-looking young man, Mother was bowled over by him. And Father was sure he'd do well in life, he was ambitious, go-ahead and hardworking.'

'Was Mansell a local man?' Kelsey asked.

'Not exactly. He'd lived here since he was a small boy but he was probably born in London towards the end of the war.'

'Is there some doubt about where he was born?'

'Yes, there is. He doesn't know who his parents were or where they lived, he doesn't even know exactly how old he is.' A V2 had fallen on a crowded London department store during the last stages of the war. Fire broke out, there was a large number of casualties, many of the bodies were unrecognizable. 'They found Tom in one of the cellars,' Miss Peplow said. 'He'd been blown down there by the blast, he got away with bumps and bruises. He was a few months old.' There had been nothing on him to identify him; no one had come forward to claim him. A Civil Defence man by the name of Mansell adopted him; he and his wife were middle-aged, childless. 'The wife was from these parts originally,' Miss Peplow added. 'After the war they came here to live; the husband got a job as a clerk. They're both dead now, they died years ago.'

She fell briefly silent. 'With Tom not knowing who he was himself, who his parents were, it seemed to make his wife and children very important to him. Diane was born after a year, Stuart seven years later. Tom was doing well in the building firm, he worked long hours. Laura was always one that liked a lot of attention, liked going out and enjoying herself, she wasn't too fond of the domestic life. She started going out without him. She made out it was with girlfriends and maybe it was at first, but it ended up with her having an affair. He was a foreigner, a Greek, over here on a business course, he was quite well-to-do. Tom hadn't the faintest idea what was going on. He trusted Laura one hundred per cent. It would never have entered his head she could be unfaithful.'

She sighed. 'Of course it all came out in the end, these things always do. Tom went berserk and attacked her. I think he would have killed her but for Diane. Diane was eight years old at the time, she was upstairs in bed, asleep.

The row woke her, she came running downstairs, crying, terrified. That pulled Tom up. He told Laura to clear out while she had the chance and think herself lucky she was still in one piece.'

She looked across at Kelsey. 'She didn't have to be told twice, she went straight round to her Greek. She rang me a few days later and told me what had happened. She didn't come to see me. Our parents were both alive then, I was living at home. She didn't want them to see the state she was in, covered with bruises.' She grimaced. 'And she didn't want them to know what she'd been up to, they were strong church folk. She left the country with her Greek not long afterwards, when he came to the end of his course.'

'Was there a divorce?'

She shook her head. 'Mansell just washed his hands of her. He had no intention of ever getting married again. And no intention of giving her a penny of his money or letting her near either of the children ever again.' She sighed deeply. 'Stuart was only a year old when she left.

'Laura wrote to me now and then from Greece. I don't know what happened between her and the boyfriend but it didn't last long. She took fright then, she began to wonder what she'd done. She wrote to Tom saying she was very sorry, begging him to forgive her, take her back. The only answer she got back was one line: I'll see you in hell first.

'I wrote and told her she could always come back home to us but she said she could never do that, she couldn't stick that kind of life, she'd rather stay out there and take her chance. She got herself a work permit, she had different bits of jobs, travel agency, tourist hotel, language school. She drifted about, she had boyfriends, one after the other. The last one was Italian, he was working in the language school. She seemed fond of him, she moved in with him, she thought something might come of it. That was about two years after Tom threw her out.

'One day she went on a trip with her Italian, on a ferry boat.' She clasped her hands tightly. 'The boat was over-crowded, a storm blew up, they capsized. Laura was drowned, the boyfriend survived. He found my address later among her things, so he wrote me what had happened, told he he'd seen to everything. He seemed a very decent sort.' She was silent for some moments. 'I went to see Tom Mansell to tell him what had happened.'

'How did he take it?'

'He didn't say anything. He got up and went over to the window. He stood there with his back to me, then he turned round and said: "Thank you for coming to tell me." His face was like stone. That was all. I didn't get to see the children. I'd never once seen them after he threw Laura out, he wouldn't let them have anything to do with any of her family. Not long afterwards he sold the house and moved away. I never saw any of them again.'

CHAPTER 19

The imposing graves of the Holroyd family, going back for four generations, occupied a prominent position in a churchyard not far from Whitethorn Common, but the funeral of Claire Margaret Holroyd took place at a crematorium some distance from Cannonbridge. If by this tactic Edgar Holroyd hoped to keep the ceremony quiet and private, to avoid throngs of sightseers, the attentions of the media, he was to be disappointed.

The small chapel was filled to overflowing on this chill, bright Wednesday morning. There was an impressive array of floral offerings, one of the most beautiful from the men at Mansell's. A cross of white lilies from Mansell himself, wreaths from the staff at Hartley's, from York House, various council departments, neighbours from Whitethorn Common, staff and students of the College of Further Education. And residents of the council estate where Harry Lingard had lived.

Outside, after the service, the Chief and Sergeant Lambert stood unobtrusively to one side, casting an eye over the scene. Lester and Diane Holroyd had travelled in the same car as Edgar. They stationed themselves now one on each side of him, over by the chapel entrance, shaking hands, speaking a few words to the mourners as they came out into the open air. Among the faces Kelsey spotted Jill Lingard and Norman Griffin, Robert Ashworth accompanying Claire's aunt, Mrs Finch; Tom Mansell and his son. Sergeant Lambert pointed out an elderly woman leaving the chapel. 'That's Mrs Locke,' he told the Chief. 'The woman that worked for the Holroyd family.' Her face was creased with sorrow and concern as she spoke to Edgar. He took both her hands in his and looked down at her with old affection.

A sizeable band of men and women from the college came over to speak to the Chief. All Claire's classmates had by now been interviewed, without one single result of any significance. A pleasant, civilized bunch, the college group appeared to the Chief as they approached. They spoke to him with earnest goodwill about the service, they inquired about the progress of the investigation, they expressed hopes for its speedy success, the lifting of the cloud that hung over the town.

'The last time I saw Claire,' one of the women said, 'on the Thursday, the last class she came to, I thought how well and happy she looked, she had a sort of bloom on her.' Some of the others chimed in, agreeing.

'She was thinking of branching out with her studies,' another woman recalled. 'She was talking about taking a course with the Open University. One of their tutors came to the college to talk to us a few weeks back, Claire was very interested.'

The Chief's attention slipped for a moment. The sight of Diane Holroyd standing by the chapel door had woken stray recollections in his brain: Diane alone, drawing no attention to herself at the inquest on Harry Lingard; later, at Harry's funeral; later again, at the inquest on Claire. Had she a taste for such happenings? Or maybe, as a nurse, she took some kind of professional interest. He was roused from his musings by the realization that the college group was about to move off again, they were bidding him goodbye.

On the way back to Cannonbridge Sergeant Lambert suddenly said, 'That business about the Open University, Claire talking about taking a course. The tutor came to the college a few weeks back, that woman said just now. Robert Ashworth told us he met Claire only once, in the third week of September, he never spoke to her again, not even on the phone. He said she told him about the tutor's visit. The third week in September's a good deal more than a few weeks back, it's more like twelve weeks ago. Ashworth must have spoken to her later than that if she told him about the tutor's visit.'

They stopped by the college a few minutes later to check when the tutor had visited the college. Tuesday, October 16, they were told. Had there been any earlier visit by one of the university tutors? During a previous term, perhaps? No, there had been nothing earlier. October 16 was the only time any tutor from the Open University had visited the college.

After the funeral Jill Lingard went to work in the afternoon; on her way home in the evening she called in at the police station and asked to speak to Chief Inspector Kelsey. Her manner was tense and brittle as she took her seat facing him across his desk. The Chief made no attempt to get things going but waited for her to reveal why she had come. She had plainly expected him to take command; when she realized he had no such intention she drew a deep breath and plunged in.

'I've been going over things in my mind, trying to remember everything about the last few weeks before Granddad died, seeing if I could come up with anything that might be of use. I did remember something Granddad said on Remembrance Sunday, when Norman and I had supper with him. Granddad mentioned a case he'd read in the paper a few days before, a pensioner who'd been robbed of his savings that he'd kept in the house. I didn't know at the time that Granddad kept any money in the house himself.' She looked earnestly at the Chief. 'Thinking about it now, I believe that could have decided him not to keep money in the house any more. I think you can stop bothering about who stole his money, I don't think there was any money in the drawer to steal.' She twisted her hands together. 'I'm sure Norman would remember Granddad saying that about the pensioner.'

'I'm sure he would,' Kelsey returned drily. 'It would be a handy thing for Norman to remember just now.'

'You don't believe me, do you?' Her voice trembled. 'You think I believe Norman took the money and I'm just trying to get him off the hook.' She shook her head fiercely. 'That isn't true, I'm not making it up, Granddad did say that.' She was silent for a moment, then she burst out: 'Norman had nothing to do with either of those deaths, he's simply not capable of anything like that.' Her manner displayed increasing agitation. 'There was never anything between Norman and Mrs Holroyd, whatever you might think, he's sworn that to me on the Bible. He was never mixed up in any of it, I'd stake my life on it.'

The Chief gave her a level look. 'Would he be likely to tell you any different?' She stared back at him, her features began to dissolve, tears trickled down her cheeks. 'Why are you crying?' the Chief demanded. 'Are you afraid he did have an affair with Claire? He did have a hand in those deaths?'

That stiffened her again. She snatched out a handkerchief and dabbed at her eyes. 'You'll never be able to pin any of it on Norman,' she declared with force, 'however hard you try. He had nothing to do with any of it. I know that for certain.'

'You weren't here that Friday evening,' the Chief said flatly. 'You were over at your brother's. You don't know first-hand one single fact about anything that happened that night.'

But she wasn't finished yet. 'You'll have to give me my

ring back sooner or later. I know now it did belong to Mrs Holroyd. Norman's told me all about it, how he bought it from her, why he couldn't tell me that was how he got it. It was all perfectly legal and above board, he didn't do anything wrong. The ring belongs to me now, I'm entitled to have it back in the end.' A look of revulsion crossed her face. 'I could never wear it again, I'd always be reminded of what happened to her. Mr Holroyd can buy it back if he wants to, he can have it for what Norman paid for it. If he doesn't want it, we'll sell it to a jeweller and buy another ring with the money.' She paused for breath.

The Chief looked openly at his watch but she was plainly not disposed to take the hint. As she opened her mouth again he raised a quelling hand. 'You've had your say, I've heard you out.' He stood up. 'I must ask you to excuse me now, I'm a busy man.' He crossed to the door and held it open.

She set her lips in a mutinous line but she rose to her feet without another word. As she went past him out into the corridor he saw her eyes were blind with tears.

Downstairs lights showed from Ashworth's cottage as Sergeant Lambert turned the car into the lane. Ashworth hadn't long been in, he was glancing through the evening paper over a glass of whisky; his manner as he admitted the two men was subdued as if some of the effects of the funeral were still with him.

The Chief got straight down to business. 'You told us you met Claire on only one occasion after you came back to Cannonbridge. That meeting took place during the third week in September and you never spoke to her again.' Ashworth made no response. 'Do you now confirm that?' the Chief demanded. 'I would advise you to think carefully before you answer.'

Ashworth gave the faintest vestige of a smile. 'I can see you know I did speak to her again,' he said wryly. 'We had lunch together once more, on October 18, a Thursday.' Two days after the tutor's visit to the college, Sergeant

Lambert registered. 'I'm certain of the date,' Ashworth added, 'because I checked it after you called here last time.' He gave another hint of a smile. 'I had a notion you might discover I hadn't told you the whole truth.'

The Chief wanted to know in what circumstances the second lunch date had come about. 'We met entirely by chance in the street,' Ashworth told him. 'It was around eleven one morning. We chatted for a minute or two, then I asked her on the spur of the moment if she'd have lunch with me and she said she would. We arranged to meet at twelve-thirty outside the library. We drove out to the same country pub where we'd had lunch the previous time. It was all very agreeable and friendly.' He gave the Chief a direct look. 'But nothing more than that, nothing in the least romantic or lover-like. I ran her home afterwards.'

'When you ran her home did you go inside the house?'

He shook his head. 'That wasn't suggested by either of us. I dropped her by the common, then I went straight on into town, to my next appointment.'

'It all sounds very innocent. Why didn't you tell us this before?'

Ashworth exhaled a long breath. 'I was afraid you might think there was more to it than there was, with me having known Claire before.'

'You assure me there was no further meeting?'

'I do.'

The Chief got to his feet. Ashworth visibly relaxed as he realized the interview was at an end. The Chief stood glancing about the room; everything clean and orderly, the furniture polished to a gleaming finish. 'You seem pretty comfortable here,' he couldn't help observing. 'You keep it a good deal better than I keep my place.'

Ashworth looked pleased at this personal note. 'I've got a first-class cleaning woman, Mrs Jowitt, she never misses a cobweb, eyes like a hawk. She pops in for an hour or two in the mornings, it's handy for her, she lives in the next cottage. She's a widow, on her own, it suits her nicely. And

I go home every weekend so there isn't time for the place to get too untidy.'

'You get off home on Friday evenings?' the Chief asked idly.

'No, it's Saturday morning. The time varies, depends what appointments I have. I get off as soon as I've finished. Once or twice it's been as early as half past ten.' As he opened the sitting-room door the Chief looked down at his outstretched arm. 'That's a nice pair of cufflinks you're wearing,' he remarked casually. 'I noticed them earlier.'

Ashworth smiled. 'Yes, they are rather nice.' He raised his wrist for the Chief to take a closer look. 'They were a twenty-first birthday present. I've quite a collection of cufflinks.'

CHAPTER 20

A female civilian clerk from the murder investigation team was waiting for the Chief when he got to his office next morning. 'I don't know if this is of any use,' she told the Chief apologetically, 'but I thought I'd mention it, just in case.' She had moved house a few months ago; one of her new neighbours was a Mrs Tighe, a gossipy woman in her sixties. Mrs Tighe had been greatly intrigued to discover she worked at the police station and had tried to get her to talk about her work whenever they chanced to meet. When the news broke of first one murder and then a second, Mrs Tighe's curiosity was powerfully sharpened and the clerk had resorted to dodging her whenever possible. Yesterday evening, however, the clerk had run into Mrs Tighe when she called in at the corner shop on her way home from work; there had been no chance of escape. Mrs Tighe had waited for her, had fallen in beside her as she set off for home.

Mrs Tighe had immediately begun to talk about the murder investigation. The clerk had said nothing but let her rattle on, only half listening. 'Afterwards, though,' she admitted, apologetic again, 'when I was doing the washing-up after supper, some of what Mrs Tighe said came back to me. I wished then I'd paid more attention, I began to think it might have been useful.'

Mrs Tighe had begun by speaking of Harry Lingard whom she had known for years. She had gone on to speak of Harry's employer, Tom Mansell—she had a nephew who had worked for Mansell but had left after falling out with Mansell. From Mansell she had gone to Mansell's family, Diane, in particular. Until Mrs Tighe's retirement twelve months ago, she had worked as a ward orderly at the Cannonbridge General Hospital, where Diane had trained as a nurse. What had come back to the clerk over her washing-up were some dark hints Mrs Tighe had dropped about Diane, implying there were things she could say if she chose about Diane and her time at the General Hospital.

It was twelve-thirty when Sergeant Lambert halted the car outside Mrs Tighe's neat semi. He had no need to press the bell; by the time the two men had walked up the front path Mrs Tighe had whisked the door open and appeared on the step, darting lively glances at them.

Nor did the Chief Inspector need to tell her who they were; she recognized him at once from his picture in the papers. She was plainly delighted to see real live detectives materialize before her. She welcomed them effusively inside, swept them into her immaculate kitchen where she at once set about making tea, producing a variety of home-made goodies—of excellent quality, Sergeant Lambert was pleased to discover. He was able to make short work of several while the Chief gave his attention to Mrs Tighe.

Kelsey had no difficulty persuading her to talk, he led her by the same conversational route she had herself taken during her homeward chat with the clerk yesterday evening. 'I believe you knew Harry Lingard,' he began.

She was off at once. Kelsey steered her smoothly towards

Mansell, for whom she appeared to cherish no very high regard. In no time at all she was once again airing her opinion of Diane. She had followed Diane's progress with interest right from the first day Diane had begun her training, she had been curious to see what kind of nurse Tom Mansell's daughter would turn out to be. Diane had been a good student, worked hard, was punctual, clean and tidy; she did well in her studies. 'But I could see she was her father's daughter all right,' Mrs Tighe added with a glint in her eye. 'She had a pretty nasty temper under all the top dressing—though she kept it well under control most of the time.' She nodded sagely. 'A bad temper's the one fault you can't afford as a nurse.'

Diane had worked in the geriatric unit after finishing her training. Mrs Tighe dropped her tone to a confidential level. 'It was one of the old women, pretty senile she was, she'd got a heavy cold at the time.' She cast her mind back. 'This would be around two and a half years ago. The old woman suddenly came up with a fine crop of bruises. No use asking her how she came by them, she couldn't speak two words of sense together. It was decided she must have slipped and fallen, though there'd been no fall reported and the bruises didn't look much like what you get from a fall —not to me, at any rate. There was no one to ask awkward questions, the old woman had no family, no friends, no one ever came to see her from one year's end to another. Anyway, her cold turned to pneumonia, she was dead within a week. There was no inquest, nothing like that—she was over ninety.

'But that didn't stop the whispering. There wasn't much doubt in anyone's mind who was responsible for the bruises, they were all sure it was Diane. But the top brass closed ranks and hushed it up. There'd been a case a couple of years before, an old man who'd come up with a lot of bruises. He wasn't quite so old and he didn't die—and he had relatives, they kicked up an almighty fuss, it got into the papers, you probably remember it. The last thing anyone wanted was another dose of that kind of publicity.

'I don't know what was said between Diane and the top brass but she was allowed to leave quietly, no inquiry, no charges, no official reprimands. The word went round she'd had to promise never to apply for work in a hospital, old people's home, children's home or home for the disabled. But of course she's not the type to sit twiddling her thumbs at home all day or spend her time going to coffee mornings, she's far too energetic. And she does like nursing. Tom Mansell soon got her that job in the factory where she is now. He can always pull a few strings.'

The route back to the police station took them along White-thorn Road. They had to halt beside the common, where minor roadworks were causing interruption to the smooth flow of traffic. The Chief gazed idly out at the sunny stretches of common, the lunch-time strollers and joggers. A few yards away, a little girl was playing with a dachs-hund, she spotted the police car and her face at once assumed a look of sharp interest; she clipped the lead on to the dog's collar and came running up to Kelsey's window. She was a chubby-faced, rosy-cheeked child of about ten years old; her hair was taken back in a long plait, tied with red ribbon. 'You're Detective Chief Inspector Kelsey,' she said in a rush. 'I read about you in the paper. I hope you catch the people who killed Mrs Holroyd, she was a very nice lady.,'

'Did you know her?' the Chief asked gently.

She nodded. 'I used to talk to her in the mornings, before I went to school, when we were both out on the common exercising our dogs.'

Kelsey sat up. 'Did Mrs Holroyd have a dog?'

'She had a puppy,' the child said. 'A lovely little grey puppy. A Norfolk terrier, Mrs Holroyd told me. I'd never seen one before, they've got drop ears. It was called Beauty. It would be about—' she screwed up her face in thought —'five months old now but I haven't seen it since—' She fell abruptly silent.

The Chief got out of the car and walked with the child

to a nearby bench. The traffic began to move again and Sergeant Lambert joined them as soon as he had pulled the car out of the line, on to the common. The child chatted in friendly fashion, all the while throwing a stick for the dachshund. She told them she lived in a side street a few minutes' walk away; she loved dogs but couldn't have one of her own—her mother was a widow, there were two younger children, the money wouldn't run to keeping pets. But she always managed to have some dog or other, belonging to a neighbour or relative, to play with and fuss over.

Kelsey asked if she could remember when she had first seen Mrs Holroyd with Beauty. She was able to pinpoint the date without difficulty. 'It was when the old man up the road had to go into hospital for a new hip joint, he asked me if I'd look after his little Scottie while he was away. Of course I said I would. He told me to make a note of the date when he'd be going in: October 15. I can show you where I wrote it in my diary.

'I took the Scottie out on the common early next morning after I got him, so that would be October 16, that was the first time I saw Mrs Holroyd out with her puppy. The Scottie and the puppy made friends and Mrs Holroyd started talking to me. I'd often see her about but I'd never spoken to her before and I'd never seen her out that early before. I always used to think how pretty she was and what lovely clothes she had—though she always wore an old raincoat and old shoes when she exercised Beauty.'

The Chief didn't interrupt with questions and she went chattering on. 'She told me they always had dogs at home when she was little, and she had an auntie who kept dogs. But she hadn't had one herself since she left school, not till she got Beauty. Her husband didn't really like dogs, he'd never been used to them.

'I said didn't her husband mind her having Beauty. She laughed and said she never asked him about it, she got the puppy while her husband was away. I asked her if he was cross when he came back and found the puppy but she said no, he was very good about it, he didn't mind it staying if she promised to keep it out of his way. She said that was easy to manage, it was a big enough house.'

A sudden inspiration lit a glow in her eyes. 'If Mr Holroyd doesn't want the puppy now, I could look after it till he finds another home for it.' She gazed pleadingly up at the Chief. 'Beauty knows me, it wouldn't be like going to a stranger, I'd take very good care of her.' The glow faded as another thought occurred to her. 'But I expect he's found a home for Beauty already.' A church clock struck the quarter, she jumped to her feet. 'I have to go, I mustn't be late for school.'

They drove straight to the council offices to see if they could catch Edgar Holroyd but they were out of luck, Edgar was out on inspection calls, he wouldn't be back till late afternoon. But the Chief was able to leave a message with an assistant on his way out of the office for lunch, asking Edgar to meet them at Fairbourne immediately after work. The assistant walked with them along the deserted corridor towards the exit. 'This has been a terrible time for Mr Holroyd,' he said. 'He's beginning to look a little better since he came back to work. I suppose it helps to take his mind off what happened.' He gave a wry smile. 'I can't get used to the idea that we'll never see Harry Lingard in the department again. He could be a right barrack-room lawyer but there was usually a lot of horse-sense in what he had to say. I always thought he'd be a good man to have on your side.' He grimaced. 'Better not let Mr Holroyd catch me saying that, he was no fan of Harry's.'

'No?' Kelsey said.

'He and Harry couldn't help rubbing each other up the wrong way, they saw things from different angles. It got so Mr Holroyd wouldn't deal with Harry any more. When he showed up with another of his complaints it was usually me that had to deal with him—not that I minded, I quite liked the old codger, he was a bonny fighter for anything he believed in.'

'He really got under Mr Holroyd's skin?' Kelsey said.

'He certainly did. Mr Holroyd even persuaded himself it was Harry tipped the scales against him a couple of years back when the number one job in the department was up for grabs.'

'What could Harry have had to do with that?'

'He had one of his campaigns going at the time, he was firing off letters every week to the local paper. They always printed them, they loved Harry down at the paper, he was always good copy. Mr Holroyd was certain it was one particular letter, where Harry had listed all the cock-ups and blunders the department had made over the previous twelve months, that put paid to his getting the top job. I didn't see it that way myself, I thought it was because Mr Holroyd was on the young side, the man who landed the job is quite a bit older.'

The lights were on in Fairbourne when Lambert pulled up by the common shortly after five-thirty. The Chief waved aside Edgar's offer of tea and got straight down to business. 'I understand your wife owned a puppy,' he began.

'That's right,' Edgar confirmed. 'A little grey pup. Beauty, its name was. It was given to her while I was away at a conference in October.'

'Where is the pup now?'

'I have no idea. I assumed Claire took it with her when she left. I've certainly never laid eyes on it since.'

'Did she make any mention of it in the note she left?'

He thought back. 'Not that I can recall, but she may have done.'

'What about its things—basket, dish and so on?'

'They're still here. Claire wouldn't need to take anything like that, May Finch has any amount of that kind of stuff, she's always kept dogs.'

'May we see its things?'

'Certainly. They're out in the garage.' He took them out to the garage, a large brick structure, solidly built a good many years ago, fitted out with built-in cupboards and drawers. He opened a cupboard. Propped on its side on the lowest shelf was a basket, with a grey blanket folded beside it. Ranged on higher shelves was an orderly array of items for feeding, bathing, grooming, training. Higher still, a folded long-sleeved overall and headscarf. 'Claire wore those when she groomed the pup,' Edgar explained. 'She always did that out in the garden.'

'Were these things always kept out here?' the Chief asked.

Edgar shook his head. 'They were kept in a room in the basement, next to the garden; that was where the pup lived. It never came up into the house. I brought its things over here after Claire left. I thought I'd decorate the basement room while she was away, it hadn't been done for some time.' His voice shook. 'I thought it would be a nice surprise for her when she got back.' He took them back into the house through a side entrance leading directly into the basement and turned the handle of the first door opening off a passage, revealing a room freshly painted: pale yellow walls, white woodwork; a sink unit in one corner, an ample provision of shelves and cupboards.

'I had nothing to do with the pup myself,' he said as he closed the door and took them along the passage, past the workshop, storerooms, up a flight of stairs into the main part of the house. 'I've never had anything to do with dogs, I don't know the first thing about them. My father would never allow one inside the house, he thought them unhygienic.'

'Did you mind your wife bringing a pup home?' Kelsey asked.

Edgar managed the ghost of a smile. 'I wasn't given the chance to mind. I always knew Claire would have liked a dog of her own, but she knew right from the start what my thoughts were about that and she'd never pressed it. I must admit I was surprised when I got back from the conference and found Beauty already installed, gear and everything.'

'Was your wife apologetic?'

'Far from it. She was delighted with the pup. She was sure I'd get fond of it in no time at all, I wouldn't be able to help myself. I told her I'd no intention of trying. The pup could stay if she promised to keep it out of my way, never let it up into the house. She agreed at once, and she kept faithfully to her bargain.' His face grew bleak. 'What a fuss for a grown man to make about a tiny animal. It hardly bears thinking about now.'

'Did she say who gave her the pup?'

'Yes, it was some woman from one of her classes. I don't remember if she mentioned the woman's name but it wouldn't have meant anything to me. The woman had several pups to give away, she wasn't selling them—they weren't pedigree, nothing like that, she just wanted them to go to good homes. Some of the other students said they'd have one—and of course Claire couldn't resist the offer.' He looked across at Kelsey. 'It gave her such pleasure.' Tears glittered in his eyes.

'You made no mention of the dog at the time your wife's body was found,' the Chief pointed out.

'It never crossed my mind. I doubt if I even remembered its existence.' Exhaustion began to show in Edgar's face. 'I can only suppose it must have run off somewhere. It could have been knocked down by a car, could have been killed. Or some youngster may have come across it and taken it home.' He closed his eyes. 'It could be that whoever killed Claire also disposed of the dog.'

'Was the pup wearing a collar?' Kelsey asked. 'Giving name and address?'

'I'm afraid I can't say,' Edgar answered. 'I scarcely ever set eyes on the pup.'

The Chief switched to another matter. 'In your professional dealings with Harry Lingard, how would you describe your attitude to him?'

Edgar seemed thrown by the sudden change of tack. 'I would hope I was always fair-minded and courteous,' he replied after a moment.

'Would you say you ever displayed animosity?'

'Certainly not,' he responded with a return of energy. 'He could be difficult but we're well used to that in the department, patience is something you learn early on.'

'Did you always deal with Lingard yourself?'

'I used to. But he came in one day when I was very busy and one of my assistants dealt with him, I thought he handled him very well. He nearly always dealt with him after that.'

When they got back into the car the Chief sat slumped in his seat; fatigue and staleness were creeping up on him again, he was strongly tempted to call it a day. But training and habit wouldn't allow it. Check everything, he had been taught, years ago. Most thoroughly of all, check those things you are certain don't need checking. As soon as they reached the station he set a team to work phoning down the list of Claire's classmates and lecturers, to check if one of them had indeed given her the puppy.

Half an hour went by. Not only had the team failed to discover any woman who had given away puppies, they hadn't even come upon anyone who could recollect such an offer ever having been made. They continued to slog their way through the remaining names but the Chief no longer had any faith that the list would come up with the goods. Too late this evening to start ringing round pet shops to make inquiries, they would all be closed. But not too late to begin phoning every dog-breeder and kennels within a fifty-mile radius. He set a second squad to work. Twenty minutes later one of the squad located a woman who bred Norfolk terriers—she ran boarding kennels out in the country, forty miles from Cannonbridge.

The Chief seized the phone and spoke to the breeder. Yes, she had sold a litter of Norfolk terrier pups in October. Pedigree animals, registered with the Kennel Club; three months old at the time she advertised them. She went off to fetch her record book, returning shortly to read out the names of the buyers. The fourth name was a Mrs Finch; she had taken a grizzled bitch pup by the name of Hampden Grey Beauty.

Could she recall what Mrs Finch looked like? Indeed she could. A very good-looking woman, late twenties; beautiful curly hair, golden chestnut.

Did she have a note of Mrs Finch's address? Yes again. She always insisted on the address, she would never part with a pup unless she had it. She read it out. The Chief closed his eyes as he heard it: Aunt May Finch's address. 'Could we come over tomorrow morning to have a word?' he asked.

'Come as early as you like,' she invited cheerfully. 'We're always up well ahead of any lark.'

By eight-fifteen next morning they had covered the forty miles to the kennels. The owner was a vigorous-looking woman in her fifties, already hard at work, but happy to break off to talk to them over mugs of steaming coffee.

Mrs Finch had called without an appointment in the early afternoon of Thursday, October 11. She was accompanied by a man whom she had taken to be Mrs Finch's husband, though she couldn't recall that that had ever been stated. She had put the pair down as honeymooners, they were very lovey-dovey. She couldn't remember what car they had arrived in.

Had Mrs Finch used the man's Christian name at all? Yes, she had, she had used it more than once. She puckered her brow but the name eluded her. When the Chief produced a photograph of Claire she identified it without hesitation as Mrs Finch. He saw that the photograph rang no other bells with her, she appeared to know nothing of the murder investigation. She showed intelligent interest but no untoward curiosity, she didn't ask what all this was about.

Could she describe the man who had accompanied Mrs Finch? She did her best but couldn't summon him up as clearly as she could Mrs Finch. It was Mrs Finch who had taken the lead throughout, Mrs Finch she had dealt with —except when it came to the matter of payment. It was the man who had paid for the puppy, in cash—it was clearly by way of being a present to Mrs Finch. To the best of her recollection the man was on the tall side, well built, reasonably good-looking. Around the same age as Mrs Finch,

maybe a year or two younger. She couldn't recall his colouring or any distinctive features. She suddenly snapped her
fingers. 'I nearly had it then! His name.' She paused, shook
her head ruefully. 'It's gone again.'

At the Chief's request she took them along to see some
of her terriers. 'This is one I kept from the same litter as
Hampden Grey Beauty,' she said as she showed them a
drop-eared bitch some five months old, with a rough grey
coat, straight and wiry. An engaging little creature, bright
and affectionate; it seemed active and fearless.

The breeder walked with them to the car when they left,
she stood watching as they got in and Lambert switched
on the engine. He was about to move off when she suddenly
darted forward and rapped on the Chief's window; he
wound it down. She stooped to speak to him, smiling
broadly. 'I've got it—the man's name. It was Lester, I'm
certain of it.'

CHAPTER 21

The moment they got back to Cannonbridge the Chief rang
Mansell's yard to summon Lester Holroyd to the police
station. Lester began to demur. He had appointments, he
couldn't simply abandon everything. Wouldn't this afternoon do? No, he was told brusquely, it wouldn't do. He
could either come now, under his own steam or someone
would be despatched to fetch him. That changed his tune,
he came along without further ado and was taken to an
interview room. The Chief kicked off with a single abrupt
question: Did he ever wear cufflinks? The cuffs on the shirt
Lester was wearing were fastened with buttons.

Surprise flashed across his face. His look sharply
expressed the thought: Have I been snatched from my
duties to discuss cufflinks? But a glance at the chief's
unbending countenance kept him from voicing any such
query. 'Yes, I do wear them,' he answered. 'Not for work,

but if I'm going out, evenings or weekends, when I want to look smart.'

The Chief moved rapidly to another matter. 'The relationship between you and Claire, when precisely did it end?'

'When she left Mansell's in June.' He made a dismissive gesture. 'It was no more than a silly flirtation.'

'Did you have any contact with Claire after she left Mansell's?' the Chief pressed him.

'None at all.'

The Chief winged his next question like a dart. 'Then how come we find you buying Claire a pup on October 11?'

That brought him up with a jolt, he could say nothing.

'You lashed out a fair sum for a pedigree pup,' the Chief pursued. 'And another sum, I've no doubt, for its gear. All for a trifling flirtation?'

Lester moved his shoulders. 'OK,' he said with an attempt at lightness. 'There was a bit more to it than I've told you. And it did go on for a while after she left the office. It went on till the middle of October. Edgar had to go off to a conference, he was going to be away the best part of a week. I fixed it so I could be out of the office a good part of the time. I was supposed to be looking at possible sites in different parts of the county, I do a lot of that kind of thing, it was easy enough to fix.'

Now he had fairly got started he showed no reluctance to continue. 'We had a few marvellous days together.' He stared back into that rose-coloured time. 'It was buying the pup put paid to it all in the end. We'd driven well out into the country, to be on the safe side. It was on the Thursday, our last day, Edgar was due back on the Friday. It was a glorious day, we had a first-class lunch, we both felt on top of the world. We were driving round afterwards and we saw the sign for the kennels, saying Norfolk Terriers. Claire asked me to stop. She said Norfolks were charming little dogs, she'd love to have one. Of course I said I'd buy her one. We went along to a shop afterwards and bought all the gear.

'Claire behaved in a much more relaxed way that day. I could see by the way the dog-breeder woman looked at us she thought we were newly-weds. But I woke up that night in a cold sweat thinking about it, I realized just how close to the wind we'd been sailing, if it went on we'd simply slide into disaster. I knew there and then it had got to stop. We both valued our marriages, neither of us had the slightest wish for a divorce.'

He stared at the wall. 'It was madness, really, all along. Looking back on it, I can see it was sheer lunacy. But at the time . . .' He gave his head a slow shake, then took up his tale again. 'I'd arranged to see Claire again on the Monday afternoon. I made up my mind I'd tell her then we'd have to finish. I didn't know how she'd take it so I decided to say Diane was starting to get suspicious, I knew that would pull Claire up short.'

'Was your wife starting to get suspicious?' Kelsey put in.

'No, not really. She had asked one or two questions but I was able to get round them all right. Anyway, as it turned out, I didn't have to say anything about Diane to Claire, I didn't have to do any persuading. Claire had been thinking things over herself during the weekend, she'd come to very much the same conclusion. We agreed to make a clean break. She shed a few tears but it was all perfectly friendly, no arguments or quarrelling.' He gave the Chief a level look. 'We both stuck to the agreement one hundred per cent. There was no more contact after that Monday. October 15 was the date, I checked it after you spoke to me last time. We never even exchanged glances at the Acorn dinner-dance a week or two later.'

All that could square, Sergeant Lambert thought, with what Robert Ashworth had told them about his chance meeting in the street with Claire on Thursday, October 18. She could have been in a very vulnerable state three days after the break with Lester, very much in need of a friendly arm around her, particularly the arm of a man she had once loved.

'I expected it to be a terrible wrench,' Lester added,

'breaking it off like that. But it wasn't. I just felt very relieved it was all over. I must have been suppressing a whole lot of guilt towards Diane—and towards Edgar. I realized Claire had probably been doing much the same thing.'

'During the time Claire worked in Mansell's office,' Kelsey said, 'did you ever see any sign that either of the Mansells was interested in her?' Lester looked uncomfortable but said nothing. 'Did Claire ever say anything to you?' Kelsey persisted. 'About either of them?'

'As a matter of fact she did,' Lester replied after some further hesitation. 'One of the reasons she decided to stop working at Mansell's was because Stuart had started eyeing her, trying to chat her up.'

'Stuart?' the Chief interrupted. 'What about his father?'

Lester shook his head. 'She never said anything about Tom. She said she'd done her best to discourage Stuart, treat it as a joke, but it didn't seem to be working, he didn't seem to want to get the message. I suggested I might have a word with him.' He gave a rueful half-smile. 'I could well remember the way I'd carried on myself as a lad, hanging round Hartley's when Claire worked there. But she wouldn't let me speak to him, she didn't want to make something out of it. She'd been thinking of leaving anyway because of the situation between the two of us, she was afraid someone might spot what was going on. The Stuart business just made her mind up for her a bit more quickly. As far as I know that was the end of it, she certainly never mentioned Stuart to me again after she left the office.'

When Lester had departed back to the yard the Chief sat in silence for some moments, then he looked across at Lambert. 'The question now,' he said, 'is what happened to the pup.'

A small saloon car was drawn up near the front door when Sergeant Lambert drove up to Lester Holroyd's house fifteen minutes later. As the two policemen got out of their vehicle the front door was snatched open, revealing Diane, wearing outdoor clothes and a far from welcoming expression. 'Lester's not here,' she declared belligerently by way of greeting. 'He's at work—where you might expect him to be at this time of day.'

'It's not your husband we've come to see,' the Chief told her soothingly. 'It's you we'd like a word with.'

She eyed him ungraciously. 'I'm just off out to the shops. Couldn't you make it another time? Tomorrow morning? Around nine?'

The Chief could be equally unbudging. 'It had better be now, we won't keep you many minutes.'

She let out a noisy sigh and held the door wide to admit them. 'All right then.' She urged them into the sitting-room, plonked herself down opposite them. 'Get on with it, then,' she commanded.

The Chief plunged straight in. 'Do you know what happened to Claire's puppy?'

Her brows came together in a fierce frown. 'Puppy? I didn't even know she had a puppy. I haven't the faintest idea what happened to it.' She made to rise from her seat.

The Chief waved her down again. 'Did you ever see the puppy here?'

She blew out an irritated breath. 'As I've no idea what the creature looked like, how can I possibly say if I ever saw it anywhere?'

'A bitch puppy,' the Chief supplied. 'Norfolk terrier. Rough grey coat, drop ears.'

She shook her head briskly. 'I never saw any pup like that here—or anywhere else, for that matter. What on earth would Claire's dog be doing here? I never saw much of Claire at the best of times, I saw nothing at all of her in the last few months.' Again she made to rise.

This time the Chief didn't stop her. He got to his feet himself and stood facing her. 'Would you mind if we took a quick shufti round the place?'

She uttered a loud groan. 'You'll do it whether I mind or not. Be as quick as you can.'

The shufti was as rapid as they could make it but sharply comprehensive for all that. It yielded nothing.

Again they found a small car—a coupé this time—drawn up by the front door when they arrived at their next port of call, Tom Mansell's dwelling. Lambert's ring brought the housekeeper from the kitchen; her manner was as relaxed and amiable as before. The Chief declined her offer to take them into the sitting-room, they remained standing in the spacious hall while the Chief spoke to her. This time he employed a slight variation in framing his opening question. He asked: 'Did you ever see a small bitch puppy on these premises?' Again he described the terrier. The housekeeper shook her head. 'Or any article that might have belonged to such a pup?' the Chief added. 'Collar? Lead?' Again she shook her head. She looked as if she would have liked to ask what all this was about but she didn't voice the question. 'All right if we take a look round?' the Chief asked.

She wasn't at all happy about that. 'I don't know that I can take it on myself—' She broke off at the sound of movement from the upper floor. 'That's Stuart,' she told the Chief. 'He's just popped back for some books he forgot this morning—this is one of his days at the college.' A moment later Stuart came bounding down the stairs, clutching some books. He halted abruptly at the sight of the little group in the hall, then he continued down. The housekeeper returned to her kitchen and the Chief had a word with Stuart. He put his question in much the same way as he had put it to Diane: had Stuart any idea what had happened to Claire Holroyd's dog? And he got back very much the same reply: Stuart didn't even know Claire had owned a dog, let alone what had happened to it. Yet again the Chief gave a description of the terrier. No, Stuart knew nothing of it, he had certainly never seen it on these premises. His manner was easy and courteous.

The Chief asked when he had last seen Claire. Stuart thought back. 'I saw her in town once or twice after she stopped working in the office. And she was at the Acorn dinner-dance.'

Had he spoken to her on any of these occasions? He shook his head. 'Did you like her?' the Chief wanted to know.

'She was all right.'

'No more than all right?' Stuart made no reply.

'I understand you liked her well enough to give her a birthday present.'

Stuart made a dismissive gesture. 'It wasn't a proper present, it was just a leg-pull, a silly joke. I hope I've grown up a bit since then. I thought Claire was a bit snooty and stand-offish. I thought I'd play a joke on her, take her down a peg. I had a brooch, a prize I'd won at a fair, it looked pretty good till you gave it a closer look. I did it up in a box, fancy paper and ribbon. It was a childish trick. I'm not very proud of it.'

'How did you know it was her birthday?'

'I can't remember now. I suppose I heard somebody mention it.'

The Chief changed tack. 'Friday, November 16, did you go out at all that evening?'

'You asked me that before,' Stuart answered with composure. 'I told you no, I didn't go out.'

'You didn't take it into your head to pop out for a breath of air after your studying? Take a car for a runaround? Past Whitethorn Common, maybe?'

He shook his head, appearing unruffled. 'I didn't leave the house at all that evening.'

'You can't prove that.'

'No.' He smiled slightly. 'Any more than you can prove I did leave the house.'

'If at any time you were out driving and you came across Claire on foot, would you stop and offer her a lift?'

'Yes, I expect I would.'

'Did you in fact ever do that?'

'I may have done. I can't really remember.'

The Chief executed another swift change of direction. 'Did you receive a phone call that Friday evening from your sister Diane?' He shook his head. 'Did your father receive a phone call from Diane?' Again he shook his head. 'How would you know if you were up in your room?' He made no reply. There was a brief silence, then the Chief asked: 'Would you say you'd do anything for your sister?'

'Yes, I guess so,' 'Stuart answered. 'Anything within reason.' He directed a steady look at the Chief. 'And within the bounds of law.' Another brief silence. Stuart looked at his watch. 'I have a class at twelve,' he said. 'I'd rather not be late.'

'We'll let you get off, then,' the Chief responded. 'All right if we take a look round before we go? The housekeeper didn't know if she ought to let us.'

'That's all right, go ahead.' Stuart waved a hand. 'Go anywhere you like. I'll have a word with the housekeeper.'

This time the look-round was a little more prolonged but once again it yielded nothing of consequence.

When Sergeant Lambert halted the car outside the Griffins' cottage, Mrs Griffin was upstairs in her bedroom standing before the long mirror of her wardrobe, holding her new dance-dress against herself, peering with anxious concentration at the effect of the brightly coloured pattern in conjunction with her skin and hair. Particularly her hair—a warm brown beginning to be touched with grey. The ring of the doorbell broke in on her musings. Still clutching the dress, she hurried downstairs. 'Oh, it's you again,' she exclaimed without enthusiasm at the sight of the two policemen. 'What is it this time? Norman's not here, he's at work.'

'It isn't Norman we've come to see,' the Chief explained in soothing-syrup tones. 'We'd very much appreciate a word with your good self.'

'Oh, very well then, I suppose you'd better come in,' she responded grudgingly. 'Though what all this is in aid of, I'm sure I don't know.' She took them along to the sitting-room. 'Is Norman supposed to have done something or not?' she demanded with some irritation. 'Though I'll lay good money you're not going to tell me.' She would certainly have won her bet, the Chief didn't enlighten her. Instead he remarked, 'That's a very pretty dress you've got there, if you don't mind my saying so. Beautiful colours.'

'Oh, do you think so?' She perked up at once. 'I bought it specially for the dance tonight but I was beginning to wonder if it wasn't a bit on the young side for me. It's a special occasion at the club, the golden jubilee, I'd like to look my best.' She crossed over to a mirror above the fireplace, stared into it, touched her hair. 'I've got an appointment at the salon this afternoon. I've been wondering whether to have my hair touched up. Not a proper dye, Norman wouldn't like that. Just a bit of a tint.' She turned her head towards the Chief. 'What do you think? Would it make me look younger? Or older? That's always the risk. I wouldn't want to look like mutton got up as lamb.'

'I think a tint would be fine,' the Chief pronounced heartily. 'Touch of auburn. Or chestnut. Something along those lines. Knock ten years off your age.'

Her face lit up. 'Right then, that's what I'll do.' She frowned. 'Auburn? Or chestnut?' She darted a glance at Lambert. 'You're a smart-looking young fellow, you ought to know what's what. Which would you recommend?'

'Auburn,' Lambert bounced back at her without hesitation. 'It would go with your eyes and skin. You'll be the belle of the ball.'

She glowed with pleasure. 'I had a bit of auburn in it as a girl.' She laid the dress carefully over the back of the sofa, insisted on bringing in a tray of tea and finally got round to asking in what way she could help them.

'A very simple question,' the Chief told her. 'Did you ever see Claire Holroyd's puppy on these premises?'

Simple or not, it astounded her. 'Mrs Holroyd's puppy?' she echoed. 'What in the name of goodness would Mrs Holroyd's puppy be doing here?' The Chief didn't answer that. Once again he gave a description of the terrier. Mrs Griffin was emphatic she had never seen such a creature about the place. Had she ever seen a collar or lead that

might belong to such a puppy? Again she was equally definite, she never had. She added after a moment, 'I don't
know why you should think they could be here, I only ever
saw Mrs Holroyd here a couple of times.'

The Chief felt the hair rise along his scalp. 'When would
that be?' His tone was as casual as he could make it.

She moved her shoulders. 'I couldn't say now, it wasn't
all that recently. You can ask Norman, if it's important, he
might remember.'

'What did Mrs Holroyd want?'

'I don't know, I didn't ask her. She just said she'd like
to speak to Norman. I took it to be something to do with
the office.'

They had previously made a search of the dwelling but
the Chief asked—on the you-never-know principle—if they
might take a quick look round now. Mrs Griffin's mood
was still mellow and she raised no objection. Once again
the look-round yielded nothing.

Still unflaggingly adhering to the rule of never overlooking
anything, however unpromising, the Chief called next at
the terrace house Jill Lingard shared. Jill was at work but
one of the other girls was at home, awash with the miseries
of a streaming cold. She expressed no surprise at the visit
or at the Chief's questions, she appeared in no condition
to feel surprised at anything but sat swathed in woollies,
sunk into an easy chair before the gas-fire, sipping hot her-
bal tea in between bouts of coughing, sneezing, blowing her
nose. No, she had never seen any puppy in the house, never
seen any collar or lead. She made no protest when the
Chief asked if he might look round. Nor did she attempt to
accompany them but remained huddled in her chair while
they carried out their swift and fruitless search.

There was no sign of life from Ashworth's cottage; they
continued on to the next cottage where Ashworth's cleaning
woman, Mrs Jowitt, was clearing away after her solitary
lunch. The appearance of two policemen on her doorstep

plainly provided a stimulating interlude in her day. She was greatly intrigued when the Chief produced his warrant card but he saw with satisfaction that neither his name nor his face meant anything to her. Yes, she could spare the time to talk to them, she wasn't due at her afternoon job till two-thirty. She invited them to stop inside, gave them tea from her best china cups.

This time the Chief adopted a somewhat different approach. 'We're looking for a missing puppy,' he told her. He described the terrier. 'We think it might have got out this way.' Her face shone with lively interest, she was charmed by the notion of two stalwart police officers careering about the countryside in search of a lost pet. Had she seen anything of the puppy? Or come across any of its belongings? A collar? Or lead?

She shook her head with regret. Nothing she would have liked better than to be able to point them in a direction which would reveal the poor creature, whining and terri- fied, crouching in some bosky retreat.

The Chief got to his feet, thanked her warmly for her time, the delicious tea. 'I believe you put in a few hours at the cottage next door,' he remarked casually on the way out. 'I remember Mr Ashworth mentioning it the other day when we were chatting. He said how well you looked after him.'

She was delighted at that. Yes, she did work for Mr Ashworth. She had done her stint next door this morning, as usual.

Kelsey paused in the hallway. 'I suppose it wouldn't do any harm to have a quick look round Mr Ashworth's garden while we're over here. Any sheds or outhouses next door the pup could have got into?'

Indeed there were. She was growing more interested by the minute, more eager to be helpful. The garden was quite a size, there was a shrubbery, any number of places where a weary animal might bed itself down. 'I'll fetch the key,' she offered. 'You might want to take a look inside the house as well.'

'You and I will go round the garden,' the Chief told her in a matey fashion when they reached the cottage. 'Sergeant Lambert can nip inside for a dekko.' Mrs Jowitt accompanied the Chief happily on his tour, pointing out likely hiding-places. When they joined Lambert again, inside the cottage, the Sergeant indicated to the Chief by an infinitesimal shake of his head that his dekko had once again produced nothing.

The Chief stood glancing about with an admiring eye. 'Lovely old place,' he said appreciatively. 'You keep it beautifully.' He picked up a framed photograph from the top of a bureau. 'Mr Ashworth's family?' Mrs Jowitt nodded. 'Must be lonely for him here on his own during the week,' the Chief added. She didn't reply to that but he noted the gleam in her eye. 'Some men might get up to tricks,' he remarked lightly as he replaced the photograph. 'But I'm sure Mr Ashworth isn't one of them.'

She gave a sharply knowing glance. 'That's just where you could be wrong.'

'Is that so?' He allowed scepticism to colour his tone.

'I wasn't born yesterday,' she avowed with energy. 'I can put two and two together as well as the next one.' She faced him squarely. 'I was running the vacuum cleaner round upstairs, one morning a month or two back. What do you think I found on the carpet in Mr Ashworth's bedroom?' She paused dramatically. 'A lady's earring!' The Chief permitted his eyes to widen. 'Worth a bob or two if I'm any judge,' she added with conviction. 'I know a bit of quality when I see it.'

'What did the earring look like?' the Chief asked carelessly.

'It looked old to me, antique, you might say. Gold, set with pearls. I'll stake my life they were the real thing. Nothing flashy, good style, very neat. Not very big, sort of a new moon shape. It fitted close to the ear.' She put up a finger to her ear, drew a crescent curve along the lobe. She smiled. 'I don't mind admitting I tried it on in front of the mirror —it had a clip fastening. Suited me a treat. I wished I could have had a pair like that to wear to my niece's wedding, she was getting married next day. They'd have looked lovely with my good suit and the new hat I'd bought.'

'What did you do with the earring?' Kelsey asked.

'I brought it down here and left it in the middle of that table over there, where Mr Ashworth would be sure to see it when he came in. I didn't leave a note or anything, I wouldn't want to embarrass him. The earring was gone next morning when I came in. Mr Ashworth never said a word about it and I never said anything either.'

'It was a month or two back that you found the earring?'

'I can tell you the exact date. My niece got married on the Saturday, October 20. It was the day before that when I found the earring. That makes it the Friday morning, October 19.'

CHAPTER 22

The Chief had two appointments on Friday afternoon, the first to record an interview at the regional TV studio, making a fresh appeal for information and giving some account of the investigation; the interview would go out after the early-evening news, would be repeated later in the evening. His second appointment was with the local radio station. The interview there—along much the same lines —would be broadcast live, repeated later in the evening.

After he got back to the police station at the end of the afternoon the Chief had a phone call from the Fraud Squad to inform him they were now satisfied there were sufficient grounds to warrant taking the next step in relation to Tom Mansell's business activities. They intended moving in on Mansell first thing on Monday morning, going through his books, records, accounts.

At half past five the Chief set off for Fairbourne to catch Edgar Holroyd when he came in from work. Edgar had got in just ahead of them, he was garaging his car when they drove up. As soon as they were inside the house the Chief asked if he might look through Claire's jewellery; he offered no explanation. Edgar seemed about to ask if something fresh had come up but a glance at the Chief's unforth-coming countenance halted the words on his lips. He went off to fetch the casket.

He stood watching in silence as Kelsey began to look through the contents, coming very soon upon a small velvet-covered box which opened to reveal a pair of elegant gold Victorian earrings with a clip fastening. Not very large, crescent-shaped, set with pearls. The Chief studied them, then he replaced them and closed the casket, making no comment; again Edgar looked as if he would ask a question, again he refrained.

The Chief sat looking up at him. He had a question of his own to ask but he hesitated before framing it, striving for some way to lessen its grievous force. But he could think of none so he went ahead with what delicacy he could muster: had Edgar any reason to suppose Claire had at any time been on an intimate footing with his brother Lester?

It took a moment for the full impact of the question to strike Edgar. He reeled slightly, steadied himself against the back of a chair. A look of astounded anger flashed across his face. 'That's a vile suggestion!' he exclaimed with vehemence. 'There's not a shred of truth in it!' He made a fierce gesture of repudiation. 'Claire could never have done such a thing to me. Or Lester. My own brother! Never! Never! Never!' His face was convulsed. The Chief let it go and stood up to leave. He didn't disclose that Lester had admitted the affair.

Robert Ashworth was in his sitting-room watching the news over a drink when his doorbell rang. 'I've just seen you on TV,' he told the Chief as he admitted them. 'You came across very well.'

Kelsey brushed that aside and got down to business. 'You told us that the last time you had any contact with Claire was on Thursday, October 18.'

'That's right,' Ashworth confirmed.

'You took her to lunch, ran her home afterwards.'

'That's right,' Ashworth said again.

'Did you ever bring her here to this cottage? That day or any other day?'

He shook his head. 'She never set foot in the cottage.'

'Then how come she dropped one of her earrings on the carpet in your bedroom?'

There was a brief silence, then Ashworth said, 'I see you've been talking to Mrs Jowitt.' He got to his feet and began to pace about the room. 'Claire *was* here. It was that same day, October 18. I didn't run her straight home after lunch, I had to call in here to pick up some papers. Claire was rather taken with the cottage, she asked if she could see over it. I suppose we were here about ten minutes—I couldn't stay long, I had to get back for an appointment. Then I drove her home, I dropped her by the common. Next day, Friday, when I got home in the evening, I found one of her earrings on that table over there. I rang Claire on the Monday morning—October 22, that would be—to tell her about the earring. I said I'd be out that way on business in the afternoon, I could drop it in. She said that would be fine, she'd be at home. I didn't go in when I called, neither of us suggested it. I wouldn't have had the time, in any case. I gave her the earring and went straight off to my next appointment.'

He halted by the fireplace, began to move things about on the mantelshelf. 'I did try to phone her three or four times after Harry Lingard's body was found. I wondered how she'd been affected by the discovery, all the commotion, if she'd been very upset, living so close. I never got any reply. I thought maybe she'd started some course at the college or she might have got herself a job. In any case I'd probably run across her in the street again before long.' He lapsed into silence.

'Were you aware,' the Chief asked with a matter-of-fact air, 'that at the time of her death Claire was in the early stages of pregnancy?'

Ashworth stopped his fidgeting. He remained where he was, his back to the Chief, looking down at his hands motionless on the mantelshelf. 'No, I didn't know,' he said in tones of great sadness. 'She would have been so pleased. Did she know she was pregnant?'

The Chief didn't answer that but executed a swift change of direction. 'When your earlier relationship with Claire ended some years ago, you left Cannonbridge soon afterwards. How long after that did you get married?'

Ashworth half turned to look at him. 'Four or five months,' he answered.

'Would you say you married on the rebound?'

Ashworth moved his shoulders. 'Possibly. But it's worked out all right.'

'Is your marriage in trouble?' Ashworth hesitated. 'We can find out without much difficulty,' the Chief said.

Ashworth resumed his pacing. 'We've had our ups and downs, the same as any couple, but we're not in any trouble now. The marriage works as well as most. My wife wasn't too keen on moving here, we did have arguments over that. She thought I accepted this job without properly consulting her. She'd prefer to stay down that end of the country, it's her home town, all her own family are down there. She thought I could have found an equally good job down there if I'd put my mind to it and I wouldn't have had to uproot the children.' He halted. 'But she's got over all that now, we've settled everything between us. When I was home last weekend she agreed to move here when I've found a house. She's not a woman to go back on her word.' He gestured at the photograph on the bureau. 'We have two fine children, we owe it to them to make the marriage work.'

'When you came across Claire in the street that Thursday morning, October 18, did she tell you she'd broken off a relationship with another man a few days before?'

Ashworth shook his head. 'She said nothing about that.' He resumed his pacing.

'She could have been more than ready to find consolation elsewhere,' Kelsey continued. 'In the arms, perhaps, of someone she'd been close to years ago. Were there other meetings with Claire you still haven't told us about? Was it your child she was carrying?'

Ashworth came to an abrupt stop, he swung round to face the Chief. 'It most certainly was not my child! I never went to bed with Claire. Never at any time. Not years ago and not this time round.' Perspiration gleamed on his forehead.

'I put it to you,' the Chief pursued, 'that you saw more of Claire after you came back to Cannonbridge than you're still willing to admit.' Ashworth began to shake his head but the Chief went on. 'I put it to you that you saw her very shortly before she died. Did she tell you then she'd discovered she was pregnant? Pregnant by you?'

'You've got this all wrong,' Ashworth said in tones of vociferous protest. 'None of it happened.'

'Did she tell you she was ready to leave her husband?' the Chief continued inexorably. 'Was she pressing you for marriage? Did you refuse? Did you tell her you didn't want to end your marriage, didn't want to lose your children? Was there a quarrel? Did you lose your head? Did you strike her?'

'There was never any quarrel,' Ashworth retorted. 'Never any question of marriage. Her pregnancy was nothing to do with me, I know nothing about it. We had only a couple of friendly meetings, no more. You're trying to make something terrible out of them. I know nothing at all about her murder. I had nothing to do with it.' He dropped into a chair. He looked pale and shaken. 'This is like some horrible nightmare.'

'Where were you that Friday evening?' Kelsey pressed him. 'November 16?'

'I expect I was here all evening,' Ashworth said. 'I'm usually here in the evening.'

'Is there anyone who can vouch for that?'

'I shouldn't think so. I can't particularly recall that evening but I'd more than likely be here by myself.'

The Chief didn't let up. 'You knew Harry Lingard from

the old days at Calthrop's. Did you come across him that Friday evening?'

Ashworth shook his head with energy. 'I certainly did not.'

There was a long pause, then the Chief got to his feet. 'Anything else you remember,' he said. 'Anything you haven't yet told us, anything you'd like to get off your chest, we're always ready to listen. Any time, day or night.'

By the time the two policemen got back to the station the number of calls coming in had risen again in response to the Chief's TV and radio interviews. The usual mix of callers: the disturbed, the notoriety-seekers, jokers, mischief-makers—and the genuine would-be-helpfuls; every one to be meticulously dealt with. It was turned nine before the Chief called a halt for the night.

The wind had veered to the north. Feathery flakes of snow were drifting down as he let himself into his flat. He was pretty hungry but too tired to eat just yet. He would lie down on the sofa for ten minutes, close his eyes.

When he woke he was stiff and cramped, ravenously hungry; everything was deathly quiet. He looked at his watch, blinked his eyes wide open in disbelief, looked again: his watch showed twenty minutes to six. He levered himself up and crossed to the window, drew aside a curtain and peered out.

Diamond bright under the street lamps, a heavy mantle of snow lay over road and pavements, driveways and gardens, shrouding rooftops and hedges, the line of parked cars.

CHAPTER 23

The Chief was in his office early, showered and shaved. He had cooked himself a vast breakfast and greatly enjoyed it; he felt buoyantly cheerful again, ready for anything.

The calls continued to come in. Two personal calls, half an hour apart, lit a sparkle in the Chief's eye. The first was from a woman in her forties, a single parent, a tenant on the council estate where Harry Lingard had lived. She came marching in a few minutes after eight, a big, hefty woman, grim-faced and steely-eyed, accompanied by her two offspring, a girl of thirteen with the same strapping build, the same air of granite resolution, and a slim, slight boy of twelve, wearing a hangdog expression.

Left to himself the boy would have uttered never a word. It took nudges and jabs from his mother to persuade him to open his mouth at all and prevent him thereafter from falling periodically into sheepish silences. With the aid of interjections, additions and explanations from the girl, the Chief finally pieced the tale together.

On the evening of Friday, November 16, the lad, in company with two of his mates, had decided on a little adventure. They had armed themselves with cans of spray paint and set off to ornament the walls of empty properties; one of their objectives was the old chapel in Tolladine Road. They had just got nicely started when Harry Lingard, on his freesheet round, came down the path of a nearby house and spotted them. He knew the trio, he called out their names; they took to their heels. Burdened with his satchel, Harry made no attempt to chase after them but the lad, glancing back, saw him standing under the street lamp, writing in his notebook.

The lad had raced all the way home, bursting in on his sister who was watching TV; their mother was out on her evening shift at a factory on the industrial estate. The girl demanded to know what had happened, she wouldn't be put off. The lad told her, swore her to silence. They were both certain retribution would swiftly follow in the shape of a visit from a policeman—or at the very least from Harry Lingard.

But the next day brought no visit from anyone. On the day after that Harry's body was found. After the first shocked disbelief the lad felt a surge of relief. It was going to be all right, Harry wouldn't have had time to tell the police about the spraying. Then he remembered Harry's notebook. It would surely have been found in Harry's pocket, the police would be certain to look through it, they would come upon the entry, the names. He sweated out the next day or two but still there came no heavy knock at the door. He began to breathe again.

Then the police appeals began, asking for information; in particular, information about any sighting of Harry on his round that Friday evening. The lad was able to ignore the earliest appeals without difficulty; other folk would surely have seen Harry that evening, they were bound to come forward.

Then Claire Holroyd's body was discovered, so close to where Harry had stood under the street lamp. Rumour linked the two killings. There were fresh police appeals for sightings of either victim. The lad began to have difficulty sleeping.

Yesterday evening he and his sister had seen Chief Inspector Kelsey on TV. Afterwards his sister had confronted him. 'They still haven't found anyone who saw Harry that evening at a definite time,' she'd pointed out. 'You three lads could have been the last to see him. You've got to go to the police, you've got to tell them what you know.' He couldn't face it, he refused point blank. His mother would flay him alive if she knew about the spraying. His sister was adamant. She would give him till the morning to decide.

He had scarcely opened his eyes this morning before his sister burst into his bedroom demanding to know if he'd made up his mind. He told her yes, he had: he would not be going to the police. 'Very well,' she informed him. 'If you won't do anything, then I will.' She had run downstairs to the kitchen, poured out the story to their mother.

It was the timing the Chief pounced on. Here at last they had Harry positioned a few yards from where Claire's body was found. What was needed was the precise time of that positioning. The girl had been watching a favourite TV programme that evening, she knew the exact point at which her brother had burst in. That put the time the lad reached home at around 8.55. How long would it have taken him to run home from the chapel in Tolladine Road? Would he be willing to re-run the course for them now, timed by a stopwatch?

The lad's hangdog expression vanished, his face lit up. Yes, sir! Nothing he'd like better!

The second caller was a girl of nineteen with a quiet manner, though by no means lacking confidence. She wasn't a native of Cannonbridge; she worked for a nation-wide chain of stores. She had been transferred to the Cannonbridge branch a few months ago and was living in a bedsit in a house on the edge of Cannonbridge. Her firm had recently sent her on a three-week training course. She had left Cannonbridge on Sunday, November 25, and had got back yesterday evening, when she had seen the Chief's interview on TV. As soon as Claire's photograph appeared on the screen she realized she might be in a position to help.

On the evening of Friday, November 16, she had gone straight from work to a charity event in a Cannonbridge hall. Afterwards she had caught a bus to take her back to her digs; the bus had left the centre of Cannonbridge a minute or two after eight. She had sat down on one of the two double seats facing each other by the door.

At the next stop, outside the College of Further Education, a woman got on, carrying some books; someone knocked against the woman, sending her books flying. The girl helped her to pick them up; the woman thanked her and took her seat beside her. They chatted till the woman reached her stop, by Whitethorn Common. As the bus moved off again the girl saw the woman start to cross the road towards the common.

She was shown photographs of Claire; she was certain it was the same woman. Several things about the woman had impressed her: her good looks, elegance, pleasant manner, the beautiful perfume she wore. And the impression she gave of a deep well of happiness inside her. Their chat had mainly been about the college. Claire hadn't specifically said she had attended a class there that evening; the girl assumed she had because of the books and the fact that she had boarded the bus outside the college. Claire had said nothing to contradict that impression.

She was able after some thought to describe what Claire had been wearing: a tweed coat, grey-blue, a light brown suède beret, brown leather shoulder-bag, brown leather boots. The Chief picked her up at once about the boots. Was she certain about them? When Claire's body was found she was wearing flat-heeled shoes. But the student was not to be shaken. She had particularly noticed—and admired —the boots, as Claire sat beside her: of fine brown leather, long and elegant, close-fitting, a side zip fastening, slender heels, a narrow foot. Claire had also worn brown leather gloves. She could distinctly recall her pulling them on just before she left the bus.

At nine-thirty Sergeant Lambert drove the Chief along to Fairbourne. The paint-spraying lad had re-run his course; they now had Harry Lingard standing under the lamp-post, writing in his notebook, at 8.48, as near as they could make it.

Children were already at play on Whitethorn Common, pelting each other with snowballs, their shrill voices echoing in the sparkling air. Half a dozen youngsters were busy constructing a snowman not far from the gates of Fairbourne when Lambert halted the car. Edgar Holroyd was down in his basement workshop, he answered the door promptly to Lambert's ring. The moment he saw the Chief's face he exclaimed, 'Something's come up, hasn't it?'

The Chief gave a nod in reply, waiting until they were all in the sitting-room before he enlarged. 'We now know your wife got on a bus outside the college a few minutes after eight that Friday evening. She got off the bus at her usual stop, just along the road from here, she crossed over towards the house. We've checked with the bus company, and that would have been around 8.17, give or take a minute either way.' Edgar made no reply. 'At the time she approached the house,' the Chief went on, 'she was wearing the coat and beret she was wearing when her body was found. She was also wearing knee-length boots. But when her body was found she was wearing flat-heeled shoes—in her own narrow fitting. That very strongly suggests she did reach home that evening and changed into shoes after reaching home.' Still Edgar said nothing. 'According to your own account,' the Chief continued, 'you were at home at that time on that Friday evening.'

Edgar expelled a long breath. He didn't appear unduly put out. 'I'm afraid I didn't tell you the whole truth earlier,' he acknowledged. 'I didn't see how I could. I'd said one thing to your men when they called here during the house-to-house inquiries after Harry Lingard's death. I couldn't very well tell you something else when Claire's body was found.' He gave the Chief a direct glance. 'How would it have looked to you if I'd changed my story?'

'Right, then,' the Chief responded briskly. 'Forget what you did or did not tell us before, forget your reasons for withholding the truth. The important thing now is to get at that truth. We'll have the proper story now. All of it, this time.'

Edgar looked immeasurably relieved. He plunged in at once, speaking rapidly and clearly, as if he'd been over it countless times in his mind. 'I got home around a quarter to eight. I changed my clothes, I was going to do some jobs in the garden. Everything here was as usual. Claire was out. I believed she was at her class at the college. I made myself some coffee in the kitchen. The lecturer rang a few minutes after eight, saying Claire hadn't been at the class and wanting to know about the trip. I said I'd pass on the message. I imagined Claire had decided to go to the cinema or theatre, I didn't give it another thought. I went back to the kitchen, finished my coffee. I went outside and started a job at the bottom of the garden where it's sheltered from the wind—the trees down there screen most of the house. Not long after I'd got started I found I needed a tool from the shed higher up the garden. As I went along to the shed I saw lights on in the house. I went in by the back door. The door leading into the hall was closed but as I came along I could hear Claire talking on the phone in the hall. As I opened the door I heard her say: "Very well, I'll be there," then she put the phone down. She didn't sound alarmed or upset, just businesslike. I thought it was some classmate, or someone wanting her to help at some charity do. I thought nothing of it.'

He stared back into that evening. 'She looked surprised to see me; she'd have thought I was still out at the meeting. She didn't say anything, she just looked at me. She was sitting in the chair by the phone. Her books and other things were on the table beside her. She had her coat on, and her beret, but she'd taken off her boots and put on her flat shoes—the shoes she was wearing when she was found. She kept them in the cupboard in the hall, she used to change into them when she came in, if she was wearing close-fitting boots.

'I said, just for a joke: "Be sure your sins will find you out. I know you haven't been at your class." I thought she'd smile and say: "I decided I'd go to a cinema instead." But she didn't. She looked up at me as if she was thinking very fast.' He put a hand up to his face. 'Then she started talking.' He closed his eyes. 'I couldn't believe what she was saying, I kept thinking any moment she'd stop and laugh, say it was all a joke.'

His face was very pale. 'She said she was leaving me, leaving then and there, and this time it was for good. She was going to Aunt May's, she'd stay there for the present, she would never be coming back. She'd take a few things with her, she'd send for the rest later. I was stupefied, I couldn't say a word.'

'Did she say anything about being pregnant?' the Chief put in. Edgar shook his head. 'Did she say where she'd been that evening?' Again he shook his head. 'Did she mention any other man?' Once more he shook his head. 'She just said the marriage was finished, it had been a mistake from the start. I wasn't to try to come after her, she would never change her mind.' His voice shook. 'She went upstairs. I thought I'd collapse, I sat down in one of the hall chairs. I couldn't think, it seemed like a terrible dream. Then she came down the stairs, carrying a suitcase. She said, "I'll go down and get Beauty, I'll go out by the side door." She saw her boots, where she'd left them by the hall table. She picked them up and put them in her suitcase. She stood there for a moment, expecting me to say something but I couldn't speak. She went down to the basement. I don't know how long I sat there. I couldn't believe it.'

He drew a long shaking breath. 'When I woke up next morning everything looked a lot better. I was sure she hadn't meant what she'd said, it was just one of her moods, the same as she'd had before when she'd gone off to May Finch's. The difference this time was that I'd happened to get home early, I'd caught her right in the middle of the worst part of her mood, when it must have been over her like a black cloud. That had never happened before. Every other time she'd left while I was out of the house. I was tremendously relieved. I was quite sure that was what it was. She hadn't gone for good, she'd come back when she was ready, the way she'd always done before, I was certain of it. When the police came, asking about Harry Lingard, I told them my wife was away, staying with her aunt, which was what I believed.'

He stared at the wall. 'The days went by very slowly, the way they always did when she was away. I was beginning to think it wouldn't be much longer before I got in from work one evening and there she'd be, back home again.' His head dropped. 'Then they found her.'

'Once the investigation had got properly under way,' Kelsey said, 'you must surely have realized it was vitally important for us to know at exactly what time Claire had left the house.'

Edgar looked conscience-stricken. 'I did realize that. I

knew I ought to tell you. I kept making up my mind to but every time it came to the point . . .' He shook his head. 'I couldn't do it, I was terrified of how it might look.'

'Did Claire say anything before she left about who it was she'd been speaking to on the phone when you came into the hall?'

He shook his head. 'She never mentioned it. It didn't cross my mind to ask her. Next day, when I remembered the phone call, I thought maybe she'd been phoning for a taxi to take her to May's. I remembered what she'd said: "Very well, I'll be there." That could have meant she'd be at the side of the road, in twenty minutes or whatever, when she'd put a few things together. She wouldn't have wanted him to come up to the house in case I happened to come home.'

When they left Fairbourne a few minutes later and got back into the car, the Chief gave Lambert no instructions but sat in brooding silence, watching the children building their snowman. 'If that was some classmate or charity worker on the phone to Claire that evening,' he said at last, 'that person would surely have come forward by now to tell us about the call.' No local taxi firm or driver had any record of a phone call from Claire that evening. She couldn't have been ringing her aunt; Mrs Finch was not on the phone. 'Wherever Claire spent the evening,' he said, 'she certainly wasn't at the college.'

'Robert Ashworth?' Lambert hazarded. 'Could she have been with him?'

Kelsey shook his head. 'I think it's far more likely she was with Lester Holroyd. I'm not at all sure the affair with Lester was ever broken off. Or if it was broken off, that it stayed broken.'

'You're suggesting it was Lester she was talking to on the phone?'

Kelsey shook his head again. 'I'm not suggesting it was Lester on the phone. I'm suggesting it was Lester's wife. Diane Holroyd.'

CHAPTER 24

'Diane?' Lambert echoed.

'Yes, Diane. She could have had her suspicions for some time that something was going on. Suppose she didn't stop at Melanie's flat that evening for as long as she makes out? Suppose Edgar wasn't the only one who got home early that evening? There's no one there when Diane gets home but she comes across something that confirms her suspicions. Maybe Lester and Diane had been together in the house earlier that evening and somehow Diane realizes that. Something as simple, perhaps, as smelling Claire's perfume.

'She grabs the phone, rings Fairbourne. Claire answers. She's just got in from being with Lester, she thinks she's alone in the house, she thinks Edgar is out at his meeting. Diane accuses her, she says: "I know what's been going on between you and Lester." Claire can't stop herself blurting it out, she tells Diane she's carrying Lester's child, they intend to marry. Diane says: "Is that so? You and I are going to have this out. I'm coming over right away." Claire says: "OK, come on over but don't come right up to the house. I don't want Edgar walking in on us. He doesn't know anything about this and I'd rather he didn't find out that way. You can drive on to the common. I'll be waiting for you, we can talk in the car." Diane agrees and they fix a spot.

'As Claire rings off the hall door opens and there's Edgar in his gardening clothes, he's clearly been home some time. And what is it he comes out with? He looks at her and says: "Be sure your sins will find you out." She doesn't know how much he's heard, how much he knows. Her mind is made up in a flash. She tells him she's leaving, for good. She goes upstairs, throws some things into a bag, picks up the pup, leaves the house. She walks across to the spot where Diane is sitting waiting for her.'

When the police car drove up, Diane was in the sitting-room, dealing with the array of Christmas cards, calendars, envelopes, postage stamps, lists of names and addresses, set out before her on the table. She clicked her tongue in irritation at the sound of the bell, sprang up and darted out into the hall. She snatched open the front door, groaning aloud at the sight of the two policemen. 'Not you two again! What is it this time?'

'If we might come inside,' the Chief said mildly.

'You do choose your times,' she protested loudly. 'I'm up to the eyes. I'm trying to get finished to get off out. Everywhere will be jam-packed if I don't go soon. To cap it all, I'm meeting a girlfriend for lunch.'

'Five minutes?' the Chief persisted. She swung round without another word, flounced back into the sitting-room, flung herself into an easy chair in a half-reclining posture. The two men entered the room behind her in a more decorous fashion. 'We won't waste your time,' the Chief said as he sat down. 'A few questions that need answering. On the evening of Friday, November 16, did you get home earlier than usual? Earlier than you've told us? Did you phone Claire at Fairbourne shortly before eight-thirty?'

Diane gazed belligerently up at him. 'The answer to all those questions is no,' she said tartly. 'The last time I had any contact with Claire was around May or June.'

'Did you arrange to go over to Fairbourne right away, to talk to Claire?' the Chief pressed on, as if she had answered yes instead of no.

'Why should I want to talk to her?' Diane demanded with a sharp frown. 'I'd nothing to say to her.'

'You might have wanted to talk about her relationship with your husband.'

She sat bolt upright. 'I didn't know anything about the relationship while Claire was alive. I never had the slightest inkling of it. The first I knew of it was a few days ago.

Lester sat me down and told me there was something he wanted to get off his chest. He'd had a bit of a fling with Claire. It didn't last long, it never amounted to much, it was over well before she died.' She grimaced. 'I wasn't best pleased to hear about it but it's water under the bridge now, we've put it behind us.' She jumped up to get a cigarette, lit it, inhaled deeply. She didn't return to her chair but stood leaning against the wall, regarding the Chief with an unwavering eye.

'I put it to you,' the Chief said, 'that you did get home earlier than usual that evening. It was then that you found out about the relationship, one way or another. You did phone Claire, to say you were going straight over to Fairbourne to have it out with her.'

'That's all poppycock,' Diane retorted.

The Chief ignored that. 'When you put down the phone after speaking to Claire, did you then ring someone else? To put that person in the picture? Your father, perhaps? Or Stuart? Or Norman Griffin?'

'I did not ring my father,' she flung back at him. 'I didn't ring Stuart. Or Norman. I didn't ring anyone. I was lying flat out in the dark on Melanie's sofa, fast asleep.'

'You didn't feel too good the rest of that weekend,' the Chief went on. 'You were pretty washed out, you had to force yourself back to work on the Monday morning.'

'A migraine often takes me that way,' she maintained. 'It's sometimes the best part of a week before I feel right again.'

'You felt well enough on the Wednesday to attend the inquest on Harry Lingard,' the Chief pointed out. 'And the inquest on Claire, a couple of weeks after that. As well as both their funerals.'

'Why wouldn't I go to both their funerals?' she snapped back. 'People would have had something to say if I didn't go to Claire's—you included, I've no doubt. I went to Harry's because I knew him, I liked him, he was a bit of a character.' She stubbed out her half-smoked cigarette and at once lit another. 'As for the inquests, I'm a nurse, it would be strange if I didn't take an interest in such happenings.'

After a moment's silence she added more calmly, 'I can't pretend I ever liked Claire. It seems I was right not to trust her, she had no scruples about making a play for my husband.' She blew out a long stream of smoke. 'But I never hated her, I never wished her harm. I'm sorry she's dead, I'm sorry she died such a horrible death. If I could wave a wand to bring her back right now, I'd wave it.'

She looked the Chief in the eye. 'You can keep coming back here till you're blue in the face but you'll be wasting your time. I had nothing to do with either of those deaths, directly or indirectly. I know nothing whatever about them. And neither, to the best of my knowledge, does Lester. Or any member of my family.'

For all that she had been out dancing till well after midnight, Mrs Griffin had made an early start on this bright, snow-white morning. She had already tracked out to the shops and back when the police car halted outside her cottage. She expressed neither surprise nor irritation when she opened the door to the two men. She greeted them with a cheerful smile. 'Norman's not here,' she told them. 'He's had to go to work this morning. They're pushing contract dates at the yard, it's all systems go out there just now.'

The Chief didn't disclose that she was the one they'd come to see. 'As long as we're here,' he said casually, 'perhaps you wouldn't mind if we came inside for a moment. One or two little details we'd like to get clear.'

She stood back at once to admit them. 'Come on in,' she invited. 'Always glad to help when I can.' She flashed a warm smile at Lambert. 'You can see I took your advice.' She put up a hand and primped her hair, now a fetching shade of auburn. 'It was a great success.' She took them into the kitchen where she had been unpacking her shopping. She sat them down, bustled about putting things away, making tea. She raised no objection when the Chief asked her to cast her mind back to Friday, November 16, run through for them how she had spent that evening.

She answered readily. She had gone to her social club, she went every Friday evening for the olde-tyme dancing. She was able to recall that particular Friday clearly, there had been a presentation to the club secretary before the dancing started. When she left the house just after seven, Norman was in his workshop. She had got back around one in the morning, she had found Norman still up, watching a film on TV.

'I always tell him not to wait up,' she said. 'And I always find him still up when I get in. He's a good son, none better. He does sometimes pay attention to what I tell him.' She laughed. 'I saw he'd changed his clothes all right, when I got back that evening.' The Chief cocked an inquiring eye. 'He had his good jacket and trousers on when I left the house,' she explained. 'I asked him if he was thinking of going out but he said no, he'd be working on his radios. I told him he ought to change out of his good things. When I got back I saw he'd got some old working clothes on. It would have been a shame to mess up good things. Norman always buys himself good stuff for best, he likes to look smart. The trousers were brand new. He's had the jacket a year or two but it still looks very nice. It's Harris tweed, you can't get better than that.'

'Indeed you can't,' the Chief agreed heartily. 'I like a good Harris tweed myself. Mind if I take a look at it?'

She was delighted at his interest. She took them up to Norman's bedroom and produced the jacket; the Chief duly admired it. 'Of course it's been to the cleaner's since that evening,' she said chattily. 'The trousers, too. Norman's very fussy about his things. He took them along to the cleaner's himself, he wanted them done for my brother's silver wedding party. Lovely do, it was, all the family together for once. More than thirty of us, all told. Proper sit-down dinner at a posh restaurant. Must have cost my brother a fortune, but it was worth every penny.'

'When would that be?' the Chief asked idly as they went downstairs again.

'It was on the Saturday,' she answered promptly. 'November 24. Couldn't forget that date. It'll be a long time before we have another evening like that one.'

Neither Tom Mansell nor his son was in the yard when Sergeant Lambert drove in; Lester Holroyd was also out. But Norman Griffin was there, getting into his van. He set his jaw at the sight of the two policemen. The Chief took him over to a quiet corner and tackled him without delay. 'You told us you never left the house that Friday evening, November 16.' Norman gave a nod. 'You stick to that? You never set foot outside the house at all, after you got in from work?'

Norman hesitated. 'More or less.'

'More or less?' the Chief echoed. 'What kind of answer is that? Either you set foot outside or you did not.'

'I did nip out to the corner shop for a paper, not long after my mother went out, but that was all. I wasn't gone ten minutes. I don't call that going out.'

The Chief didn't argue. 'Were you still wearing your good clothes?'

'Yes, I was.'

'Why did you change out of them later that evening?'

'I didn't want to get them dirty, working on my radios.'

The Chief brushed aside that explanation. 'Did you change into working things in order to scrub out a van?'

Norman's eyebrows shot up. 'I never scrubbed out any van that evening.'

'You told us earlier you drove into the yard around knocking-off time that Friday evening. Tom Mansell was here. He told you the van he'd been driving that day had been playing him up, he wanted you to sell it at the Saturday car auction, pick up a replacement.'

'That's right,' Norman confirmed.

The Chief regarded him for some moments. Their efforts to get hold of the van Norman had sold at auction had met with no success; the van had already been shipped abroad. 'I'm going to put to you a somewhat different scenario,'

Kelsey said. 'There was no conversation about vans with Mansell here that Friday. But some such conversation did take place later that evening at your own house, after Mansell turned up on your doorstep in one of the firm's vans.'

Norman opened his mouth to speak but the Chief silenced him with a gesture. 'The van Mansell drove to your house had just been given a pretty good clean but Mansell told you to go over it again, pronto, inside and out, as thoroughly as possible. You were to sell it at the auction next day, bring back another as near to it as you could find. You were to keep the replacement as your regular van, he'd be taking your current van away with him, driving home in it.'

Norman looked steadily back at him. 'I don't know where you came by that tale but it's a load of codswallop. It happened the way I told you before.' The Chief let that go and returned to the matter of Norman's change of clothes. Why had he put on his good clothes in the first place? 'I had intended to go along to the pub for an hour or two,' Norman explained. 'Then I changed my mind.'

'Perhaps you were intending to meet someone?' the Chief hazarded. 'Someone special, worth dressing up for. Maybe you did actually go out to meet that person? A lady, could it be? Claire Holroyd?'

'I didn't meet any lady,' Norman responded with some heat. 'I never laid eyes on Claire that evening. I wasn't in the habit of meeting her. We weren't on those sort of terms.'

'I understand she called at your house more than once to see you.'

Anger showed in Norman's eyes. 'You're not trying to make something out of that? She just called in a couple of times with some query from the office. Time sheets, weigh slips, that sort of thing.'

'Why not ask you about them at the office?'

'Because I was off work both times when she called here. Once with 'flu and once when I'd ricked my back.'

The Chief switched back to Tom Mansell and the van. 'When Mansell turned up here that Friday evening did he give you a load of stuff to get rid of? Did he tell you to be sure to get rid of every last bit of it? Get rid of it piecemeal on your way to the car auction? Skips, tips, rivers, canals, flooded quarries—anywhere as long as it never surfaced again?'

Norman kept a hold on himself with a visible effort. All he said was: 'Tom Mansell never gave me anything to get rid of, that night or any night.'

The Chief swept on. 'Maybe it was all wrapped up in plastic bags. Did you take a squint inside, after he'd gone? Did you find a suitcase? A satchel? A shoulder-bag, a stack of freesheets? A dead pup? Smaller stuff, too: money, watches, jewellery? A garnet ring? Did you think: What a waste to dump all that. Who'd be any the wiser if I pocketed some of it? You helped yourself to the money, you couldn't resist the ring.'

Norman's eyes blazed back at him. 'There was never any stuff in plastic bags, no stuff of any kind, no money, no rings, watches, bags, freesheets, no dead pup. I was never given anything to get rid of. None of it ever happened, you've dreamed the whole thing up. Go ahead and try to prove any of it, you'll have your work cut out.'

'You knew Claire had a puppy?'

Norman hesitated. 'Yes, I did,' he acknowledged after a moment. 'I'd seen her with it on the common.'

'Did you ever come across the puppy, on or after that Friday evening? Alive or dead? Did you come across any of its belongings?'

Norman had got himself under control again by now. 'No, I did not,' he replied curtly. He looked at his watch. 'Is this going on much longer? I'm holding up an urgent job.'

The Chief let him go. Then he went across to the office and spoke to a clerk. Yes, Lester Holroyd had come in a few minutes ago, he was in the inner office; she went in to speak to him. Lester came out at once. He was very busy but he could spare a few minutes. He took them into the inner office, told the clerk they didn't want to be disturbed.

The Chief began by asking him about the sale of one van and the purchase of another. Lester answered readily and fully, his account varied in not one single particular from that given them by Norman. It was Lester who had looked out the registration document, arranged for the thousand pounds in cash—on Mansell's instructions; he was adamant this was during the afternoon of Friday, November 16.

The Chief turned abruptly to another matter. 'We have fresh information about Claire's movements that Friday evening, very solid information.' Lester sat motionless. 'We know now without any doubt that Claire boarded a bus outside the college a few minutes after eight. She got off the bus by the common, she went into Fairbourne. She was carrying books but it's been clear all along she wasn't at the college that evening.' Lester stared at him as if hypnotized. 'The question is,' Kelsey said, 'where was Claire during the time she was supposed to have been at her class? Was she with you? Was the affair very far from over? Was it still very much alive?'

There was a tense silence. All at once Lester's face crumpled, he sagged in his chair. 'You're right,' he said. 'She was with me.' The words came tumbling out. 'We did break off the affair, the way I told you, in the middle of October. But I did see her that Friday evening. She rang me here on the Friday morning, she said she had to see me, it was very important. Could I meet her that evening? I said I would.' He halted, he seemed on the verge of tears.

'Better tell us everything,' the Chief urged. 'No good coming out with it in dribs and drabs.'

Lester rallied somewhat, he shifted into a more upright position. 'Yes, I will,' he agreed with fervour. 'I want to tell you. It's been keeping me awake at night.'

CHAPTER 25

'You met Claire that evening?' Kelsey prompted. 'Then what?'

Lester closed his eyes. 'It was cold and windy. I didn't fancy driving up into the hills or to one of our other places. I decided to chance it and take her home. I'd never done that before but I thought it was only going to be this one time, it would be perfectly safe, she'd be gone long before Diane got in from work. I could see Claire was strung up, very pleased about something, but she didn't tell me what it was till we got into the house. Then she told me she was pregnant. She was quite certain, she'd carried out tests two mornings running, it was positive both times. She reckoned it had happened while Edgar was away at his conference that time, just before we split up. She was absolutely overjoyed, she couldn't stop smiling, but it frightened the life out of me. I felt as if someone had thrown a bucket of cold water over me.

'She talked as if there could be no doubt about the next step: divorces all round, the pair of us marrying, setting up house together. She said: "You do see, this puts everything on an entirely different footing."' He made a despairing gesture. 'None of the practical implications seemed to cross her mind for an instant. If I went along with what she wanted I could kiss goodbye to my job, taking over the new yard, I'd lose my house, even the car I was driving. Claire didn't have a penny of her own and Edgar was hardly likely to shell out in the circumstances.'

He gave the Chief a direct look. 'I make no bones about it, I was horrified. I'd never had the slightest intention of leaving Diane. But I couldn't come right out and say all that point blank. I couldn't spoil her moment, she was so overjoyed. I just told her it had been a bit of a shock, it would take some thinking over, it wouldn't do to make decisions in a hurry. It was possible she might decide not to go through with the pregnancy.

'She said she wasn't surprised that thought had occurred to me. It would occur to a good many men in my position, but she was positive I'd very soon come to feel as pleased about it as she was.' He looked across at Kelsey. 'She was so confident, so happy.' He drew a long, sighing breath. 'It was no time to start up an argument. I had one thought in my head: she must get off somewhere, out of the way, till she'd come down from cloud nine and got to grips with the hard facts of the situation. Somewhere where she wouldn't be tempted to open her mouth and spill the beans to Edgar.

'I said why didn't she go to her Aunt May's for a week or two, think things over quietly. I knew she'd gone there before when she'd wanted to duck out for a while. Edgar wouldn't think it was anything different this time. She had no need to tell her aunt anything about it. If she did decide on a termination, she could arrange it quietly from there, not a soul need ever know. Any money she needed, just let me know.

'She said at once there was no question of a termination, she'd waited too long for a child even to consider that. But she thought all the same it was a good idea to go to May's, she'd rather not stay under the same roof as Edgar, trying to behave as if everything was as usual. It was a pity she couldn't go straight off to May's there and then.

'I said why not go there and then, if that was what she wanted. She'd told me earlier Edgar was at a council meeting, he wouldn't be home before ten. I said I could run her out to Fairbourne right away, she could pack a few things, leave Edgar a note to say she was off to May's for a week or two. She'd be out of the house well before Edgar got in and I'd run her straight over to May's.

'She was tempted but then she said no, it wouldn't be fair to her aunt. She couldn't ring May to say she was coming, May isn't on the phone. Apparently May is always up at the crack of dawn, in bed by nine. By the time we got over there she'd be sound asleep. Every other time Claire had gone to May's it was always in the morning. It would be making too much of a drama out of it to turn up on her doorstep and have to get her up out of bed. And it wouldn't be a very good idea to have me drive her over there. May would guess there was something going on, it wasn't just one of Claire's usual fits of low spirits. It would be best all round if she went to May's on the Monday morning after Edgar had gone to work. So that was how we left it.

'I dropped her near the college just before eight, so she could get the bus home. I'd intended going back home, going out on a security run around nine. But after I dropped Claire I felt too restless to go home, everything she'd told me was going round in my head. I decided to go straight off on the run. I was out longer than usual, I went further afield. I got home around ten. Diane came in soon afterwards.

'When I didn't hear anything from Claire I was very relieved, I was sure it meant she'd decided on an abortion. I thought she'd get in touch with me as soon as she got back from May's, let me know what had happened, what the money situation was. I was sure that would be the end of it and we could forget the whole thing.'

He put a hand up to his face. 'Then she was found.' He looked ready to weep. 'It was a staggering shock. I couldn't believe it. In my mind I'd got her over at May's and all the time . . .' He lapsed into shuddering silence. It was some moments before he succeeded in getting a grip on himself. 'I was terrified it would all come out about our relationship. I couldn't face Edgar. I knew I ought to go to see him. I tried more than once, but I couldn't do it. I did manage to go to the funeral, that took me all my time. I spoke to Edgar there. I've no idea what I said, it was like a nightmare, I couldn't look him in the eyes. I only got through it because it was in public. I could never have faced him in private.' His voice shook. 'I hope to God he need never know the whole truth, it would kill him. He worshipped Claire. He would have laid down his life for her.'

His eyes were tormented. 'I'm not very proud of any of

it. I'm still trying to come to terms with it all. It was only after her death I really saw just how shamefully I'd behaved from start to finish. I've told Diane something but nowhere near the whole of it. She'd never forgive me, never in a million years. It would be the end of everything between us.'

'That thought must have crossed your mind the moment Claire told you she was pregnant,' Kelsey said. 'If the truth came out you stood to lose everything.' Lester's look was now sharply alert. 'You've no proof worth tuppence you were out on a security run that evening.'

'That's where you're wrong,' Lester retorted. 'I can prove it. I can prove it in a way that will stand up in a court of law. I didn't think of it when you spoke to me before because you asked me then if I'd seen or spoken to anyone and that was what I was trying to remember.' One of the stops he had made on his run that evening was at a site thirty-five miles from Cannonbridge where Mansell's were putting up flats. A load of aggregate had been ordered for delivery to the site on Friday afternoon—there was no Saturday working on that site at the time—to be ready for use first thing on Monday morning in the concrete mix for covering an underfloor heating system. The load hadn't arrived by knocking-off time, the driver had been delayed by traffic. At the foreman's request a labourer who lived not far from the site stayed on to take delivery of the load.

'When I got to the site,' Lester went on, 'I took a look at the aggregate. I saw at once it was the wrong grade, too coarse.' First thing next morning he rang the firm to get the mistake rectified in time for Monday's start—no small demand on a Saturday morning but he had been insistent and the mistake was rectified. He could produce the paperwork to substantiate what he had told them and they could also check with the firm involved.

There was a silence during which the Chief digested all this; Lester began to look more relaxed. Then Kelsey said, 'You're very anxious your wife shouldn't know the whole truth about your relationship with Claire. Are you so sure she doesn't know the whole of it already?'

Lester jerked back in his seat. 'She couldn't possibly know! She could never have kept quiet if she'd found out!'

'Claire could have changed her mind on the bus going home,' the Chief pointed out. 'She could have decided she couldn't face staying in Fairbourne over the weekend after all. She knew you intended going straight home after you dropped her. Maybe she decided to ring you the moment she got in, ask you to come over to Fairbourne right away, drive her over to May's, as you suggested.

'But it wasn't you that picked up the receiver at the other end when she phoned your house. You were out on your site run. Diane could have come home early that evening, she could have come across some trace of Claire in the house, something that confirmed her suspicions. Suddenly the phone rings. It's Claire on the other end.'

Lester's face was ashen. 'It's not possible.'

'When Diane came in at her usual time,' the Chief added, 'that could have been the second time that evening she'd driven home, the first time could have been a couple of hours earlier.' Lester was no longer capable of speech, he sat shaking his head in horrified silence. The Chief stood up. 'What time are you expecting Tom Mansell back?' he asked.

Lester gazed blankly up at him. 'Oh—Mansell,' he said after a moment. 'I'm afraid I've no idea. He could be back any minute. Or it could be another hour or more.' He didn't go with them to the door but stayed sunk in his seat with a face like death.

CHAPTER 26

'Not much point hanging on here, waiting for Mansell to show up,' Kelsey said as they got back into the car. 'We could be stuck here the rest of the morning.'

Lambert frowned as a thought struck him. 'Suppose Claire did change her mind on the bus? She doesn't fancy spending the weekend at Fairbourne but neither does she want to disturb Aunt May. It isn't Lester Holroyd she decides to ring when she gets in, it's Robert Ashworth.'

'Ashworth?' The Chief's tone was highly sceptical.

Lambert pressed on. 'She knows there's a spare bedroom at the cottage, she can stay the night strictly on an old-friends basis. All she need tell Ashworth is that she's had a tiff with Edgar, she wants to clear out for a while, she'll be off to Aunt May's in the morning. She phones Ashworth the moment she gets in, tells him the tale, asks if he'll come over right away, wait nearby. He says yes at once, he jumps at the chance to do her a favour. He's probably been seeing more of her after she broke up with Lester than he's ever admitted to us. She could have found him a comfort, nothing more, but he's been falling for her again; his own marriage is in a pretty dicey state. He's overjoyed at her phone call, he reads all kinds of hopeful signs into it: her marriage is breaking up, he's the one she's turning to.

'They've just about settled the arrangement for him to pick her up, Claire's about to ring off when she hears her husband's footsteps along the passage. She has a split second to decide what to do. Stick to what she's arranged with Ashworth and go now? Or cancel the arrangement, stay at Fairbourne over the weekend, leave later. She decides she'll go now. She tells Ashworth: "Very well, I'll be there." She puts down the phone.

'Later, when she comes out of the house with her suitcase and the pup, she finds Ashworth waiting for her as arranged. Off they go to the cottage. She's strung up now, after the confrontation with Edgar. When she phoned Ashworth she had no intention of telling him the whole story of her affair with Lester but now she's so full of it all she can't stop herself. By the time they get to the cottage it all starts to come pouring out.

'Ashworth is poleaxed. Here she is, telling him she's pregnant by another man and overjoyed about it. She's talking

happily of divorce, marrying Lester—it's the first he knows
of the affair. He realizes she's just treating him as a father
confessor, making use of him to cadge a bed for the night,
then she'll be off, out of his life again. He's overwhelmed
with jealousy and rage. It's the second time in his life she's
suddenly given him the go-by. It's more than he can take.
He turns on her.' He came to a full stop and sat eyeing the
Chief. All he got in reply was a non-committal grunt. 'It
does seem,' Lambert added, 'as if Ashworth only made a
serious attempt to patch up his own marriage after Claire
was dead, out of the picture for ever.'

The Chief sat with his lips thrust out, pondering. 'I suppose it's a possibility,' he said at last. He sat pondering a
little longer, then he glanced at his watch. His manner
grew suddenly brisk. 'Right, then! We'd better get cracking.
Ashworth goes off home on a Saturday morning. Stop at
the first phone-box, we'll give Calthrop's a ring.'

The girl in Calthrop's did her best to be helpful. 'We
don't expect Mr Ashworth in the office again today,' she
told the Chief. 'He went out some time ago on a couple of
calls. He'll be off home as soon as he's through.' She didn't
know where the calls had taken Mr Ashworth. The Chief
left a message, in case Ashworth was in touch with the office
again during the morning, asking him to call in at the police
station before he left for home.

'He might stop by at his cottage on the way home,' Lambert said as they came out of the phone-box.

'Worth a try,' the Chief agreed. He said nothing on the
way to the cottage but sat gazing out at the snowy landscape
sparkling in the sunshine. There was no sign of life at the
cottage, no answer to rings and knocks. They went along
to Mrs Jowitt's and found her at home. Her manner today
was markedly different from yesterday. It was plain she had
seen the Chief on last evening's TV, she looked up at him
now with an expression of mingled fascination and re-
proach. He didn't waste time in explanation but fired
his question: Did she know if Mr Ashworth had left for
home?

Yes, Mr Ashworth had left. He had called in at his cottage not fifteen minutes since, picked up his things and left. The Chief thanked her and turned to go. But if he had finished with Mrs Jowitt, she had by no means finished with him. 'Is it about that earring I found?' she asked in a rush. 'I've been thinking about it.' She gazed up at him with bright, knowing eyes. 'I'm positive Mr Ashworth had a woman at the cottage again, after that.' She paused, expecting questions. She got none, there was no need, it would have taken an armoured regiment to stop her coming out now with everything she had on her mind.

'I could smell the perfume,' she declared with relish. 'I've got a very keen sense of smell.' She rolled her eyes. 'Beautiful perfume, the sort that costs the earth. French, of course, you can always tell. A lady I used to work for at one time, managing director's wife, she always used that selfsame perfume. I'd know it anywhere.' She gave the Chief a look charged with significance. 'I could smell it at the cottage that morning when I found the earring. I didn't smell it again for a week or two after that, then it was there again, three or four times, over about ten days or a fortnight. I've never smelt it at the cottage since.'

When they got back to the yard the Chief was far from pleased to learn that Mansell and his son had still not returned. 'Pull into a lay-by,' the Chief directed as Lambert drove out again through the gates. When they reached the lay-by the Chief sat in slumped silence, eyes closed, the frustration emanating from him almost tangible. Lambert stared out at the snow-covered fields, the traffic slipping by. A minibus turned into the lay-by, passengers descended. One of them, an elderly woman, glanced across at the police car. Her eyes met Lambert's, she gave him a friendly smile. He watched her walk away up the road. Something about her put him in mind of Mrs Locke, the woman who had worked at Fairbourne. His thoughts began to rove over their conversation on the morning of the inquest on Claire Holroyd.

'Always very different in their natures, Edgar and Lester,' Mrs Locke had said. 'You'd scarcely take them for brothers. Lester would give away any toy to another child who fancied it, he never valued his things, never took care of them. What he didn't give away got broken or lost. But not Edgar. Even as a small child Edgar valued everything he was given, looked after it, cherished it. Once something was his it was his for ever.'

Lambert turned to look at the Chief. Kelsey still lay back with his eyes closed but he gave no impression of resting; his brow was furrowed, he chewed his lips. 'Can you really see Edgar Holroyd just sitting there?' Lambert asked. 'Watching his wife go upstairs to pack a bag? Not even wanting to know the reason she'd suddenly decided to clear out for good? Not raising a finger to stop her?'

The Chief's eyes flashed open, the furrows vanished from his brow, he sat bolt upright. 'You're right!' he declared with energy. 'I can't see it.'

There was an electric silence. 'And the pup,' Lambert added. 'What shred of evidence is there to say the pup ever left Fairbourne?'

An icy ripple ran along Kelsey's spine. He turned his head and looked at Lambert. 'Come to that,' he said slowly, 'what shred of evidence is there to say Claire Holroyd ever left Fairbourne alive?'

CHAPTER 27

A few minutes after the Chief came bounding up the steps of the police station, ready to set all wheels in motion, a detective-constable from the murder team came along to see him. A woman had called in at the station an hour ago, in response to the Chief's TV appeal for information. She was a respectable widow, living near the council estate where Harry Lingard had lived; she had known Harry for years. 'I don't know if this is of any use,' she had told the constable, 'but the Chief Inspector did say not to be afraid to come forward. Any little thing might help.'

All her married life she had been a collector in a modest way of porcelain and glass. After her husband died she had found it increasingly difficult to manage and had from time to time sold items from her collection to help pay the bills. She had tried various methods of sale but had found selling them to Harry as good as any. He was always discreet, he gave her a very fair price and it was cash on the nail; no delay, no uncertainty, no commission to pay.

On Tuesday, November 13, she had called on Harry at about six in the evening, taking him a porcelain figurine. He had offered her three hundred pounds, which she had accepted. Harry went along to his bedroom for the money, as he always did. When he came back he gave her only two hundred pounds. He told her, 'That's pretty well cleaned me out. I'll call in tomorrow evening with the other hundred.' He explained that he'd recently decided not to keep any quantity of cash in the house any more as it was getting too risky; he would in future get what he wanted from the bank as it was needed.

The following evening, November 14, Harry called round to give her the hundred pounds in notes. She was certain of the date, she had gone out next morning and paid a bill from the money. She produced a receipted electricity bill showing a cash payment and the date: November 15.

It was almost one-thirty when the police vehicles turned into Whitethorn Road. The common was deserted in the lunch-hour, except for some lads larking about in the sunshine. The snowman was finished now, rakishly cheerful in his bright green scarf and stovepipe hat.

At the sound of the doorbell Edgar Holroyd came along from the kitchen where he had been clearing away his lunch things. He listened courteously as the Chief produced his search warrant, he gazed expressionlessly out at the vehicles drawing up, policemen in overalls and gumboots jumping down, taking out tools and equipment. 'I was going down to my workshop,' he told the Chief. 'I'm in the middle of a tricky piece of work. All right if I get on with it?' The Chief made no objection. A flick of his eyes despatched a constable to accompany Edgar, stay with him.

The lads on the common ceased their skylarking. They exchanged excited whispers and darted silently about, seeking vantage-points to observe what was going on, but the thick screen of trees kept them from seeing in.

The police split into squads to cover the entire property, inside and out, in simultaneous searches. At no point did Edgar break off from his labours in the workshop to watch what was going forward. He made no comment, behaving as if he were alone on the premises, applying himself assiduously to the job in hand.

In the neighbourhood of the common the bush telegraph was at work. Other youngsters appeared, agog with curiosity, adults began to stop by. Before long a small crowd had gathered, kept back by constables. There was no disorder, no unseemly noise or levity.

The interior of the house was soon dealt with; it yielded nothing. Men went through the outbuildings with no better result. Both squads joined forces with the garden contingent, engaged in systematic quartering of the grounds. The blanket of snow made it impossible to see if there had been any recent disturbance of the ground, they had to resort to rods, thrusting them down into the earth. Where the rods met with resistance, digging took place. Time after time the digging revealed nothing more than a boulder, a piece of ancient timber, the remains of an old brick path or the stony relics of some long-demolished wall or rockery.

The Chief returned to the house and mounted the stairs to a window overlooking the front garden. He sent a sweeping glance over the terrain, then he moved in turn to side windows, a rear window, repeating from each the same ranging scrutiny. He returned to one of the side windows and stared intently down. Close to the boundary wall, under a heavy mantle of snow, stood what he took to be a sizeable compost heap, neatly fenced about with chestnut paling.

He went rapidly downstairs, down into the basement, past the open door of the workshop where Edgar still bent over his task, out into the crisp, bright air. Inside a few minutes he had men removing the chestnut fencing, taking the compost heap carefully apart, down to ground level. They found nothing.

They began to thrust rods into the patch of earth. A few moments later one of the men straightened himself to look across at the Chief with a meaningful glance before thrusting down his rod again, a little further along, and again, still further along. He straightened up again and gave the Chief a decisive nod.

They began to dig with the utmost care. As soon as the first spade broke the ground it was clear the earth had been recently disturbed. The Chief at once halted the proceedings. He went swiftly back into the house, along to the workshop. Edgar had reached a delicate moment in his work, he didn't look up as the Chief came striding in. 'If you'd be good enough to leave that,' the Chief said without preamble, 'I'd like you to come outside.'

Edgar set down the tool he was holding. He rolled down his sleeves without haste, put on his jacket. Neither man spoke as Edgar followed the Chief out into the garden, over to the site of the compost heap. The Chief stationed himself at Edgar's side; in silence he signalled to the men to resume their careful digging. Edgar stood watching with a face wiped clear of expression.

In the first fifteen inches they found nothing. Then the spades uncovered a bundle of male clothing: jacket, trousers, shoes. All old, all bearing traces of soil, bracken, grass, cobwebs. Rolled up inside the jacket, a smaller bundle of male clothing: underwear, socks, shirt.

Edgar stood silent, motionless, as the men lifted out a folded bedspread of tapestry-weave cotton, buttercup yellow, with traces of dust and cobwebs, particles of gravel embedded in the weave; a tag in one corner carried a laundry mark. Beneath the bedspread, a bedroom rug, pale blue, slightly stained with blood. And a scarlet satchel with the black-and-white *Bazaar* logo, half full of freesheet copies bearing the date: Thursday, November 15.

CHAPTER 28

Crammed into the satchel on top of the freesheets was a jumble of articles: woollen mittens with fragments of twigs, leaves, grass, adhering; a pigskin wallet holding eighty-five pounds in notes; a man's white handkerchief, ring of keys, tagged car keys, a leather purse containing some ten pounds in coins; a gold wristwatch engraved on the back with Harold Lingard's name and the date of his seventieth birthday. Regimental badge, signet ring engraved with entwined initials: HWL. Ballpoint pen, pocket notebook, its last entry dated Friday, November 16, 8.47 p.m., giving details of the spray-painting episode, the names and addresses of the three boys involved.

Edgar made no move, no sound.

Next came a suitcase holding female clothing and personal items, among them a pair of brown leather knee-length boots, brown leather gloves. Beside the suitcase, a shoulder-bag containing cosmetic items, a handkerchief with the initial C embroidered in one corner, a combination purse-wallet holding ninety pounds in used notes, some four pounds in coins; a lady's gold wristwatch, gold ring set with a solitaire diamond, wedding ring engraved inside with initials and the date of Claire Holroyd's wedding. A centre compartment in the shoulder-bag unzipped to disclose house keys, cheque-book and bank card in the name of Mrs C. Holroyd.

When the Chief ran his fingers over the inside of the bag he discovered a long, zipped pocket discreetly set into the back of the centre compartment. Inside were pedigree papers relating to Hampden Grey Beauty, two hundred pounds in new twenty-pound notes numbered in sequence and a small diary.

The diary opened at the last week in September, where a folded paper had been slipped between the pages—a receipt dated September 28 from the jeweller who had called on the Chief Inspector, acknowledging a cash deposit on a pair of gold cufflinks. The diary page carried an entry for September 28: *Pd. dep. L's Xmas pres. Collect end Nov.*

The Chief glanced rapidly through the other pages. The last two entries were for Thursday and Friday, November 15 and 16. Thursday's entry consisted of a single word written in block capitals: POSITIVE! Friday's entry read: *And again, POSITIVE!!!*

Still Edgar neither stirred nor spoke. As if, Sergeant Lambert thought, seeing the blank gaze Edgar levelled at the proceedings, a shutter had slipped down between his brain and the intolerable reality of what was taking place a few feet away.

He displayed no sign of emotion as three further objects were lifted from the pit: a cold chisel, ball-peen hammer, a length of iron piping. The chisel and hammer were large and heavy, the rounded end of the hammer stained and caked with blood and hair, fragments of bone and tissue. The chisel was similarly stained and caked, with the addition of tattered strands of wool, brown and white. The iron piping was clean and dry.

At the very bottom of the pit they came upon a bag made of heavy-duty, clear plastic, securely tied at the mouth with a length of stout cord. Visible through the plastic was the body of a grizzle-haired pup. In with the body, a collar and lead.

The pup's head had been brutally smashed in by ferocious blows, possibly delivered from outside the bag with the length of iron piping, after the drowsy animal had been fastened into the bag alive.

CHAPTER 29

The arrest of Edgar John Holroyd for the murders of Harold William Lingard and Claire Margaret Holroyd took place in the Fairbourne sitting-room. The Chief administered the prescribed caution. The formal charging would come later, at the police station.

The sombre nature of the proceedings produced a marked effect on Edgar, as if the shutter had all at once lifted from his brain. His blank expression vanished, a look of tortured anxiety swept across his face before the Chief had reached the end of the regulation utterances. Edgar opened his mouth to speak, a torrent of words ready to come spilling out. But the Chief raised a hand to silence him till he had finished. The instant the Chief ceased speaking, Edgar burst into an agitated outpouring.

'I was in the garden, I saw the lights go on in the house. I went up, went inside. Claire was in the hall, sitting in a chair. She'd taken off her boots, put on her shoes, she was taking off her beret. She wasn't on the phone, that wasn't true—the only phone call that evening was from the college lecturer.'

He began to wring his hands. 'She looked startled when she saw me. I said, for a joke: "Be sure your sins will find you out. I know you haven't been at your class." She didn't smile, she looked up at me, cold as ice. She said: "Then you'd better know it all. I have a lover, I'm pregnant by him. I'm leaving you, for good this time."' His voice shook. 'I couldn't take it in, I was paralysed. She said: "Don't you want to know whose child it is? It's Lester's child." It was like some frightful nightmare, I couldn't speak.

'She was like a hanging judge. She said I'd no right to marry her, I must have known all along I was never likely to father a child.' His eyes burned into Kelsey. 'She'd found out from Lester. He had mumps as a child and I'd caught them from him, nursing him. He had them mildly, I took them very badly.' He gave a terrible bark of a laugh. 'Mumps! Even the word is ludicrous! I never took any tests, I had a good idea what they'd tell me. I didn't want to know for certain, I was sure I'd be a bachelor all my days, there was never anyone before Claire. I couldn't believe it when she said she'd marry me. I knew she wanted children, I knew I ought to tell her, I ought to take a test. But I couldn't risk losing her. As long as I didn't know for certain, I could tell myself there was always a chance of children.'

He pressed a hand to his forehead. 'She said I'd deceived and cheated her from the start. If she'd known the truth she'd never for one moment have considered marrying me. I'd let her go on, month after month, believing it was her fault she never got pregnant, I'd watched her go into depressions because of it, she could never forgive me for that. She had as much right to happiness, to children, as any other woman. She wanted to marry Lester but if things didn't work out that way she was still going to keep the child, whatever happened. She was going over to May Finch's, she went upstairs to pack a bag.'

His face was ghastly. 'Then I was standing in the door-way of the bedroom. She'd packed her bag, it was by the bed. She was sitting on the stool in front of the dressing-table, tidying her hair.' He stared back into that moment etched into his brain. 'She saw me in the mirror, she saw the hammer in my hand. She gave a little gasp, she half got up from the stool.' His voice shuddered into silence.

He tilted back his head, closed his eyes. 'I was coming out of the house in Tolladine Road, walking to the gate. I'd left the car down the alleyway, out of sight. I was carrying the bedspread I'd wrapped her in. I couldn't see out because of the trees. I stopped to listen, I couldn't hear anyone about.'

He opened his eyes. 'I went out through the gate—and there was Harry Lingard, under the lamp-post, writing in a notebook. He looked over and saw me, he saw the bed-spread under my arm.'

He drew a shaking breath. 'Neither of us spoke. I went off down the alleyway and got into the car. I came back here, got the chisel from the workshop and went back out again, on to the common. I waited behind some bushes till he came along.'

Dusk had fallen by the time they set off for the police station, leaving a forensic team still at work inside the house. The crowd outside had swollen now.

Edgar had fallen into an apathetic silence. His face looked old and grey, set in deep lines. He took his seat in the rear of the car, between the Chief and Lambert. He seemed unaware of the clicking cameras, the murmur that ran through the throng as the driver turned out through the gate.

The evening was cold and still. Under the street lamps the common lay white and shining. Edgar suddenly began to speak again. 'If it had been any other man on God's earth—' His voice broke. 'Ashworth I could have understood. But Lester! My own brother! That I'd brought up, given up my youth for.' He fell briefly silent. 'I couldn't believe what I'd done, I tried to close my mind to it, pretend none of it had happened, she'd just gone to May's the way she'd done before, she'd be back, one of the days.' He began to weep silently.

They were nearing the centre of town, everywhere brilliantly lit, pavements thronged, lamp-posts hung with spangled decorations. A brass band, grouped round a tall fir decked with festive lights, played the old familiar carols with rousing fervour. In the busy shopping streets the windows blazed with colour, glittered with tinsel. This year's crop of children pressed their faces up against the glass, dreaming of the joys to come.